MURDER
ON SEA

A gripping cozy crime mystery full of twists

JANE ADAMS

A Rina Martin Mystery Book 1

Revised edition 2021
Joffe Books, London
www.joffebooks.com

First published by Severn House Publishers Ltd
in Great Britain in 2007

Cover art by Dee Dee Book Covers

ISBN: 978-1-80405-001-9

PROLOGUE

February was not a month that McGregor associated with weddings. He assumed that most people would prefer to be married when the weather was warm enough for the light-weight froth and frills that most brides of his acquaintance deemed essential for the ushering in of connubial bliss.

He might have guessed that Naomi would do things differently.

Cliff View had been licensed for weddings almost as soon as the licences had become available, and the wonderful Art Deco building, with its views of the ocean and rolling countryside, had been turned into the perfect venue for celebration. The ceremony could be carried out in the Summer Lounge, a high-ceilinged room, one wall of which was entirely made up of window which gave on to a generous terrace and formal garden. The reception would then take place in any one of four rooms set aside for dining and cel-ebrating, each with its own bar, and guests could, of course, stay over in the hotel.

McGregor had gone for one of the little B&Bs down the hill, as the prices for a one-night stay at Cliff View had caused him to blanch. He had to admit though, it was a lovely place. Warm rooms substituted for summer sun and bride and attendants flitted like so many bright butterflies among the equally gaudy guests. Mac, in his sober grey suit, the lightest and brightest of his limited collection, felt distinctly drab.

'I'm so glad you could come.'

Alec grasped his hand, beaming like a loon, Mac thought, not that he could blame him. Mac studied Alec's radiant bride and felt a flush of deep envy. 'Naomi, you look wonderful,' he said sincerely. 'Truly lovely.'

'Thanks, Mac.' She leaned in to kiss him and he was astonished as ever at how delicately she managed to land the kiss on his cheek. On the odd occasion he was called upon to deliver a kiss, he could be guaranteed to fumble it, and *he* was able to see.

'We are *really* glad you could make it,' she told him. 'I didn't know if you would.'

'Couldn't miss this now, could I?' he said. 'Alec's been asking you for so long I'd about given up hope.'

Alec laughed and Naomi reached and clasped his arm. 'I hear you're back at work?'

'I start on Monday. Frantham-on-Sea. I hear it's quiet this time of year.'

Alec laughed. 'I hear it's quiet any time of year.'

'Suits me,' Mac said and an awkward silence fell. There was so much that could not, would not be said. Then the couple were called away and McGregor watched them go, mingling with the joyous crowd.

He almost *hadn't* come. But he had wanted to see these two wed and in the end that desire had won. Just.

He and Alec had gone into the police force together, done their basic training at the same time and Alec was about the closest thing Mac had to a long-term friend. Naomi, though a later addition, was a woman he had always liked a lot. OK, if he were honest, a woman he wished he'd had the nerve to ask out before Alec got to her.

But still, he almost hadn't come. Just back off long-term sick leave and now about to transfer to a place where he was unknown, Mac had been unsure about the wedding, knowing so many of his former colleagues would be present. He had been so relieved to find himself seated at a table with friends of the bride and groom who were not associated with the force. Grateful and, at the same time, oddly put out as he realized that Alec or Naomi—or probably both—had known how awkward it would be for him. They had recognized what Mac saw as his weakness.

A waiter offered him another drink and he selected a fruit juice from the glasses on the tray. He'd had a glass of champagne for the toasts and sipped it sparingly, worried that even a small amount of alcohol would break his carefully maintained control.

He could not countenance that. Not now. He glanced round, noting familiar faces among the crowd. A man he had worked with for fifteen years caught his eye and raised his glass in awkward acknowledgement, then turned away.

I'm a leper, Mac thought, deciding he would find Naomi and say goodbye.

A leper; six months off sick. *Stress*, it said on his records. His superintendent had been at pains to say that no one blamed him and that everyone understood. A case like that— no leads, no closure—it could get to anyone.

And Mac knew the truth of that. He watched hungrily as guests laughed and joked and teased and as the two small- est bridesmaids, dressed like lilac fairies, floated by. Twins, he noted; small blonde twins with their long hair streaming out behind them as they ran.

He did not need to close his eyes to see that small, pale face. Eyes staring upwards at the darkening sky as though she still saw the moon rising and the stars prick through the black.

Mac swallowed hard, trying not to see her long fair hair darkened by the tide, flowing out across the sand, and the blue eyes, sightless now, just staring at the stars.

ONE

February had arrived on the wings of a vengeful wind that whipped off the ocean and flung a chill flurry of salt-tanged rain into the face of any soul wilful enough to venture out. Rina Martin, with sixty-three winters behind her, was not about to be driven inside by this one.

She marched sturdily along the promenade, the little wicker trolley with its uneven wheels ticking along behind her and the crepe soles of her embroidered leather boots squeaking slightly on the smooth slabs of fancy stonework the council had laid in the autumn to define the new pedestrian area. Rina had no truck with bad weather. In her opinion, it should be dealt with the same way as anything that misbehaved and that didn't respond to either a stern telling off or a quick slap on the legs: it should be stoically ignored.

Anyway, this morning she was a woman on a mission and a little bit of weather certainly wasn't going to slow her down. There were, unfortunately, some things that even Rina could not be stoical about and which she certainly could not ignore, and the break-in at number 42 Newell Street fell firmly into that category. What was more, Rina was determined to make certain no one else ignored it either.

Rina wheeled sharp left at the end of the promenade and dragged her little trolley up the three steps that led to the big double doors. There was a newly installed ramp at the side of the steps which would have been somewhat kinder to the wheels, but Rina was in no mood for concessions. The doors of the police station, which faced directly on to a distinctly grey and irritable sea view, were firmly shut against the chill weather. Rina had expected that. What she had not expected at eight o'clock in the morning—a weekday morning at that—was to find them still locked.

'Well, really!' Rina hammered on the wooden door, bringing a response a few minutes later as the bolt was drawn back and a very young and slightly blemished face topped with a shock of bright red hair poked out.

'Oh!' The head was rapidly withdrawn. 'It's you, Miss Martin.'

Rina ignored the usual mistake; calling her Miss instead of Mrs seemed to be a common fault among the young and at this moment she had other, more important things to occupy her mind. She marched across to the desk and hammered on that too.

'Frank Baker, don't you dare try to run away from me. You get back here.'

Behind her, the red-haired and spotty boy stifled a giggle. Rina turned just long enough to stare him into silence then removed her attention back to the desk sergeant who was reluctantly returning to his post.

'It's the third this week,' she told him.

'Um, third what?'

'Oh, for goodness' sake. Third burglary. In our street. The third. I want to know what you're doing about it?'

Frank Baker looked askance. 'Third?' he said. 'Look, I'm sorry, Mrs Martin, I've only just come on. I've not had time to consult . . .'

'Third,' Rina reaffirmed. She unfastened her coat and unwound one loop of scarf from around her neck. She was wearing two and they were a little too much in the warmth of the station foyer, but the Peters sisters had started knitting again and Rina didn't like to hurt feelings by choosing one woollen offering over another. 'We had *one* patrol car round last night and poor Mrs Freer had to call a locksmith out herself to secure her back door. All your lot wanted to do was nail a bit of wood over the broken pane. What good, I ask you, would that have done?'

'I'm sure our officers would have left the place secure—' Frank Baker began.

'And how, pray, would she have been able to get out to the bins? Or let the cat into the yard? Mrs Freer walks with a frame, Frank Baker, as well you know. You can't expect her to trek all the way round from the front every time she wants to put a bit of rubbish out.'

'I'm sure, if she'd asked, they'd have called a locksmith for her, Mrs Martin.' Frank felt he ought to defend his colleagues even though as yet he had no idea what had been going on and, come to that, did not actually know Mrs Freer from Adam.

'Oh, would they indeed? They were there barely half an hour. Long enough to drink tea, then they were off, called to some night club or other. Tell me, Frank Baker, what's more important? An old lady scared half out of her wits after some thug broke into her house or some idiots who have drunk too much and got themselves into a fight?'

Frank knew he was on to a loser but he had to try. 'Mrs Martin, if the officers were called to an affray, then—'

'An affray, you call it? I call it drunken louts. If they want to beat seven shades out of one another, I say let them get on with it. Call an ambulance when they're done if you really must and charge them for the privilege. I ask again, which is more important, Frank?'

Frank Baker leaned across the counter, a dangerous move even if it was intended to be a reassuring one. 'Look, Mrs Martin . . . Rina . . . I'll get someone out this morning, I promise. We're not forgetting our other duties, you know.'

'I should hope not,' Rina told him calmly. 'I expect you to keep your word, Frank Baker, and whoever you send to see Mrs Freer, you'd better tell them to call on me as well.'

Rina took her leave, sweeping out of the foyer and pausing in the doorway to fasten her coat and re-loop her scarf. It was, she felt, her duty to allow some of the stiflingly warm air out and a little of the chill back in, just to reinforce the depth of her displeasure.

She jogged the wicker trolley back down the steps, aware that Frank Baker's gaze was fixed upon her right until the point that the door slammed shut. *Seeing her off the premises*, Rina thought. Then, with the storm front of her outrage somewhat spent, she walked back up the promenade, into the face of the gusting wind.

* * *

'That woman!' Frank breathed.

The red-headed probationer who had opened the door to the redoubtable Mrs Martin now stared at his sergeant.

'Is she really married? Poor bugger.'

'Hey, I'll not have you speak ill,' Frank told him. 'That's my job. Widowed she was. Years since.'

'He die to get away, did he?' The probationer was risking displeasure, he knew, but he couldn't help himself.

'Get on with you. She's a good woman . . . once you break through the barricades. A very *determinedly* good woman.' He frowned and glanced through the entries in the day book that he really should have read long before Rina arrived that morning. 'She's right, though. It is the third break-in of the week in that road.'

'Druggies, probably,' the probationer mooted.

'Maybe. Report says nothing was taken this time. The old lady screamed and they ran away. She was lucky,' he added seriously. 'They could have turned nasty on her.' He paused, checking the duty roster and glancing up thoughtfully at the probationer. 'Now, who shall we give this little job to?'

'Sir, I don't think . . .' The colour had drained from his already pale face, leaving only blemishes and freckles behind.

Frank chuckled. 'Don't worry, lad, I wasn't going to throw you to the lions. I think I'll have a chat with Inspector Eden, suggest our new boy go and do the honours. Get a feel for the local population, like.'

'Oh.' The red-headed young man smiled and the colour returned, rising like a tie from his rather thin neck. 'Inspector McGregor,' he said. 'Nice one.'

'I don't need your approval, lad,' Frank told him as he retreated into the back office in search of his Chief Inspector. 'You just stand there and watch the door.'

TWO

Peverill House was at the best end of Newell Street, in that it was the end closest to the promenade. The houses at this end of the road were mostly Edwardian, three storeys plus attic rooms and basements, many of which had now been converted into flats. Others survived as B&Bs, though this early in the year guests were few and far between and hopeful 'vacancy' signs swung like invitational flags beneath painted names like Sea View and Ships Lodge.

The lower end, as the locals called it—the end furthest away from the sea—had suffered most at the hands of town planners. The eighties had seen a new road built that crossed Newell St, cutting in half what had once been a long and elegant row and destroying three of the tall town houses Rina so admired. A decade later, further planning outrages had demolished more as tiny boxes—designated affordable housing—had been built in their stead. Rina had never understood the logic of demolishing perfectly good houses, which could be easily converted to provide flats for a half-dozen or more tenants and throwing up in their stead these flimsy rabbit hutches that the planners declared were family homes. A scant fifteen years on, they looked tired and unkempt and many of those at the furthest end of the street were now boarded up and unoccupied. Rina had heard rumours that they too were now scheduled for demolition and that a large supermarket chain was hoping to redevelop the site. It was at this far end of the road that the three most recent burglaries had occurred and Rina could not help but wonder what on earth the thieves had hoped to find. No one down at the lower end owned anything worth stealing, surely. The unfortunate Mrs Freer certainly did not.

Rina climbed the steps at the front of Peverill Lodge, bumping the now full wicker trolley unceremoniously in her wake. The sign above the door announced that Peverill was a guest house, but no wooden vacancy flag ever swung in the stiff breeze in front of Rina Martin's door. Rina's guests came to stay and stayed. If a vacancy should happen to arise, then it was rapidly filled by someone on Rina's informal but jealously guarded 'waiting list'.

She let herself in and allowed the heavy door with its stained glass panels of green and blue to slam shut behind her. She listened; all was still quiet, despite it being after nine.

She pulled the trolley through to the kitchen and, before removing her coat, filled the kettle and set it on the stove, fixing the whistle firmly in place.

Rina's kettle was the household wake-up call. Rina herself was an early riser, always had been, but she was perfectly willing to make allowance for the habits of her guests. For most of them, a lifetime of late nights and equally late mornings had become ingrained and she had found that few of them were capable of sensible conversation much before ten. Breakfast, a communal affair, was generally acceptable from about half past nine.

Kettle on, she slipped out of her coat and went back to the hall to place it in the tall wooden closet beside the door. Rina's hall was hung with pictures of her guests, mostly from their glory days. The Montmorency twins when they had made their one brief but cherished appearance on Broadway. The Peters sisters perched like bright-clad birds on the edge of a grand piano. The Great Stupendo, and the same guest in

his incarnation as Marvello, flanked a large poster advertising Rina and the late Mr Martin on Brighton Pier. True, she and her husband were never a headline act, but they always worked and, since his unfortunate death, Rina had proudly maintained that claim.

She touched the poster fondly, smiling as she recalled just how young they had been back then. She'd look a little silly now, she thought, in the skimpy corset and red feathers that had passed for a costume in her husband's knife-throwing days, but she had done it justice back then.

Later, she'd joined a touring company, played small walk-on parts and then small speaking parts and then lead roles but that had been without her beloved Fred. Five years after she had taken his name, Fred had been taken from her and Rina had never found another man to match him.

The kettle had begun to scream by the time she re-entered the kitchen. She held the door wide so that the piercing whistle should screech through the rest of the sleeping house, and was satisfied to hear the bump and clatter of waking guests as she took it from the stove and filled the first tea pot. A second kettle would ensure that any stay-abeds would rise in due course.

Then she set a large griddle pan across two burners on the stove and left it to warm while she found the bacon, sausages and eggs in the fridge and the fresh-baked bread from her wicker trolley. It still felt faintly warm, despite the chill wind on the home journey.

She paused again to examine one last poster. This one hung in the kitchen above a large wooden settle against the longest wall. It was a picture of Rina, though she thought of it almost as an image of the kitchen god. After all, the role in which she was depicted in this rather grand black and white photograph had been her last and greatest—the role that had paid for this house.

'Lydia Marchant,' Rina said, her tone of quiet satisfaction very different from the harridan's voice she had used to flagellate poor Sergeant Baker that morning. '*Lydia Marchant*

Investigates. A run of a full ten years and two rival channels on the television. Something to be proud of, eh, Fred?' And now cable and satellite channels reprised her role on a daily basis and dubbed it into a dozen different languages around the world. Such franchises brought nice little cheques dropping on to her doormat with satisfying regularity.

A contented look on her face that Frank Baker would have been astonished to see, Rina laid bacon and sausage on the griddle pan and filled her second pot with tea as the first of her morning guests started to arrive.

THREE

Mac had made no comment when requested to visit Mrs Freer—a job he could reasonably have expected to be handed off to uniform. It had quickly become apparent that any rules of engagement learned in his previous postings simply did not apply here. Chief Inspector Eden was not one for set roles and not much of one for rules and regulations—or, Mac had noted, for paperwork, Eden's desk being piled high with files and letters and Post-it notes. He was getting used to being told 'it's probably on the desk' whenever he wanted something that should have been in a filing cabinet.

At first, Mac had assumed that such overt muddle would be reflected in the running of the small HQ, perched at the end of the promenade, but he had quickly learned better. Eden knew exactly what was on his desk and in which archaeological layer it resided. Mac's attempts to casually remove at least the odd stack of misplaced files to their proper resting place had been greeted with amusement and, he soon realized, a small degree of disdain.

Despite this, Mac was already starting to like Eden and his cohorts; to admire the town of Frantham, any part of which could be reached by shanks' pony within a quarter-hour or so.

In fact, if he had any complaint then Mac would have to admit that he was bored. Deeply bored.

He had walked from the police station to Newell Street, hardly a stretch and a pleasant walk even on such a blustery day. He found number 42 and, there being no bell and only a letterbox without a knocker, he rapped, rather too gently, on the door.

Mrs Freer was a frail, elderly lady, he had been told, and he had no wish to startle her. Unfortunately, no one had told him that Mrs Freer was deaf. Five minutes of increasingly loud knocking and the old lady finally came to the door.

'Who are you?'

She sounded scared, he thought. 'I'm a police officer,' he told her.

'A what?'

'A police officer.' He raised his voice, struck by the difficulty of sounding gentle and reassuring at the same time as having to shout.

'Oh? I see.'

Mac heard a chain being fastened and the door cracked open just a few inches. He was ready with his ID card. 'Look, Mrs Freer. This is who I am.'

She took her time, examining the card and then studying him, and finally she opened the door and allowed him to come inside.

Mac paused on the threshold and wished he'd taken a deeper breath of fresh air. The house smelled stale and old and reminded him faintly of school dinners and men's urinals. The carpet in the hall was sticky underfoot and he was forced to wait, trying not to adhere, until the elderly resident manoeuvred her walking frame in the too narrow hall and led the slow way back into the kitchen at the other end of the hall.

'You'll be wanting tea.'

'No, no thank you. I'm fine.'

She filled the kettle anyway and he reminded himself that she couldn't hear. 'I said, no. It's all right. Please don't trouble.'

She fumbled with the kettle plug, her obviously wet hands in such close contact with electricity causing Mac to wince and reach out to help. She ignored the gesture, fumbled the plug home and then took hold of her frame once more. Thus supported, she scrutinized Mac for a second time.

'Have you caught them then?'

'Er, no. I'm sorry.' He backed off and sat down at the Formica-topped table. 'I wondered if you had anything to add to what you told the officers last night.'

'Are you Scottish? Your name is Scottish. You don't sound Scottish.'

'My family,' Mac said. 'I was born and raised in England.'

She nodded. 'I went to Scotland on my honeymoon,' she told him. 'We liked to travel. Though not like the young people do nowadays. Getting on planes the way we used to catch buses.' She barked with laughter. 'What a life, eh?'

Mac smiled. 'I suppose it is,' he agreed, not really sure what he was supposed to say.

Mrs Freer eased herself across the kitchen floor and Mac realized that she had not in fact switched the kettle on. He wondered if he should remind her, before she got too far away from it and had to make another awkward turn, then he decided not. He really didn't want any tea. The kitchen was cleaner than the hall but it smelled no sweeter and, frankly, Mac had endured his share of unclean tea in his uniformed days. He could do without now. He waited until Mrs Freer had struggled to the table and lowered herself into a chair before asking again if there was anything more she remembered.

She considered the question thoughtfully, nodding to herself as though some inner dialogue was going on that Mac was not party to. Finally she said, 'There were two of them. Only one came in, but I know there was another outside. It was late, well after ten, so they probably thought I'd be asleep upstairs, but I've not used the upstairs, you see, not in years. The Red Cross lady came and had my bed brought down and things fixed up for me so I could cope. They put a special shower in the cupboard in the hall, special handles and such, but mostly I just have a lick and a promise in the kitchen sink.' She smiled at Mac. 'You don't need so much washing and brushing at my age.'

Mac was doubly glad he had refused the tea. 'And so, what happened? I know you told the officers last night, but sometimes in the fresh light of day . . .'

She nodded again. 'I've had a bit of time to think,' she said. 'I'm sure there was two of them. I went and had a look outside this morning and there's footprints in the flower bed. Two lots.'

'May I take a look?'

She started to get up and Mac waved her back to her seat. 'Don't worry. I can manage—that is, if you don't mind?' He was suddenly afraid that he might have offended the old lady's sensibilities.

'No, you go on, take a look.'

The lock on the back door was new and the surround had been reinforced but the tool marks where it had been forced were still clear. Mac wondered if anyone had photographed them or if anyone was due to come and fingerprint. There had been no reference in the initial report to either possibility.

The yard was tiny, with a few slabs, a wheelie bin and a flower bed maybe three feet by two, unexpectedly well planted with winter pansies. Closer inspection revealed that she was right about the footprints.

Mac may only have lived in Frantham for a couple of weeks but he was already learning to read the weather and as he had walked along the promenade had taken note of the bruised rain clouds collecting out at sea. Another hour and the footprints would be history, washed away by the torrential rain he had read in the clouds. Mac returned to the kitchen and asked if she had a dustbin bag. More out of hope than expectation he photographed the prints with his mobile phone and then covered the footprints with sections of torn bag, weighting it down with garden pebbles.

Mrs Freer listened closely as he explained what he had done. She nodded sagely but Mac could see in her eyes that she had about as much of hope as he did that anything would come of it.

'There have been three burglaries in the street,' she told him. 'This week alone. Last week it was Gala Crescent on the Jubilee Estate. Last week and the week before.' She gave gentle emphasis to the 'and'. 'Nothing seems to have been done.' She shrugged frail shoulders. 'Children,' she said.

'Children?'

'They were young things, the two that broke in here. Just children. What were they doing out so late at night?'

'Children?' Mac frowned, realizing he was repeating himself. 'Could you guess how old they were?'

The frail shoulders lifted again. It looked to Mac as though it cost her to make even so slight a movement. 'Still in school,' she said. 'Teenagers. Thirteen or fourteen or so, I'd say. The boy in the kitchen looked no more than that. Scared to death he was.'

Of you? Mac thought. 'What did you do?'

'Oh.' Mrs Freer was nonchalant. 'I started to tell those officers last night but they had to rush away. Young people, always rushing, they get on planes, you know, the way my generation used to get on buses.'

Mac nodded. This was obviously something that impressed her. 'You were going to tell the officers what?' he asked.

'That I showed them my gun,' Mrs Freer told him.

FOUR

Several thoughts skidded through Mac's mind at that point. *Does she mean a real gun? Should he call for backup? Where is it now?* He settled for voicing that final thought.

'Um, Mrs Freer, where is the gun? Can I see it?'

She started to get up but then flopped back down in the chair. 'Oh, be a dear and get it for me, will you? I don't feel so good today; it's taking a lot of getting around. I expect it's because I had such an interrupted night.'

'Of course,' Mac told her. 'Where . . . ?'

She flapped a bony, fragile-looking hand back towards the hall. 'In the other room, dear. Under my pillow.'

'Under your . . .' *This is surreal*, Mac thought. A sudden worry struck him that, if by some quirk the gun was real, he might have to arrest this fragile pensioner. Reluctantly, he made his way into the living room, now converted into a bed-sitting room. The curtains were half open, allowing only a slant of grey light to infiltrate. Mac took in the threadbare carpet and the ageing furniture. The television resembled the one his parents had nursed through years of faithful service before its final demise. The old lady's bed was tucked between the window and the couch and draped with a crocheted blanket and, somewhat to his surprise, a thick and puffy duvet dressed in a very smart purple cover.

For a moment, Mac was taken aback by the very clean nature of the crisp white linen sheets and pillowcases. 'Clean linen and winter pansies,' Mac muttered. 'Who takes care of that, then?' He twitched the pillows aside and stepped back.

'Oh boy.'

Gingerly he lifted the very real revolver from its place beneath the plump white pillow and checked the chamber. To his profound relief it was empty. Mac's knowledge of guns was not vast, but he reckoned the snub-nosed little revolver was probably a .38 and, holding it up to what light managed to get in through the window, read the Smith & Wesson name, much worn but still clearly engraved.

Returning to the kitchen, he laid it down gently on the table. 'You do know that it's illegal to own this, don't you?'

Again that airy wave of the hand. 'Oh, stuff and non-sense, my dear. My husband had it decommissioned long ago. Filed through a pin or some such, I don't really remember what he said.'

'I'll have to take it away, have it examined, just to make sure,' Mac told her gently. 'Mrs Freer, tell me, have you threatened anyone else with this?'

'Not for years,' she told him. 'There's never really been the need.'

* * *

Mac needed a cup of tea the next time it was offered. The same type of pansies as he had seen in Mrs Freer's garden were growing happily in large terracotta pots by the door to Peverill Lodge and the pin-neat woman who greeted him at the door had Mac guessing that she must be the provider of clean sheets as well. She looked vaguely familiar, Mac thought, but he couldn't place where he might have seen her before.

'Mrs Martin?'

'Yes.'

'DI McGregor. I've just come from speaking with Mrs Freer.'

She raised an eyebrow and then took his identification from him, inclining it towards the daylight, the better to see.

'Come in,' she ordered, standing back from the door. 'I hope you don't mind talking in the kitchen but we're getting lunch. Would you like some tea?'

'Thank you, I would.' Rina Martin led him through a spotless hall and into a large and sparkling kitchen. The scent of herbs and what his hungry stomach identified as fresh tomato sauce reminded him that he had eaten very little at breakfast and it was now well after one o'clock.

From somewhere off the hall he could hear a piano being played and two pretty if slightly wavery voices singing. A tall man with a mane of steel-grey curls stood beside the kitchen range, stirring a pot from which the enticing fragrance issued. A second man, this one smaller, plumper and rather bald, washed salad at the Belfast sink.

'That smells good.' Mac couldn't help himself.

Rina Martin turned and raised an eyebrow. She gestured towards the taller man. 'Mr Matthew Montmorency,' she said, 'and Mr Steven Montmorency. This is Detective Inspector Sebastian McGregor. Please, do sit down. You make the place look untidy.'

Mac sat down with alacrity. Making the place untidy was, he felt, probably a sin around here. Matthew Montmorency inclined his grey head. 'Pleased to meet you.'

'Apparently,' Rina said, 'Inspector McGregor has just come from interviewing Mrs Freer.'

'That poor woman!' Steven Montmorency spoke this time. 'First her husband going off like that and then all this— and it's not as if she has any health left.'

'Quite.' Rina silenced him.

'Gone off?' Mac asked.

'He died,' Rina said quietly. 'Steven has something of an aversion to speaking about death.'

'Oh, I see. Was it recent?'

Rina shook her head. 'No, it must be seven years ago, eight maybe. But they'd been together since she was sixteen and he wasn't much older. It was a terrible blow.'

Mac nodded. 'It must have been. Mrs Martin, do you know Mrs Freer well?'

'Well enough. I call in twice a week and see if she needs anything. She has a care package, or so they call it, and a woman comes to do shopping and pay bills and the like. But there are some things she doesn't like her to get. Personal things, you know.'

Mac didn't know but he wasn't sure he was going to ask.

'I wash her sheets and keep the bed nice.' Rina shook her head. 'There's not much I can do about the house—she's too proud to let me or anyone else clean and scrub for her—but I think if she can at least sleep in clean sheets, that's something.'

'And the flowers?'

Rina shrugged. 'Hearts ease. Did you know that was the old name for pansies?'

Mac replied honestly that he hadn't known that.

'It's a good name. They do ease the heart, I think. Such cheerful little plants. She doesn't get out into the back yard much at this time of year but at least she can see something colourful from the kitchen window.'

'That's nice of you,' Mac said. 'Mrs Martin, this might seem like a strange thing to ask, but did you know Mrs Freer had a gun?'

Steven Montmorency laughed. 'Oh, that old thing,' he said. He piled the washed salad into a spinner and began to turn the handle. 'Of course we knew. She keeps it under her pillow.'

'It doesn't work,' Rina said. 'I made sure of that the first time I saw it. But it made her feel better to have it so I left well alone. You can only interfere so much in other people's affairs.'

'I've had to have it removed,' Mac told her reluctantly. 'When she showed it to me, I had to call uniform and get them to take it away, just to be sure.'

Steven tutted. 'Now what will she do?'

'Had to be done, Steven,' Matthew returned. 'We kept telling her it wasn't a good idea.'

'What do you mean *we* kept telling her? *You* wouldn't set foot in the place. You said it stank.'

'I never did.'

'Boys, please! If you must quarrel then take it outside.' Rina turned her attention back to Mac. 'What can you do?' she said. 'Brothers always quarrel and I'm sure twins are worse.'

'Twins? I . . .'

A tiny, almost imperceptible shake of the head came from Rina and Mac trailed off. 'Right,' he said, and decided to return to safer ground. 'The gun. Do you know where she got it from?'

'I would imagine,' Rina replied, 'that it belonged to her husband. Matthew, make the tea, would you, I think the kettle is about to screech. Her husband was a member of the local gun club. Years ago that must have been, but she once showed me trophies he had won. I believe he competed all over the country.'

'It looked to be quite an old gun,' Mac mused.

'Smith & Wesson, thirty-eight, snub-nosed. At one time it was standard US police issue.'

Mac stared at her. This day was just getting too weird. What was it with elderly ladies in Frantham? Did they all belong to some local militia he hadn't been told about?

'*Lydia Marchant Investigates*,' Steven Montmorency informed him proudly, pointing to the far wall.

Puzzled, Mac got up to see. 'Oh, yes.' Suddenly it all became clear. That vague sense of familiarity he had noted when Rina Martin had let him in. The way she knew about the gun. Well, now it made a little more sense. He studied the black and white publicity shot, comparing it with the woman who faced him across the expanse of scrubbed wooden table.

'Research?'

Rina nodded. 'Weapons of one sort or another showed up in the scripts on a regular basis. I always thought I had a duty to get the detail right, even if the stories were sometimes frankly unbelievable.'

Mac laughed. 'My mother loved the series,' he said. 'My aunt too.'

'Not you?' Rina's mouth twitched in a half-smile.

'Mrs Martin, frankly, I can't watch whodunnits of any kind. They feel too much like homework.'

Rina laughed then and the stern face was transformed. Mac caught a glimpse of a much younger, much gentler woman. 'You were very successful,' he commented. 'The series ran for years.'

'More than ten,' she agreed.

'You can catch it on satellite and cable most days,' Matthew Montmorency told him. 'And sometimes they show it in the afternoons on proper television. Rina, darling, will you set an extra place for our guest? He's been salivating ever since he came in and if we wait for him to go the pasta will be ruined.'

Mac had been going to refuse but it rapidly became clear that he had no say in the matter—and besides, he was hungry. He'd never had much of an appetite until coming to Frantham and, as his last posting had also been coastal, he didn't think he could blame the sea air. Maybe it was all the walking he'd done. His petrol bill had dropped almost to nothing in the past couple of weeks, while his food consumption had rocketed.

The table in the dining room was set with blue and white china, heavy, old-fashioned cutlery and an odd assortment of pretty but uncoordinated glasses clustered about a large, cut-glass jug. He found himself seated between two women of

Rina's age, he guessed, though they could have been anything from fifty to seventy. Carefully applied make-up and a light blonde rinse to take the edge off the grey confused the issue for Mac, who was not all that good at guessing a woman's age anytime.

These two obviously *were* sisters and probably real twins, or at least very close in age. Rina introduced them as Eliza and Bethany Peters as she directed Mac to his seat and placed a basket of fresh rolls on the table, instructing him to help himself.

'Where's Tim?' Rina asked.

'Marvello is rehearsing,' said Matthew Montmorency, rolling his eyes in theatrical despair.

'Marvello?' Rina looked worried. 'I thought the booking was for The Great Stupendo? I can't see them wanting a mind-reading act at a children's party. Steven, fetch him down, will you, and tell him to hurry.'

Steven Montmorency exited. He had, Mac noted, an odd, shuffling walk, as though his knees hurt if he bent them too much. By contrast, his twin loped along, evoking, to Mac's mind, some large breed of long-haired hound. A saluki, perhaps.

The Peters sisters, by contrast, were more the Yorkshire terrier type, not that they were yappy or shrill, but fussy and effusive as they ensured he was comfortable, and competed with each other to get him the best bread roll and the prettiest glass for his water.

Rina met his gaze and shook her head indulgently. 'We don't have too many guests,' she said.

Steven returned, carrying the tea tray and followed by a tall, ascetic-looking man that Mac guessed must be Marvello—or Stupendo. He paused for a moment in the doorway, allowing time for everyone to take note of his arrival. When no one did, he pursed his lips and wandered over to his seat, opposite Mac. He looked younger than the others, Mac thought. Too thin, too tall and too spare, dressed entirely in black. Mac remembered what Rina had said about a children's party and struggled with the image.

'I'm told you're a policeman,' Marvello said. 'I'm Tim, otherwise known as Marvello or The Great Stupendo.'

'DI McGregor, otherwise known as Mac. And you are a magician?'

'So I'm told, yes.' The studied moroseness of his words was spoiled by the sudden smile. It reached his eyes, sparking life into the drawn and sallow face. 'Actually, I think of myself more as a mentalist than a magician, you know, like Derren Brown.'

Mac nodded. 'Thanks,' he said as a heaped bowl of pasta and a second of salad were paced before him. 'I've seen him on the TV.'

Tim laughed. 'Unfortunately, my agent doesn't share my vision. He keeps getting me bookings more suited to Coco the clown.' He dug a fork into his bowl and twirled it enthusiastically, then shrugged. 'But it's all work, I suppose. Pays the bills.' He shoved the loaded fork into his mouth and Mac followed his lead, soon eating with the same silent enthusiasm as the rest gathered about the table. Food in the Rina Martin household was, Mac realized, something to be dealt with in all seriousness and given full regard as one of the important things in life. Like clean sheets and winter pansies.

Marvello finished first, then took a bread roll and proceeded to stuff it full of salad. He consumed that and started on another. How, Mac wondered, could he eat that much and still be so stick thin?

'So, any leads on these burglaries?' Marvello asked between bites of overfilled roll.

Mac shook his head. 'Mrs Freer said she thought the boys were young, maybe fourteen. That doesn't really tally with what our other witnesses have said. I'm going to re-interview the other victims this afternoon.'

'Well, we all wish you good luck with that,' Matthew Montmorency said. 'I doubt you'll get much help from the Jubilee.'

'Jubilee?'

'The Jubilee Estate,' Rina said.

25

'Ah, Gala Crescent. Yes, of course. Though there have been two more on this road as well, I believe.'

'True,' Matthew went on, 'but it'll be kids from the Jubilee responsible, you mark my words.'

Marvello grimaced. 'Matthew has a few prejudices,' he said.

'It isn't prejudice if it's true,' Matthew insisted.

'Well, I'll be looking at all possibilities,' Mac assured them. 'I don't yet know the Jubilee Estate well. I'm new to the area; you'll have to give me time to get the lie of the land.'

'New?' Rina asked.

'New job, yes. I arrived two weeks ago.'

'And do you like it here?'

'So far, yes I do.'

'Is it very different from your last position?'

'It's quiet,' he said. 'I was told it would be when I applied.'

'Quiet except for this mini crime wave of ours,' Rina reminded him sternly.

Mac nodded. 'Apart from that.'

'Well.' Rina stood and began to stack the crockery. 'I'm sure you'll soon have that sorted, won't you?'

Would I dare not? Mac thought.

FIVE

Mac arrived back at the police station just before they shut up shop at five. Cover, from that point in the evening, had to come all the way from Dorchester or Weymouth.

'Had a busy day, I hear?' DI Eden emerged from his office, coffee mug in hand that exuded fumes of more than hot coffee.

'It's been eventful,' Mac agreed.

'Find anything new, apart from one armed and dangerous old lady?' He guffawed loudly and took a swig from his mug. 'Come on through.'

Mac followed Eden into the warm office, shedding coat and scarf and gloves. He took a seat in one of the two old-fashioned captain's chairs. Eden took the other. 'Any news on the weapon?' he asked.

'Non-functional,' Eden confirmed.

'Good, but she still can't go round waving it at people.'

'People who should not be breaking into her house,' Eden observed. 'But no, it isn't a good idea.'

Mac remarked to himself, not for the first time, that his boss was fond of understatement. 'I went back and re-interviewed the earlier victims. Or at least, those who were home and willing to talk.'

'How many did you find?'

'Well, I talked to a Mrs Emmet on Gala Crescent and also to Julie Harper.'

'First and second burglaries, right?'

Mac nodded. 'The Bakers, victims of the third break-in, were out but seem to have acquired a very large dog.'

Eden laughed again. 'Anything new?'

A lot of abuse, but that wasn't new. 'I gained the impression that both Mrs Emmet and Julie Harper had a good idea who might be responsible but—'

'But they weren't saying. It'll be local kids. We had a spate of this before.' He delved into one of the precarious stacks of paperwork piled on the left-hand side of his desk, produced a list. 'PlayStation and games, mobile phone, a bit of cash. Kids.'

'Could be drugs related.'

Eden shook his head. 'Not round here,' he said. 'We just don't get it. The other two though, now I'm not so sure that was just kids after toys.'

Mac agreed. 'Neither of the householders on Newell Street were at home. The neighbours came out and had a look at me, wanted to know what I wanted and then, when they found out who I was, they asked what I was doing about it.'

Eden nodded. 'That sounds about right. Oh, don't be fooled, the whole of the Jubilee Estate would have known your business from the moment you set foot on Gala Crescent, but on the whole they've a policy of not talking to coppers. It's a different picture on Newell Street. Different attitude.'

'It's an odd road,' Mac said thoughtfully. 'Those big houses up at the top end and then—what are they—housing association down the other end?'

'Run by the Alderman Calvin Trust, yes. So is the old folks' home. You see that?'

'Circular thing? Ugly yellow brick?'

'That'll be the one. Don't know how the planners got away with it.' Eden sounded disgusted. 'Palms greased somewhere along the line, must have been. That's the only excuse I can think of for allowing anyone to build such cheap-skate rubbish. Any nosy neighbours have anything useful to tell?'

'Useful? No, I don't think so. A lot of talk about kids hanging about and some complaints about motorbikes on the wasteland. They seemed to connect the two.'

Eden nodded. 'Wasteland to the back of the tin huts?'

'Tin huts?'

'Oh,' Eden amended, 'that's what the locals call them, seeing as most started out that way and some are little better even now. Small industrial units, some little bits of manufacturing. There's a local carpenter, painter and decorator, pair of brothers that make specialist machine tools, that sort of thing. Go and take a look tomorrow. You can check out the bike riders too. Take Andy with you; do him good to get outside.'

Andy, Mac recollected, was the red-haired probationer, on attachment from Dorchester but to what purpose Mac had yet to work out. 'I had an interesting encounter with Rina Martin,' he said.

'We thought you might enjoy that,' Eden said.

'You know her well?'

'Everyone *knows* Rina. Know her well? No, I don't think I do but she usually has her finger on the local pulse. What did she have to say?'

Mac thought through what he had gleaned from the post-lunch conversation. Rina and the others had been free with their opinions, true, but out of the general discussion had come some interesting points. 'She'd agree with us,' Mac said at last. 'That the robberies were different. That it was probably local kids on the Jubilee that robbed the properties on Gala Crescent, opportunists out for what they already knew was there. The three break-ins on Newell were more speculative, somehow. Or at least the first two were. Mrs Freer was certain that the two who tried to get into her house were young, not more than fourteen or so, and they scared easily.'

'Easily? The gun would have been enough, surely, even if it was an old lady holding it. *I'd* have left in a hurry, I can tell you.'

'Hmm, maybe. But what was taken was a little different too. Sure, on the second robbery they took a games machine, but the search was more systematic. They looked for money and jewellery, didn't just grab what was in plain view.'

'I'd agree,' Eden said. 'The other oddity was the passports. The second robbery. Mr and Mrs Green. Both retired but not too badly off. They were planning a couple of weeks in Spain, to get away from our wonderful British winter. Kids wouldn't bother with passports. No one would bother with passports unless they had the means to sell them on.' He rummaged for another list. 'Passports, some bits of jewellery, nothing exceptionally valuable but some of it sentimental. Nothing distinctive enough that it would be hard to shift. Mobile phone, cash and a few bits of silver. The Greens had more cash in the house than usual because of the planned holiday. They were intending to get it changed the following day.'

'And someone knew.'

'Anyone could have known. They were excited about their holiday. Talked to neighbours, told friends in the local pub. People do.'

Mac nodded. 'The pub,' he said.

'I asked. The Railway. And yes, a couple of the other victims drink there too, but so does half the Jubilee Estate and most of the bottom end of Newell Street too. It's closest.'

'Might be worth a look though.'

'Feel free.' Eden eased himself out of his chair. Mac had heard that he was once quite an athlete but that must have been a while ago, before the belly grew large enough to cover his belt buckle and he acquired the jowls that took a full second or two to catch up with the movement of his head. Eden still thought like a policeman, Mac thought, but he was starting to act like one already retired, not someone who still had four months to go.

He'd heard rumours that bad health had brought Eden to this backwater posting. Welcome to Frantham-on-Sea, rest home for worn-out coppers.

He followed Eden's lead and made for the door, bidding goodnight to the other two inhabitants, the desk sergeant and Andy the probationer, informing the latter that he was with Mac in the morning, working the burglary case. He could almost see the red hair wilt.

* * *

Mac made his slow way home, stopping off at the convenience store for essentials. He had managed to get a flat overlooking the promenade, but only on a temporary contract. From Easter onwards it was let out to holidaymakers at extortionate weekly rates and Mac would have to find something permanent by then. He had started to look in a half-hearted sort of way, but even the knowledge that his let had less than a month to run was not enough to spur him on.

His flat was on the top floor of a house like Peverill Lodge. The view was spectacular, taking in the whole of Frantham Bay. Mac could see Marlborough Head rising above the undercliff, and the posh side of town and Druidston Point, known locally as Druston, marking the boundary to his left. Beyond that, just hidden from view by the point, was the small harbour and the 'old town', the remnants of Frantham village as it once had been.

Mac deposited his shopping on the table—living room and kitchen combined in the one area—and drew the curtains, pausing to observe the cold grey ocean in the fast fading light. He glanced reflexively towards Marlborough Head. Twice now, late in the evening, he had seen lights close to Marlborough, where the cliff jutted farthest out into the sea, guarding the bay, and he had wondered who might be daft enough to be out in a boat so close to the rocks at the base of the cliffs and so late at night. He had meant to mention it to Eden, ask if the coastguard patrolled and if that would account for the lights, but he kept forgetting.

He put the kettle on to boil and set about preparing his evening meal, thanking the god of microwaves and ready meals. *I'd like a drink*, he thought. *A glass of wine. The shop sold wine. I could pop back.*

Immediately he dismissed the thought. He hadn't drunk in months, not since . . . not since the days after the child had died, when he had collapsed in upon himself so completely and utterly that the remnants of self could be confined easily within a whisky glass.

Mac was not a drinker, never had been until then, and it appalled him now how easy it had been to take on that role. The microwave pinged and he removed the steaming dish, glancing back at the cardboard sleeve to check what it was he was eating before he committed himself. He stood beside the microwave, fork in hand, eating from the dish, trying to decide if his scratch meal did in fact resemble salmon in anything more than colour, and finally depositing what was left in the bin. He washed his fork and put it back in the kitchen drawer. Washing-up thus dealt with, he made some instant coffee and switched on the television, settled on the lumpy sofa for yet another night in front of the television then stared grimly at the flickering pictures and wondered where his life had gone.

SIX

The phone ringing at five to seven woke Mac just before the alarm was due to go off. He struggled from sleep, that five-minute discrepancy making an unaccountable amount of difference to his body clock.

'Hello. McGregor.' He sat up, listened, swung his legs out of bed. 'I'm on my way.'

Mac replaced the receiver and stared hard at the phone. 'Shit!' The uncarpeted floor was cold beneath his feet. He struggled into his clothes and grabbed his coat from where he had left it on the back of the chair. Should he take his car? No, it would take as long to retrieve it from where it was parked at the back of the police station as it would to walk down to the bottom end of Newell Street. Slamming the door hard, Mac ran down the stairs.

Outside Mrs Freer's little house were three police vehicles. One was scientific support. Two men clad in white coveralls stood beside the front door. Eden kept them company. He waved Mac over.

'She's dead?' Mac was incredulous.

'Found less than an hour ago. The woman who comes to get her up in the morning, she comes early. She's got a half-dozen to see first thing and Mrs Freer likes to be first.'

'Where is she now, the care worker?'

Eden pointed towards one of the police vehicles. A young woman in police uniform sat in the back seat with an older woman huddled in a grey tweed coat. She was crying, handkerchief alternately clamped to her mouth or dabbing furiously at her eyes.

'Is the doctor in there already? He got here fast.'

'Not anyone from the rota,' Eden said, referring to the list of medics available for crime-scene consultation. 'The care worker, Mrs Healey, knew there was a doctor living just up the road. She ran out of the house and fetched him here but it must have been obvious there was nothing he could do. He's talking to the crime-scene coordinator but he's confirmed death and given us a very approximate time. The old woman was lying on the floor and he reckons she was cold. We got a liver temp when the CSI arrived and we've got an estimate for about midnight, give or take.'

Mac nodded. 'How did she die?'

Eden took a deep breath. 'Some bastard beat her around the face and head. Then they ripped the place apart. I think we can make a guess what they were after.'

Mac swallowed the lump that had suddenly risen to fill his throat. He looked away.

Eden moved closer. 'Not your fault,' he said quietly. 'So get that out of your mind right now. This was not your fault.'

But it is, Mac thought. *It is. Just like the last time.*

* * *

The doctor emerged a few minutes later, shaken and pale. He had given all the information he could and handed over to the crime-scene coordinator. The two white-clad CSIs went inside. Uniformed officers took their place beside the door and Eden led Mac to one of the waiting cars. 'Might as well be warm,' he said. 'I've sent Andy to get us some coffee. I don't imagine you've had anything.'

Mac shook his head. 'I came straight here.'

'Well, nothing much we can do until the SOCOs have completed their bit and uniform let us in.'

'What about the care worker? Should I go and talk to her?'

'Already taken care of. I've got DS Birch seeing to that. She'll take her back to Dorchester, take a formal statement. Sally's a good girl. We were colleagues in my last job, though she was just a humble PC then.' He grinned, showing oddly white teeth. False, Mac thought. 'Not that our Sally was ever humble. You could never accuse her of being a shrinking violet.'

Mac sat back in the back seat and rubbed his eyes. 'So,' he asked, 'what do you want me to do?'

'Drink your coffee when Andy brings it and then just wait.'

'Neighbours?'

'Uniform were first on scene. They've got it covered and we're expecting reinforcements from Dorchester and Weymouth later. I'll have to organize a press call. You want to handle that?'

Although phrased as a question, Mac realized what response was actually expected. He winced inwardly. He hadn't done a press conference since . . . 'OK,' he agreed. 'I can take care of that.'

For a perverse moment, Mac resented that he had been dragged out of bed in such a hurry only to find himself without any useful task. He rebuked himself for even allowing the thought. A woman was dead; what was a little inconvenience compared to that? He knew from experience that he'd be busy soon enough. Eden was right: take time, drink coffee, discuss what little they knew.

'No disturbance in the night?'

'Nothing reported. Next door heard a bit of a bang around eleven, but didn't investigate further. The walls are thin but Mrs Freer lived downstairs and there's a hallway between the living room and the house next door. That would deaden most of the sound, I'd have thought.'

'And the bang was from downstairs?'

Eden laughed. 'Mrs Briggs says she couldn't tell. Mr Briggs argued that it must have been, seeing as how his neighbour can't get upstairs. My guess is they feel guilty for not investigating and it's better for the conscience not to be sure.'

'And the search, it was throughout the house?'

Eden nodded. 'Whoever it was turned the place over upstairs and down. It's a mess.'

'How did they get in?'

'Jimmied the back door, same as last time. It must have made a noise. The doorframe had been reinforced. It would have gone with a hell of a crack.'

'You think that's what the neighbours heard?'

'It could have been,' Eden agreed, 'but they were both adamant the bang came from inside the house and they've got a point. They were in the living room. Front of the house, all doors closed and the TV on, watching some action film or other, all loud noises and explosions.' He shrugged. 'I suggest you have another go later, let the implications sink in. Helpless old lady beaten to death only yards away while they watched the telly; thinking about that might jog their memories.'

'Or add what they *think* they might have heard. Think they *should* have heard,' Mac commented.

'Ay, well there's that too. Ah, here's Andy with the coffee. You took your time,' he growled as the red-haired boy opened the door.'

'Had to wait for the café to open, boss.'

He handed Eden and Mac tall, insulated cups, topped off with plastic lids. He hovered.

'Something else?' Eden asked.

'Er, no. I suppose not.'

'Then go and make yourself useful somewhere,' Eden told him.

'I think he wanted to be paid,' Mac observed wryly as the young man scurried off, cheeks as flame red as his hair.

Eden removed the plastic and took a long swig. 'Bugger, that's hot. Ay, well we don't always get what we hope for, do we?'

* * *

It was another hour before the body was ready to be removed and Mac and Eden allowed inside the house. Sharp sea air blowing through the hall had not entirely eliminated the stale odours that clung to the carpet and infiltrated the plaster and wallpaper, but another smell overlaid them now. Blood, death and a smell that told Mac that Mrs Freer had lost control of her bowels. Mac followed the designated path and entered the living room from where he had taken the handgun the day before. Mrs Freer lay in the narrow gap between her bed and the back of the sofa. The sofa had been eased aside to allow access but Mac could see the dents in the worn carpet where its castors had sat and noted the lighter patch of green that had been hidden from view and the tread of feet. The carpet hadn't been olive after all. Drawers had been pulled out from the wall unit and the contents emptied on to the floor. Paper and trinkets scattered and flung and the two easy chairs pushed aside, their seats ripped and slashed as though the intruder thought the old lady might have hidden something inside. The sofa had been treated in a similar fashion and its foam innards poked out obscenely through deep incisions in its back.

Mac realized he had been delaying the moment. Eden had already crossed the room and knelt now, close to the body, talking to the photographer and one of the CSIs. Mac came over to join him, steeling himself before he looked down. Before—for Mac, life was all made up of 'before' and 'after' the death of the child. 'Before', he had faced the dead with, if not equanimity, at least a degree of professional detachment. And after? Well, this was the first one 'after'. The first of the dead. He forced himself to look down and then to kneel beside the older detective, aware that other eyes watched him; others wondered what was causing him to delay. Even if they weren't, Mac felt that they must be.

He listened as Eden and the photographer discussed additional shots, distracting his mind with detail as his gaze took in the state of the body lying at his feet. Mrs Freer's head had been snapped back at an angle not possible in life. Mac didn't need to be told that her neck was broken. She stared at him, chin too high, back of the head too close to the opposite shoulder, so that she seemed to be straining to look back at someone standing behind her. Blood had pooled beside the ruined mouth, the fragile cheek broken by a blow that had caved it inward. Hair matted with blood.

'He must have grabbed her arms,' Eden said. 'Look at the bruising.'

Black marks stood out against white skin. Old flesh bruised easily, Mac thought, but even allowing for that the grip must have been cruelly strong.

Abruptly he stood up, marched outside, no longer caring who noticed or who commented. He stood outside the door trying to breathe, though his chest felt so tight that he could draw no air into his lungs and a red haze came down across his eyes.

No, he couldn't faint. He couldn't shame himself quite so completely.

Someone took his arm and he heard Eden's voice, felt himself being tugged slowly away from the door. Eden got him into the car and handed him what was left of the now cold coffee.

'Drink it up, caffeine will help. Or at least, that's what I tell myself.'

Automatically, Mac moved to obey, grimacing at the chilled and sour taste. 'I'm sorry,' he said. 'I don't know what happened.'

Eden held up a hand to silence him. 'It's the first one, isn't it? First time since that little girl.'

Mac blinked. 'You know about that? Of course you do. Everyone knows.'

'Not everyone, but I read your file and then I made a few discreet phone calls. I like to know who I'm working with.'

Mac laughed harshly.

'And you know what everyone told me? To a man they said that you were a good copper. The right sort. That you blamed yourself for summat no one could help. Lad, you could have had an army on that beach and that bastard still would have done the same. There'd still have been blood on the sand and that little girl lying dead. Only thing you did wrong, that is if we're going to be finding fault, is that you didn't get off after him fast enough.'

'I went to her,' Mac said. 'I wanted to see if . . .'

'If a miracle had happened and you could do anything to save her. Lad, it would have been obvious to a blind man that she was dead even before she hit the ground, but you know, I suspect that most of us would have done the same. What you did was misjudged, but it was human and I'd rather work with a human being anytime.'

Mac swallowed the last of the coffee. 'Thanks,' he said.

'What for? You ready to go back inside?'

Mac nodded.

'You take the upstairs, see what else she had, and I'll supervise the removal.'

'I'm all right now,' Mac protested.

'I don't doubt that you are,' Eden told him. 'Just to make sure, you'll be attending the autopsy, but for now . . .'

Mac nodded and got out of the car, waited while Eden eased his bulk through the door.

'Next of kin,' he asked, slipping back into the minutiae that kept his thinking under control.

'Next thing we've got to find,' Eden said.

* * *

The bedrooms had been layered in dust. In places, Mac could still make out the strata. Thick fluff settling to the bottom and clinging to the carpet; progressively finer sprinklings powdered over time, creating a veil of spider-silk grey across the boxes and the bed, the dressing table and the matching lamps that stood on white bedside tables either side of a pine bed.

A quick glance into the second room told him that it had been used for storage and, judging from the uncarpeted floor and magnolia walls, it had most likely always been that way. The intruder who had killed Mrs Freer—always supposing, Mac reminded himself, that there had only been the one— had rampaged through this tiny back bedroom. Mac guessed he'd soon realized there was nothing to find and that much of the damage—torn photographs, smashed glass, blankets pulled from the airing cupboard and slashed with the same ferocity evidenced by the sofa downstairs—had been actions of spite and frustration.

He picked up one of the torn blankets, sniffed. It smelled of age and mould. Damp and chill came out of the walls and rose from the uncarpeted floor. Mrs Freer didn't use the upstairs of her house; she probably didn't bother to heat it either. He'd noticed a gas fire in the living room and a small halogen heater in the kitchen. It was likely she just managed with those.

He wondered if Rina was responsible for the kitchen heater. Then he realized he'd have to be the one to break the news.

The bedroom had seen less ferocious treatment. The dust strata settled on the bed was still largely intact. Pink candlewick showed through the cobweb grey. The bed was still made and Mac wondered how many years it had waited like that, for sleepers who would no longer settle there.

The curtains were drawn and Mac tugged them open, setting off a cascade of dust that attacked his throat and eyes. He coughed spasmodically, rubbed his eyes with hands that he realized, belatedly, were filthy and grimed with more of what he was trying to wipe out. Rapid blinking produced tears and washed the worst of the grittiness away, bringing a modicum of relief.

Mac peered out of the dirty window, gazed down into the street. The funeral ambulance had arrived but scientific support had gone. Across the street a uniformed officer continued with his questions. Mac glanced sideways, towards the top end of the street, and wondered if he would, after all, be the one to tell Rina or if her antennae would be twitching even now.

The room was a little brighter now and Mac finished his search. Drawers had been pulled out here as they had downstairs but the ransack here was tidy in comparison. Drawers had been placed on the floor, their contents rifled, but not tipped out. Mac stooped to look. There was little to see—a box of matches, a paperback romance, a photograph. He looked more closely at the picture of the young couple, smartly dressed and gazing out with confidence at the camera. He turned it over. Written on the back in a tidy hand were the words *Trip to Edinburgh*. He remembered what Mrs Freer had told him about their travels.

'Honeymoon?' he wondered aloud. She had been a pretty woman. Mac closed his eyes to block the unbidden image of the body downstairs.

He checked the wardrobe. Old clothes, mostly male. A couple of winter coats and a pair of shoes. The drawers in the chest beside the window were empty. Mac noted that, apart from the top one, they had not even been pulled out. The dust was largely undisturbed.

Two searchers, Mac thought. Two people. One angry and vindictive and the second whose heart was not fully in it. *Find the second*, Mac thought. Find the second and they would break the case. The other one would tough it out. He might boast though.

Mac made his slow way downstairs and joined Eden in the living room. The photographer was finishing up, recording where the body had lain. Mac studied the blood stains, frowned.

'She fell on her right side first,' he said. 'Then was rolled on to her left?'

Eden nodded. 'That's the way I read it, and the scene coordinator suspects the same. Maybe he knocked her down, left her to bleed long enough for that patch to form, then he either rolled her or . . .'

Mac shook his head. 'If he'd rolled her, the two blood pools would be closer. He picked her up, hit her in the face and dropped her down again. She fell on her left side and that's how we found her.'

Eden nodded, his jaw working as though he chewed on this new insight. Mac was surprised at how detached he now felt. He had switched into survival mode. He knew, for now anyway, that he would be all right; he could do this.

'Bastard.' Eden spat the word.

Mac didn't feel any need to reply.

SEVEN

Midday found Mac back at Rina's door.

'I saw the police cars,' she said. 'I knew you'd come. It's Mrs Freer, isn't it?'

Mac nodded.

'Come inside.' She led him not through to the kitchen this time, but into a small side room. 'Sit down,' she said, pointing to a comfortable armchair set on one side of the fireplace. Mac sat. Rina took the other chair. 'They were after the gun, I suppose.' She sounded resigned, weary.

'Nothing seems to have been taken,' he confirmed. 'It's hard to tell, the place is a mess, but we don't think there's anything missing.'

'And, of course, the gun wasn't there.'

'Mrs Martin, I had to have it checked out.' Mac was angry with himself and that anger transmitted in his voice.

Rina waved it and him aside. 'I don't imagine it would have made much difference anyway,' she said. 'It wasn't as if she could have used it and I don't suppose it would have stopped them doing . . . what did they do to her?'

'She's dead,' Mac said shortly.

'How?' Rina wasn't letting him off that easy.

Mac sighed, seeing in his mind's eye the bloody mess that had once been a face. 'Someone beat her around the head and face,' he said. 'There's no way she could have defended herself.'

Rina absorbed that silently and Mac wondered what it was about this woman that encouraged him to tell her so much.

'So, what now?' Rina asked finally. She got up from the chair and poured bottled water into an electric kettle. She set it to boil, glancing at him to ask if he'd prefer tea or coffee.

'Coffee, please.'

'I'm afraid it's only instant. Will that do?'

'Just now, anything will do,' Mac said. He watched as she unscrewed the jar, spooned the granules into two mugs, added sugar. He heard someone go past in the hall, pause by the door and then move on.

'They don't disturb me when the door is closed,' she said. She poured the water, added milk which she took from a tiny fridge beneath the shelf that supported the kettle and mugs, and set their drinks on a little table between the chairs.

'This is your sanctuary, then?' Mac smiled at his own choice of words. It sounded a little pretentious, but Rina nodded.

'We all need a space to call our own,' she said. 'I'm very fond of my curious little family and I've known most of them for more years than I care to count, but we all need a place to think and sit and ignore the world.'

Mac thought about his lonely little flat. He understood what she meant but his problem was that he had little else but space to think. He leaned forward to collect his coffee mug. 'You think of your residents as family, then.'

'In a manner of speaking.' Rina's mouth twitched. 'And as with all families, I am often irritated and affectionate in equal measure.'

Mac laughed but it occurred to him that he really wouldn't know. He didn't have what you'd call family, just people he was distantly related to. 'You all worked together?' he asked.

'At one time or another. We all performed on the same circuit. All except Tim, of course. He's far too young to remember *our* glory days.'

'So how come . . . ?'

'He's living here with all the old codgers? Oh, Tim is old in spirit if not in years, though, given time and the right breaks, he might rejuvenate.'

Mac frowned, puzzled. 'Is he any good?' he asked.

'As Marvello or Stupendo?' Rina laughed. 'Oh, very good, technically. The trouble is he hasn't a clue when it comes to performance, at least not with the audience he usually gets. I've told him many a time to sack his agent, sign up for the cruise liners where at least he'll get to do an adult show.'

'Adult?' Mac was momentarily flummoxed. Was there such a thing as pornographic magic?

Rina peered at him over the rim of her mug. 'As opposed to children,' she said sternly as she lowered it. 'He makes a bloody awful clown.'

'Ah,' Mac said, feeling himself firmly put in his place.

'And so, what now? Are you likely to catch this bastard?'

Mac blinked. Mrs Martin coming that close to swearing somehow disturbed him. He nodded. 'We'll catch him. Or them.'

'Them? Any reason to believe it was a "them"?'

'Mrs Martin . . .'

'Rina.'

'Rina, this is an active investigation and I can't . . .'

'Come off it, man. I'm hardly going to talk about it outside of this room, am I? Oh, I might discuss things with Tim, but not the others. Is there any reason to believe it was more than one person?'

Mac hesitated, then sighed. 'The night of the attempted burglary,' he began. 'When I talked to Mrs Freer, she was sure that the intruders were only young—thirteen, fourteen, not older. Do you think—?'

'That she had enough marbles to make that sort of judgement? What do you think?'

'She seemed lucid. Mostly,' Mac said.

'And you think these two came back?'

'I've no way of knowing.'

Rina sighed. 'I didn't ask you what you knew; I asked you what you thought. What *I* think is that it's unlikely. She'd scared them off once; why would they come back?'

Mac nodded. 'It's possible they bought a new batch of courage at the local off-licence,' he said. 'Or rather, that they got someone else to buy it for them.'

'It's possible. And if not?'

'Kids talk,' Mac said. 'They boast or they tell tales, or they drop hints—to other kids, not to parents or anyone who might do anything about it but . . .'

'And this would be too good a story to keep *stumm* about.' Rina sounded as though she approved of his reasoning and Mac felt unaccountably pleased. Mentally, he shook himself.

'And the "more than one" aspect?'

'I don't know. The downstairs room was torn about, the search was untidy and . . . violent. Whoever it was, they slashed the cushions, hacked at the sofa. Upstairs, whoever had gone into the bedroom had been almost careful. Disturbed stuff as little as possible. There were still layers of dust with not so much as a handprint.'

'So, two then. A thug and a follower. You'll find a fair few of those round here and not just among the younger generation.'

'I think you'll find them anywhere,' Mac said. 'It's a fairly common formation.'

'Leaders, followers and those that get out of the way,' Rina declared.

'Sorry?' She had lost Mac now.

'Society,' Rina said. 'It's made up of leaders, followers and most of the rest of us, those that get out of the way and keep their heads down.'

Mac didn't think whoever invented the saying had quite that interpretation in mind.

'Who was it said that all it took for evil to prosper was for good men to stay silent?' She shrugged. 'I don't recall the exact quote, but you get my meaning.'

'I think so, yes.' He smiled. 'But I don't see you as a woman who gets out of the way.'

'Never have,' she said. 'I don't suppose I ever will. Not till the day they put me in my box.' She smiled wryly. 'I don't suppose I've even been much of a follower either, but that's another story. What do you do now?'

'House to house, further interviews with the neighbours; we pull in anyone with a record for violence or burglary, we sift what we've got and hope something emerges.'

'And forensics?'

'SOCO are still at the scene, though Mrs Freer has been taken away. With luck there'll be prints.'

'And, of course, there will have been transfer.'

Mac raised an eyebrow.

'Locard's theory. I did my research, remember? The notion that we always take something away and leave something behind. If the search was as untidy and the attack as violent as you say, then there'll be blood and fibres. It's possible she even managed to mark the bastard.'

'It's possible. We'll know more after the post-mortem.' Mac was suddenly weary. 'My sergeant sees you as a major repository of local knowledge. Did Mrs Freer mention anyone or anything she might have had trouble with?'

Rina shook her head. 'She didn't *see* anyone to have trouble with them. Never went out, never opened her door to anyone unless she knew them. Kept her doors and windows locked. I managed to coax her out into that bit of a garden when the weather was warm enough, but she'd only sit out if I was there. "Outside" had become a frightful and frightening place but the fear was general, not specific. You should try the neighbours, though. The Robinsons, three doors down. I know they had some trouble with kids on motorbikes, she told me about it—Mrs Freer, that was, not Nora Robinson.

She wouldn't give me the time of day, never mind engage in conversation.'

'But she talked to Mrs Freer?'

Rina's head shake was rapid and assertive. 'No, no, Mrs Robinson was part of the great "outside". No, she heard them in the street, arguing with the kids. They ride their bikes over on that wasteland by the sheds. There's a footpath comes through just down from the Robinsons and the kids used it to get back on to the road. Dangerous, of course—we all complained—but the Robinsons took it personally.'

'Thanks,' Mac said. It was the second time he'd heard about kids and bikes by the sheds. Reluctantly he hauled himself out of the rather too comfortable chair. 'I'd best be off.'

'I'll see you out.'

'Oh, one other thing, nothing to do with Mrs Freer. A couple of nights now I've seen lights round by Marlborough Head. Would that be fishermen?'

Rina frowned. 'Not close in by the head, no. Boats do go out late, but the rocks round by the point . . . not a good place to be at night.'

'Thanks again.' Mac nodded. 'Probably nothing.' *Probably just a man with too much time on his hands, staring out of the window when he should be finding something better to do. Like looking for a more permanent place to live.*

EIGHT

George Parker hated the school bus. He hated the barging and the pushing and the shouts of the other kids. He loathed the way the driver yelled at them all from behind his protective screen and clearly thought they were all tarred with the same brush, as George's Nan would have said. George wanted to tell him he was different, not a trouble maker, but he figured the driver wouldn't really care anyhow. Most of all George hated the fact that his best friend Paul was off school and that someone else was bound to make a point of sitting down beside him.

'Kissed any girls lately, Georgie Porgie?' Dwayne Regis's taunt was a usual one and one of the milder that George had to endure.

Heard it before, Dwayne, George thought, but he said nothing. He pulled his bag from the seat just before Dwayne crashed down upon it. It could have been worse, George reflected. On his own Dwayne was mostly harmless. Dwayne liked to hang out with the older kids on the Jubilee. George and the others on the bus were just a passing amusement.

'So, have you?' Dwayne persisted.

'Have I what?'

'Kissed any girls?'

George glanced sidelong at him. Dwayne was grinning. No change there; Dwayne was always grinning. He grinned inanely in response to the teacher's questions, triumphantly when he managed to scare one of the younger kids, and stubbornly when hauled up in front of the Head, which for Dwayne was a far too common occurrence for it to be a threat any longer.

'I heard that's not all you bin doin'.' Dwayne's grin stretched even wider.

George shrugged. 'Don't know what you mean.'

A burst of laughter this time. Cruel, harsh. 'That ain't what I hear.'

'And what do you hear?' George tried to keep it casual but his heart seemed to have other ideas and was beating like a hammer.

'I hear you took to scaring old ladies.'

George shrugged as carelessly as he could. He turned to look fully at Dwayne, trying to ignore the stupid grin which, broad as it was, was never reflected in the cold, ice-blue eyes. 'Don't know what you mean.'

'She wet herself, did she? The old bird. Wet herself when she saw you and that other plonker? Where's he at today anyway? Stopped at home with his mummy, has he?'

'Paul's sick,' George said.

'Anyway, I hear she scared you off.'

'Still don't know what you mean.' The hammering in George's chest had grown so loud he was sure it could be heard.

Dwayne sat back in his seat and howled a mirthless laugh. 'Scared off by an old lady. Georgie Porgie ickle scaredy baby.'

George turned away and stared steadfastly out of the bus window. He could feel the colour rising to his cheeks, knew it would soon be a close match to his shock of scarlet hair. He blushed like a girl, his dad said, and somehow that thought calmed him down if only because it reminded him that he hated his dad even more than he hated Dwayne and the rest. Hated him, but managed to survive him. George drew strength from that thought.

They were only a few minutes from home now and Dwayne would get off first when they passed the Jubilee Estate. Or at least he ought to. Occasionally he'd stay on the bus for another stop, just so he could torment George for that little bit longer.

Dwayne shifted on the seat and leaned in close, so close that George could feel his breath on the back of his neck. Smell that he'd been eating those cheese crisp things that George hated. 'I know *how* she scared you off anyway,' Dwayne said. 'I hear Paul told Mark Dowling all about it.'

George spun to face the other boy. Dwayne was so close they were almost nose to nose. Paul would never tell anything to Mark Dowling.

'I hear she had a gun,' Dwayne whispered. 'True, was it, she threatened to shoot, did she, Georgie?'

The bus shuddered to a halt and Dwayne, still grinning, pushed off from his seat and barged his way along the aisle to the front of the bus. George watched him go. His heart had enlarged now, big enough to fill his chest and block his throat. The bus moved off and Dwayne waved at him from the pavement, the grin fixed and rigid.

Paul and Mark Dowling? George was chilled now. Shivering despite the bus heater that blasted hot air beneath his seat. His stop arrived a few minutes later and George stumbled to his feet, joined the queue of those getting off, as usual one of the last to leave.

Mark Dowling, George thought. The colour had drained from his face now. He could feel it slipping down from his cheeks and his neck, leaving behind his usual white, pasty skin speckled with an overgenerous spattering of freckles.

He waited until the bus moved off and then started to cross the road, his route home taking him past Mrs Freer's house. He glanced up and then stopped dead.

Police cars, tape, white-clad figures moving inside the front room. For a wild second or two, George convinced himself that this wasn't real. Someone was shooting a film—that was it. He'd see it on TV sometime and be able to say, 'Oh yeah, I saw them filming on my street.' This wasn't the old woman's house; it couldn't be.

But it was.

George felt the pavement shift beneath his feet. The world grew fuzzy round the edges. He swallowed hard to fight the sickness rising in his throat. What was happening here?

One of the policemen looked his way, his gaze quizzical and accusing. George turned and walked on down the road, crossing only when he was opposite his own house.

They know, he thought. *They must know.* The way that policeman had looked at him. Worse still, Dwayne knew and worse even than that, Mark Dowling knew.

He fumbled in his pocket for his key and stumbled inside, slamming the front door hard. It would be another hour at least before his mum got home and his sister probably wouldn't be in till after that, if she bothered coming home at all. These days she stayed over at her boyfriend's place more often than she came back here. For a brief moment George thought about phoning her. He and Karen got on better than most siblings he knew, probably because they'd both been through so much. Probably because of what had happened with their dad. Karen would go mad at him but she'd listen, try to help. George knew better than even to try and talk to his mum. Too ground down by the troubles she'd already encountered in her life, George and Karen were both careful of anything that might rub yet another hole in the thin foil she had become. Not that she'd ever been that reliable, he thought bitterly. She'd been the one to name him George.

George dropped his bag and sat down on the bottom step, reached through between the spindles to grab the phone from the hall table. He dialled Paul's number and waited impatiently, staring at the front door, half afraid the policeman who had looked at him would have followed him home.

'Yeah?' Paul didn't have the best telephone technique.

'You weren't at school.'

'Quick that, you noticing.'

'What's up with you?'

'I . . . er . . . I fell down the stairs. Mum thought I'd busted my arm, dragged me to casualty.'

Someone's there, George thought. *Listening.*

'Fell down the stairs?' he repeated.

'Yeah,' Paul told him. 'You know, like you do.'

'Yeah, I know how you do.' He closed his eyes. His mother had 'fallen down the stairs' more times than George could count. Paul knew that. The difference was, Paul's dad didn't beat him up. So who had?

'Mark Dowling?' he asked softly, scared that whoever was listening would catch the name and ask what it meant.

'Y'know.' George could hear the shrug in his friend's voice. 'These things happen. At least it's not bust.' He paused. George heard a woman's voice in the background. 'Mum says you can come round. Stop for tea. You coming?'

George breathed relief, realizing how much he didn't want to be alone.

'Thanks,' he said. 'Be right there.'

He reached back through the stair rails and dropped the phone back on the cradle. He peered cautiously out through the front-room window before opening the door and then ran full pelt to where, three doors down, Paul was waiting for him.

NINE

Tea at Paul's house had been a stilted affair. George wolfed the sausage, egg and chips with extra bread and butter that Paul's mother served up for them and drank down two mugs of the strong, sweet tea. She gave them both a can of Coke and a chocolate bar and watched anxiously from the kitchen door while the boys headed upstairs to Paul's room.

Paul had eaten almost nothing, just played with his meal and finally, reluctantly, ploughed his way through just enough to satisfy his mum before asking if they could leave the table.

'Your dad won't be home till late,' she told him. 'I'll be getting his dinner for when he comes in. You want me to do you something? You might feel more like it later.'

Paul shook his head and grunted something unintelligible. His mother sighed. 'OK, get along with the pair of you, but just you watch that arm.'

George sat down on the edge of his friend's bed and watched as he set up the computer game. Paul had got the latest *Final Fantasy* a couple of weeks before and, ordinarily, George would be almost salivating with anticipation. Today though, he saw Paul's fumbling about with the connections and taking extra time fiddling for exactly what it was:

delaying tactics so he didn't have to talk. George had been shocked by the sight of his friend. Two black eyes, purpling now at the edges, dark bruises on the back of his arm that even a parent couldn't mistake for anything other than deep finger marks and an elbow so swollen and painful that even just plugging in the connections caused him to wince.

'She knows you never fell down the stairs,' George said finally. 'Yer mum's not daft.'

Paul shrugged. 'She's hoping you'll get it out of me,' he said flatly.

'So, what do you want me to tell her when she asks?'

Paul shrugged. 'How should I know?'

'So, what *don't* you want me to tell her? That Mark Dowling beat you up?'

Paul sighed and handed the controller to George. 'Play if you want. It hurts my hand.'

George shrugged. 'Better make some noise anyway,' he said. He moved back on the bed and selected his character, sensing that he'd be more likely to get the truth out of his friend if he let him take his time and at least appeared not to be listening. That was the thing with Paul. He kept his thoughts and his feelings locked up some place even George was rarely allowed access to. It was something George didn't really understand about him. Paul's family was happy, close, nice, and yet he seemed to think he had a duty to keep himself a bit apart.

George told himself he'd love to have parents like Paul's but in his more honest moments he wasn't sure that was true. He didn't really know what that would be like and he wasn't sure that his imagination was capable of grasping it.

'Dwayne was on the bus,' he said. His thumbs shifted automatically across the control pad. 'He reckoned he knew about the old lady. That Mark Dowling knew. He said you told him.'

Out of the corner of his eye he saw Paul shrug. He came over and sat down next to George, his back against the wall, eyes fixed on the screen.

'The police are there, at the old lady's house. I saw them. I had to walk past when I got off the bus.'

'He killed her,' Paul said softly. 'He bashed her head in.'

George dropped the controller. 'He *what*?' He stared at Paul. 'How? When? How do you know? Do the police know? I mean . . .'

Paul stared straight at the screen, his body rigid, face white beneath the blackened bruising. 'I know 'cause I was there,' he said. 'He beat her up and her face was all bashed in and there was blood all over and she was just lying there on the floor and I didn't do nothing to stop him.'

George stared wide-eyed and open-mouthed, the food he had so recently eaten suddenly greasy and leaden in his belly.

'I told him about the gun,' Paul whispered. Gingerly, he fingered his damaged elbow. 'He made me tell.'

TEN

The silence between them seemed to George like a solid thing. Across the room the computer game played out a fantasy battle, dramatic music sounding softly and then ceasing as George slithered off the bed and reached to put the game on pause.

He wished that it was possible to put real life on pause. Stop it dead until you could figure out what to do.

'You went with him? Back to the old woman's house?'

'Mrs Freer,' Paul said. 'Mam says she was called Mrs Freer. I never even knew that.'

'How did Mark Dowling hear about the gun? Paul, you gotta have said something to someone for him to know about it.'

He turned, stared hard at his friend. Paul had his eyes closed but the tears still crept beneath the lids and he'd pulled his knees close to his chest, drawing in on himself.

'I never told no one,' Paul blurted. 'Someone seen us that night, when . . . when we broke in.'

'Jesus.' George crossed back to the bed, curled himself at the opposite end, his tense body a mirror image of his friend's. 'Who? We didn't see no one.'

'I don't know. Mark just said someone seen us go in then seen us leave. He was laughing at me, running away from some old woman like . . . like . . . anyway, I got mad. I said he'd have run too.'

'Mark Dowling? He don't run from anything. He's an effing psycho.'

'I tried to take it back, George—tell him I didn't mean nothing—but he wouldn't believe me. He said he wanted to know what I meant and that he'd beat it out of me if he had to.'

Looking at his friend, George figured that was exactly what Mark Dowling had done. He remembered the blows he had received at the hands of his own father, the way his dad thrashed his mum until she was begging for him to let up. He remembered how he'd stood there, watching, just too scared to intervene after that first time when he'd tried to protect her. Tried and failed. Tried and, as she'd later thrown back at him, just made it worse.

George of all people could understand how Paul had frozen, been unable to intervene, but still he couldn't stop the question falling from his mouth. 'Why'd you go with him? Why didn't you scarper, go and get help? Why didn't you come home and call the police? They might have been able to . . .'

He broke off; the bruising on Paul's face seemed now to be darkening, pinching his face closed, contorting it with pain. 'Don't you ever tell my mam,' he whispered. 'Don't you ever. I swear, you ever let on and I'll . . .'

George swallowed hard. 'She'll want to know something,' he said softly. 'Paul, she's seen your arms, your face; she knows you never fell down the stairs. She knows something's up. Besides, Mark Dowling went and killed that woman. We gotta tell someone that.'

'No!' Paul almost shouted it. Both boys stared at the door, afraid the sound would have brought Paul's mother up the stairs.

'No,' he repeated quietly. 'I'll get blamed too, won't I? You said yourself, I never done nothing to help. They'll say I might have saved her. Might have stopped him.'

'But he *killed* her, Paul.'

'And he only knew about the gun because I told him and we only knew about it because . . . because of what we did, so it's our fault too.'

George closed his eyes and leaned his head back against the wall. There was no denying their own guilt and, to be truthful, he could no longer be certain why the hell they had done what they had that night. 'We were pissed,' he said.

'That make it better?'

'No. Course it doesn't, but that's why we done it. Shaz Bates's cider.' Actually, George wasn't too sure it had been just cider. It had had a kick to it that cider didn't usually have—at least from his limited knowledge of it—and Shaz Bates's dad was known to have a well-stocked bar. It wouldn't be the first time she had mixed it. And that brought another bit of the puzzle into focus for George. Who might have seen them? Shaz was one of Mark Dowling's little gang, or at least she was on the fringes of it, her older brother being one of Dowling's friends.

'She must have been the one what seen us,' he said. 'When we left everyone at the tin huts, she said she'd have to get off home. She must have seen.'

Miserably, Paul nodded. Had they been sober, George figured, they might have thought it was odd that Shaz was leaving what was really her party so early. The Bates family had never been one to chase up the whereabouts of their numerous kids or to insist on early bed on school nights. And she'd been the one who'd said . . .

'She said I didn't have the nerve,' Paul said and George realized that this was the first time it had all made sense to him. What Shaz had *actually* said, George recalled, was that she reckoned Paul would piss himself, that he was a mammy's boy, that he didn't have what it took. George had asked what did that prove anyway; it just showed that Paul was a nice person, and everyone had jeered at that, laughed until Paul had been red in the face with shame.

George recalled the brief argument they had after leaving the sheds, Paul walking with exaggerated care across the rough ground and announcing loudly to the world that he was capable of anything.

'She keeps cash in her kitchen drawer, everyone knows that, just like me nan does, and all we have to do is get in there and—'

'*Steal* it.' George had reminded him. 'It's thieving, Paul, and she's an old woman. You don't steal from an old woman. She might *be* your nan.'

'She ain't my nan. I don't even know her.' Paul fell over, lay on his back staring up at the night sky until George hauled him back on to his feet.

'OK, then, ok. I won't take nothing. No money or nothing, just a little something or other to prove we done it.'

'We?'

'You coming with me?'

'Paul, I don't want to. It's stupid.' George had only had a swig or two of the cider cocktail. Enough to get light headed and to seem to be fitting in, but he'd lost track of how much Paul had drunk. 'It's late,' he said. 'We should be getting home.'

'I'm not a kid,' Paul had muttered angrily. 'Not a bloody kid.'

Now, sat together on Paul's bed, the memory of that fateful night became all too clear. 'It weren't your fault,' Paul said, his voice harsh with unshed tears. 'You just went with me. I'd have gone anyway.'

'No. No you wouldn't. You'd have fallen over in another ditch or forgot where you were going or summat. You wouldn't have done it on your own. I wouldn't have done it on my own neither.'

The silence thumped down between them once again and George stared at the paused screen, a small part of him wanting to pick up the controllers and beat seven shades out of the monsters, as if there was nothing wrong.

'We could talk to Karen,' he said finally. 'She'd know what to do.'

Paul shrugged and then winced. 'Maybe.' He bit his lip. 'Mam wanted to call the police. She said she thought I'd been in a fight or something. Wanted to know if I was being bullied.' He laughed harshly.

'I guess Mark Dowling would count as a bully,' George said, and for a moment they both laughed.

Paul wiped his eyes with the back of his hand. 'I don't know what to do,' he confessed.

'We talk to Karen,' George reaffirmed. 'I dunno if she'll be back tonight, but she's promised to be home tomorrow after work. We gotta talk to someone; Karen will know what to do.'

Paul nodded reluctantly but George could see the relief already dawning in his eyes. George had told Paul how it was Karen who had got them away from his dad, Karen who'd taken over when their mum had been put in hospital that last time. Karen who'd taken George and camped out in the front office of the local police station, refusing to move until they got the help they needed and then Karen who'd made sure they kept moving on and moving on until they were so far from their start point and from their dad that she felt safe enough to settle down.

George gnawed on his lower lip and glanced once more at the game screen, wishing again that it was possible to put life on pause. He had something else on his mind, something that under other circumstances he'd have wanted so much to share with Paul.

Yesterday, and then again today, he had glimpsed someone standing on the street as the bus had pulled away from school. The man had been bundled up against the rain and cold, but George was certain now that it had been his dad.

ELEVEN

Friday night, and another lonely one for Mac. He had chan-nel-surfed for a while, flicking between gardening programmes and quiz shows and a hospital drama that held his attention for ten minutes or so before the sight of so much fake blood reminded him of Mrs Freer and he abandoned it. Finally he switched off the set and wandered restlessly over to the win-dow, twitched the curtain aside and peered out into the night.

Outside the evening breeze had stiffened, beating the high tide into a frenzy and crashing waves against the sea wall. Mac watched the spray soaking the promenade and the little clouds scudding fast across a starry sky. The forecast for tomorrow had looked good but he guessed a turn in the weather was on its way.

Irritably, he let the curtain fall. He seemed to have become obsessed with weather watching since moving here. Stupid really; he'd spent almost all of his adult life living close to the sea and it had never occurred to him until now that he might have a predilection for forecasting. Perhaps it was that this southern coast seemed so much more exposed, which in itself was a foolish thought. The east coast with which he was so familiar was every bit as weather-ridden and far more prone to storms.

Knowing he'd be unable to settle, Mac wrapped himself against the cold and went out into the night. The strengthening wind battered him the moment he opened the door, grabbing at his coat and tugging at his well wound scarf. Mac wished he'd thought to get himself a hat. He'd resisted because, no matter what style he chose, he still managed to look as though he'd borrowed it as a joke. His hair fought hats, pushing them off, and his face, rather long and too heavy about the jaw, just looked even more unbalanced with something stuck to the top of his head. In his youth, people had described him as square jawed and the kindest had told him he had 'strong features'. Mac knew what that meant: you can't be handsome so settle for interesting. He lifted his gloved hand and examined his jaw line, worrying that 'square' would, when he got to Eden's age, translate into jowls.

Cold sea spray hitting him full force in the eyes encouraged him to turn off the promenade and he turned inland, unconsciously tracking back towards Newell Street and Peverill Lodge. He caught himself pausing outside Rina's imposing house, noting that a light was on in Rina's private sanctuary.

For the briefest of moments he toyed with the idea of knocking on her door, but what should he say when she answered? What excuse could he give? It had been a long time, Mac reflected painfully, since he had simply and spontaneously called to see someone just because he wanted to. A terrifyingly long time since he'd just been to see a friend.

Angry now that he was so morose; morose because he was angry and to no purpose, Mac walked swiftly on, turning left at the crossroads before he reached the lower end of Newell Street and was walking a parallel course to the promenade. Here between the houses it was sheltered and not so bitingly cold.

'Your own fault,' Mac muttered to himself. 'You've not exactly tried, have you?'

Self-consciously, he glanced around, glad that the cold had kept even the hardiest of souls inside and there was no one to hear. Up ahead of him the lights of the Railway pub twinkled enticingly. Mac drew level with it on the opposite side of the road, stared through the half opened curtains at the Friday-night crowd, recalling that the victims of two of the burglaries were regulars there.

Should he go inside? He'd been meaning to anyway, get the lie of the land, ask a few meaningful questions. Irresolute, he crossed the road and loitered on the pavement. An A-frame sign toppled over by the wind advertised a quiz night every Thursday at seven. Mac righted it, noting the smaller notice tacked alongside that appealed for new competitors.

Mac thought about it. Maybe he should go in and ask. Maybe that would be the perfect way to get involved with the local community. Maybe even a way to . . . Mac balked at the phrase 'make friends'.

A quiz team? Mac turned away. What the hell did he know about quiz teams? Irrationally irritated, he walked back the way he'd come. He was cold now, despite the coat and gloves and tightly wound scarf. His ears were stinging and his eyes running as he strode towards Newell Street. The wind had changed direction, veering so that it was directly in his face as he headed home. Mac lowered his head, blinking wind and dust and cold sea spray from his eyes.

Once inside, he closed the door against the world and hung his damp coat on the back of a chair to dry. Then, standing at the centre of his barren living room, Mac made himself a promise. Things would change, he told himself. Tomorrow he'd go along, sign up for the Thursday night battle in the Railway, make the effort, but his heart sank at the thought of it and his shoulders sagged beneath the weight of so small but heavy a decision. Sighing, Mac switched the television on and settled on the lumpy sofa, marking time until it was late enough to sleep, unreasonably eager for the working day to begin again.

* * *

George Parker was alone in his room. Karen had phoned to say she wouldn't be back that night but she'd promised to be home after work on Saturday and that she'd stay to cook Sunday lunch.

'I need to talk to you,' George told her.

'What's wrong? Is Mum OK?'

'Yeah, she's fine. It's . . . something else, but it's important, Kaz.'

He heard her stifle a small sigh. 'OK, little brother, I'll sort you out tomorrow. Promise ya.'

George stared at the portable TV he had set up on the flat-pack desk in the corner of his room. He'd done his homework, early for once. Anything to take his mind off all the other stuff. From downstairs he could hear his mother watching some late-night chat thing in the living room. She'd sit there until she was finally exhausted enough to drop off and quite often George would find her still there in the morning, the TV talking to itself, his mother oblivious on the couch. He'd taken to wandering down about midnight, covering her with a blanket so she didn't wake up cold. He never disturbed her, never. Not even to suggest she'd be more comfortable in bed. She found it so hard to sleep anyway, especially now the doctor had told her he wouldn't give her any more pills, and George would never dream of disturbing what little rest she managed to get.

He'd found an action film to watch—all loud explosions and no plot—but he was finding it hard to follow even what little story there was.

He and Paul were in deep shit this time, he thought. Worse even than when he'd had to deal with his dad. George had never thought anything could be worse than that, but now it looked like he might be back too.

* * *

Mark Dowling was alone too that night, and that in itself was unusual. Mark was not someone given to solitude; his persona depended far too heavily on the identification made by others. Alone, Mark was somewhat less than whole.

Lying on his back in the middle of a messy bed, surrounded by the remnants of a six pack he'd taken from the fridge just over an hour before, Mark Dowling was feeling remarkably pleased with himself.

TWELVE

Saturday morning saw Mac back at the murder scene, preliminary reports in hand.

He stood in the silence of Mrs Freer's hall and remembered his first visit and the difficulty the old lady had just manoeuvring her walking frame back into the kitchen. It seemed almost doubly obscene—and murder, in Mac's view, was the ultimate in obscenity—that the dead woman should have been so unable to defend herself. Would it have been better if she'd had the gun? Not that he could have just turned a blind eye, but . . . *No*, Mac thought, recalling the damage done to Mrs Freer's face and frail body. No, whoever had broken in that second time had no intention of leaving her alive or of being frightened off. Mac had no doubt that the frustration at finding the weapon gone had added to the frenzy of the attack, but it would have taken place and with the same outcome whatever.

Mac had to hope that the woman had lost consciousness after that first blow to the face and that she had known nothing more.

Report in hand, he went through to the kitchen and examined the back door. Steel screens kept out the weather and secured the entrance but the back door itself had been left open and in place. The original lock was weak and almost worthless and whoever had broken in that first time had gained entry simply by prizing open the door. A stout screwdriver could have done it, Mac thought and, looking closely at the tool marks, he guessed that was what it might turn out to be. Whoever had repaired the door had strengthened the frame and replaced the old lock with another basic one, the sort you could buy at any hardware store.

The murderer had taken a direct approach and had simply kicked in the lower panel, reached through and turned the key.

Simple.

Mac tried not to imagine the degree of fear she must have felt when she heard the splintering wood and knew that someone was forcing their way inside. Why, he wondered, didn't she have one of those alarm necklace things she could wear around her neck? His aunt had had one, although Mac remembered that getting her to keep it around her neck was another matter, and she was forever knocking it off her bedside table at night.

He bent down and studied the door more closely. There was an old bolt fitted low down, but when Mac tried it, he found it stiff and tight and so ingrained with dirt he doubted it had been shifted in years. A second bolt had been inexpertly fitted higher up. Shiny and chrome, it stood out against the grubby paintwork and though this moved more easily Mac doubted she would have bothered. She would have found it hard enough to turn the key without then struggling with a bolt, Mac thought, seeing in his mind's eye the difficulty Mrs Freer had in filling the kettle and inserting the plug into the socket on the wall.

He left the kitchen and returned to the hall. Blood drops had been found at the bottom of the stairs, dripped on to the painted wood of the skirting board and the carpet on the last tread. Drops, not spatter, the report had said, so not from Mrs Freer, even though the blood group happened to be the same. Someone had stood there and bled. The killer? Who else? Unless a visitor had cut themselves, and that seemed improbable. A visitor who had been upstairs, cut themselves and then bled on the way back down? More likely the blood belonged to that second person who had searched the upstairs rooms.

Why hadn't the killer used a knife? Mac wondered. It was something that had been troubling him since he had first seen the body, and the report now confirmed that the injuries were all blunt-force trauma, weapon as yet unknown. Looking again at the slashing wounds inflicted upon the sofa and the chair and even the mattress, Mac was struck again by the fact that the killer hadn't used a knife on Mrs Freer. Flicking through the photographs, relieved that he was, at least, managing to distance himself enough not to want to throw up, he was forcibly reminded of just how brutal and how frenzied the attack had been. Whoever had done this had really lost all sense of proportion or restraint. The injuries spoke of fury and frustration and out-and-out rage. Somehow, a knife would have almost been too precise, too considered. Whatever the killer had used to beat the old lady to death had been brought down again and again, harder and harder and with no thought or purpose to it other than to inflict more punishment and pain.

Most people backed off when their victim went down. Most creatures stopped attacking when their prey stopped moving. Whoever had done this had not been so merciful.

Glancing out through the front-room window Mac noticed a red-haired boy standing on the opposite pavement. He could have passed for a younger brother of Andy, the red-haired probationer back at the station, and Mac called to mind a comment made on the day of the murder. The police officer on watch had noted the red-haired teenager who'd got off the school bus and then stood as though stopped in his tracks by the sight of the activity.

Not that it was unusual for people to rubber-neck at a crime scene. But it was unusual for them to come back and to stand so obviously waiting to be noticed. Glancing at his watch and noting that it was almost time for him to talk to the waiting press, Mac got his things together and left the scene.

The boy still waited, trying to look nonchalant, but succeeding only in looking scared.

Mac crossed over the road. 'Hi,' he said.

The boy shrugged, then replied, 'Hi.' He shuffled his feet, staring down at them. His shoes were old, Mac noted. Scuffed and cheap and regulation black, the sort you had to wear for school and not something a kid would choose to wear on a weekend.

'Did you know her?' Mac asked. 'The old lady that was killed?'

The boy shrugged again, more eloquently this time, one shoulder rising as the other fell. It was, Mac thought, communication of sorts.

'Well, if there's anything you can tell me . . .'

The boy glanced up, briefly meeting Mac's gaze, then he looked away and a look, half relief, half irritation, crossed his face. Relief won out and Mac followed the direction of his gaze. Another boy, this one taller and with dark hair, had come out of a house three doors down from the murder scene. He stood uncertainly, staring at Mac and obviously reluctant to come over while he was there.

'See ya,' the red-haired one said and went off to join his friend. Mac watched as they went back inside the house, noting as the dark-haired boy shot a final look in his direction that his face was very badly bruised, one eye almost swollen closed. Two boys, Mac thought, thirteen or fourteen years old, and they would certainly know that Mrs Freer lived alone.

He walked down to where two uniformed officers kept the press at bay behind a very informal cordon. They all knew one another, Mac noted, hearing the chat and banter whipping back and forth across the invisible line. He had been going to ask about the boys he'd just seen but thought better of it, aware that he did not yet know which of the officers on loan to Frantham could be trusted to be discreet and which might let something slip. Andy had lived somewhere round here, Mac remembered, his family moving to Dorchester only the year before. He would probably know the boys and, of course, Rina would be able to tell him even if more regular sources could not.

The uniformed officers had noted his arrival and fallen silent and the journalists had come to expectant attention, taking their cue. Mac, the new boy, knew he had to set his parameters here and now. This meeting would establish the pattern for future conduct, define his later relations. He turned on the smile, aware that it was not a particularly brilliant one. 'DI Sebastian McGregor,' he introduced himself. 'Pleased to meet you all. Maybe you could tell me who you all are and I'll fill you in on what little we know . . .'

* * *

Tim, alias The Great Stupendo, had never been too sure he even liked kids and this afternoon had done little to change his mind.

Tim knew he didn't make a particularly convincing clown and this really wasn't the kind of gig he liked to do anyway. Truth was, he had been sort of press-ganged into it, the parents paying for this horrendously expensive sixth birthday bash being friends of one of the Montmorency twins. Tim had found himself well and truly volunteered and the only consolation was that, for a clown magician act, it was extraordinarily well paid.

Now, at three forty-five and almost at the end of his hour-long slog, Tim felt he had earned every penny of it.

'Funny time for a party,' Rina had commented. 'In my day, we had tea parties that began at four, not finished then.'

'Apparently they're having a family lunch at the hotel,' Tim told her. 'Then a party for other guests with a buffet. Then there's some kind of evening do but fortunately I'll be long gone by them.'

Rina snorted. 'I've been to less extravagant weddings,' she declared. 'And all that for a six-year-old who should be satisfied with a cake and a few friends.'

'Times are a-changing, Rina.'

'Hmm, and not for the better, in my opinion. Think about it. If you're throwing this extravaganza when the child is six, what will it expect when it hits eighteen?' Looking at the cars that had been parked outside of the hotel when he arrived, Tim figured that it would be a Mercedes at the very least.

Tim was losing his audience. Three small children sat on the floor in front of him, giggling. Another two little brats were playing tug of war with the string of fake sausages he had produced from his magic frying pan, and three more seemed engrossed in the problem of just how much iced cake and egg sandwich they could grind into the Axminster carpet.

Desperately, Tim glared down the length of the room, wondering just what it would take to attract the attention of the dozen or so adults ranged around the bar. A full-scale food fight? Right now strangulation by sausage looked a little more likely. Tim hopped off the improvised stage and grabbed the string of pink, sawdust-filled bangers from the reluctant hand of one small boy and sought to untwine the rest of the links from around the neck of his increasingly red-faced twin. The resultant howl from the first child and the choking sounds emitting from the second finally elicited a slight response from what Tim assumed must be the mother as she glanced their way, scowled at Tim and then turned her back once more.

'I know how you did that trick.'

'What?' Tim slipped fully out of clown mode now. His magic frying pan was being inspected by the oldest child at the party, a supercilious pre-teen who had previously sneered at Tim's make-up ('you don't look nothing like a proper clown'), his costume ('your trousers are too short, ha, ha, and you're wearing odd socks') and his magical prowess ('my dad could do better than that').

Tim hadn't worked out which of the absent parents was father to this particular little horror, but at this point he was past caring. He had been given his cheque in advance; let them cancel it. He snatched his magic frying pan from the child and stalked back on to the stage, then abruptly he wheeled round and peered hard at the boy, leaning in so that their noses almost touched, before recoiling as though in horror.

'What?' the boy demanded.

'Oh, probably nothing,' Tim told him. He snatched his gaze away from the child and turned the full beam of his clown smile back upon his much diminished audience, inviting a little girl of about three or four to come and see what he had in his magic hat. A sticky little hand poked about inside the black silk and she giggled up at him with her chocolate mouth.

'Nothing? Oh, we'll have to see about that.' Stupendo made several passes with his white-gloved hand then dipped into the seemingly empty hat. 'And what do we have here?' More chocolate seemed superfluous considering just how much the kids had already consumed, but that, Tim figured, was their parents' look-out. Sticky fingers reached out, still giggling for her share. Other hands joined hers and suddenly Tim found himself with an audience again.

'I know how you did that,' the older boy announced. 'It's a false bottom. That stuff was in the hat all the time. It ain't magic.'

Tim said nothing, his clown smile at odds with the look of real concern he leaned towards the boy again, swaying slightly as he examined him closely before sighing and turning away once more.

'What?' the boy demanded. 'I'll tell my dad.'

Stupendo turned his gaze back to the boy, the look of extreme pity in his eyes now unmistakable. The boy took a single step back and cast a swift, nervous glance over to where the adults sat at the far end of the room.

Sweets poured from the hat now, far more it seemed than could have been concealed in the entire depth of the hat, never mind a secret compartment. Tim selected one from the rest, bright purple wrapping that crinkled beneath his touch. He held it out towards the older boy, the broad smile he had turned upon the other children fading into sadness as he did so. Somewhat reluctantly, the child took it from him.

'Careful you don't choke,' Stupendo said solemnly.

THIRTEEN

Rina was waiting in the car park as Tim emerged from the hotel. He had changed his clothes and stowed the clown costume and props in two large orange carrier bags but traces of the make-up were still smeared across his face and his hair stood up at angles from where he'd pulled off the purple wig.

'Hello. What brings you up here?'

'Oh, a little project, let's say. How did it go?'

'Oh, it went. There was a small choking incident towards the end, but nothing serious.'

'A choking incident?'

Tim shrugged. 'I think one of the kids tried to cram in too much chocolate,' he said blithely. 'You know how it is. Parties.'

Rina pursed her lips suspiciously. She watched as Tim bent down to peer in the wing mirror and scrub ineffectually at what was left of his make-up. 'Oh, for goodness sake,' she said, producing a pack of wet wipes from her capacious bag. 'You'll ruin your skin. Here, let me.'

'Yes, Mother.' Tim stood obediently as she scrubbed.

'If I was your mother you wouldn't be doing children's parties,' she said. 'I'd have taken your career in hand long since.'

'You can always adopt me.'

'I'm not sure I'm old enough for that responsibility. Did they pay you?'

Tim patted his pocket.

'Well, I suppose that's something.'

'It's something, but seriously, Rina, I think I hate kids.'

She shook her head. 'Come along. We've got more interesting fish to fry.'

'Fry? You can fry kids? No one told me that. OK, OK, I'll behave, it's just post-traumatic-party disorder.'

'You'll get over it. We've all played bad gigs.'

'I suppose. So what's this project then?' he asked as she led him across the car park and towards the cliff path that dipped and curved across the headland. He shivered. He'd driven up here in his ancient clapped-out Ford Escort and hadn't bothered with his coat. The sweater and jacket he wore were no match for the biting wind that whipped across the open land behind the hotel.

'It'll be warmer down on the foreshore,' Rina told him. 'More sheltered, and the sun's lovely when you get out of the wind.'

'The foreshore? You mean you want to get down on to the beach? From here? *Is* there a beach down there?'

Rina sighed. 'How long have you lived here, Tim?'

'A couple of years, off and on.'

'Then it's time you explored more than the pub and the promenade.'

'I shop as well.'

'Occasionally,' Rina conceded. 'Look, just beyond that gate, there's a path down on to the under cliff just before it peters out, then from there you can get down into a small cove. That's where we're headed.'

'Mind if I ask why?'

'Oh, just curiosity. Something Mac said the other day.'

'Mac? Oh, our pet policeman. And what did he say?'

'That he saw lights, late at night, just below Marlborough Head. He wanted to know if it could be fishermen.'

'And?'

'No. I told him no.'

'And? I ask again.'

'And, I think it might be worth investigating.' They had reached the gate now. It was padlocked shut, but a stile had been built to give access on to the cliff walk.

'Investigating,' Tim said. 'Isn't that what policemen do? I mean, I'd have thought that would be more in their line.'

Rina stepped up on to the stile, her flat, lace-up shoes placed firmly on the wet and rather slimy wood. She hitched the heathery tweed of her skirt above her knees and swung one leg over the low fence then hopped down lightly on the other side.

'I mean,' Tim continued, eyeing the stile and the cliff path with equal distaste, 'I know *you* might have the credentials, Rina darling. Lydia Marchant would no doubt know exactly what to do, but you're talking to a failed clown here. We clowns are not that hot on the whole investigating thing.'

Rina eyed him with shrewdly narrowed eyes. 'And don't clowns have a sense of adventure?'

'Not failed clowns, no.'

She cocked her head on one side, sharpened her gaze.

'OK, OK.' Tim threw up his hands in mock surrender. 'I admit it. I don't like heights and I especially don't like cliffs and I really, really don't like anything that's going to drop me into freezing cold sea water and, even worse than that, freezing cold sea water with vicious rocks concealed just below the surface. I mean, is that nature's idea of a bad joke or what? You fall, you think, "Oh, I'll be all right, it's only water," but no, mother nature makes it freezing cold and like concrete when you fall into it off a cliff and then, just when you think you might have got away with the fall, the rocks get you.'

'Quite,' Rina said. 'Come along.' She turned away from him, strode out along the cliff top looking perfectly at ease in her brogues and heather skirt and old waxed coat. Tim watched, noting with a sudden surge of irritation mixed with great affection the way the sun turned her steel-grey, close-cropped hair almost to gold before taking a deep slow breath and easing himself gingerly over the stile.

* * *

'These shoes are not made for cliff climbing,' Tim complained as he slipped for the fourth time.

'Which is why you are going down first,' Rina told him. 'See, it's not so bad now, is it?'

Tim didn't comment, concentrating on the placing of his feet on the loose and slippery surface. The 'path' down from the top of the cliff consisted of wet mud and gravel in a combination designed for neck-breaking and he clung eagerly to the tussocks of grass on either side of the increasingly steep slope, hoping against hope that he would not end up sliding on his backside the rest of the way down. It wasn't so bad here though, he had to admit that. Worst had been those first few steps over the grass-concealed edge. He had clung pathetically to Rina's gloved hand and then to the outgrowths of plant and ageing root as he lowered himself down, still not convinced that this slit in the side of the cliff could ever be defined by the gratefully solid word 'path'.

'You're almost there,' Rina told him. 'I think.'

'What do you mean, you think?'

'Well, it is a little while since I came down here. There may be a bit further to go than I remember.'

Tim groaned. 'Rina, this is torture.'

'Is it? I thought it would be a lovely way to spend the afternoon.'

Tim just groaned again, but he was happy to hear that she at least had the grace to sound a little breathless. She had been right after all: they were almost down although the disadvantage of that was that the path now turned and Tim found himself peering down between his feet at a horrifyingly vertiginous view of the ocean.

'Deep breaths, deep breaths.'

'Yes,' Rina agreed. 'It does help if you keep breathing.'

Then, after what seemed like hours, Tim stood with his feet firmly planted on solid ground.

'Pretty here, isn't it?' Rina suggested, pushing her way past him and going to stand as close to the lapping water as she could without wetting her toes.

Tim looked around. Behind them the cliff rose to block out any view of the hotel or the upper part of the path or even the sky. The beach was no more than twenty yards long, he estimated, and about ten wide at the most. Boulder strewn and wild, freezing cold despite Rina's assurances that it would be more sheltered here, and pungent with the smell of what he hoped was only rotting sea weed.

'Delightful,' he said. 'Rina, can we just get out of here? I'm half frozen.'

'It isn't cold,' she said. 'It's bracing.'

'You,' he pointed out, 'are wearing a coat and, no doubt, about a dozen layers underneath. What are we looking for anyway?'

'Signs of use,' she said. 'Signs that someone might have been here recently. There's a little cave, if I remember right, just back that way.'

'Rina, I think the tide's coming in.'

'Of course it is, but we've got another ten minutes or so. Plenty of time to collect evidence.'

'Evidence of what?' Tim wanted to know.

Rina's steely glance told him it should be obvious. 'Smuggling, of course.'

FOURTEEN

'Smuggling?' Tim said sceptically. Rina was already marching off towards the far end of the little beach. 'Does our pet policeman know you're doing this?'

'No, of course not. There didn't seem much point telling him unless we had something *to* tell.'

'And are we *likely* to have anything to tell him? I mean, smuggling, Rina, that's a bit melodramatic, isn't it?'

'It wouldn't be the first time along this coast. For that matter, it wouldn't be the first time here. Five or so years ago it was cigarettes, I believe, and a year or so after that it was illegal immigrants.'

'You're kidding me. I didn't think anything happened round here.'

'As I said, you don't open your eyes. But think about it, Tim, this coastline is riddled with little coves and beaches, most of them so off the beaten track that the tourists don't find them and quite a few that even the locals don't know are there. This, for instance: you can only get down here from the landward side when the tide goes right out and, as you can see from the wet stones, it doesn't go out very far or stay out for very long.'

Tim cast a worried glance back at the water. It seemed to have crept further back up the beach even as they had stood there. 'We're not going to be long, are we?'

'No, Tim, we're not going to be long. I'm well aware of what the tide is doing. This, however, stays above the water line even at the spring tides.'

Tim turned his attention back to Rina. Curious, he joined her at what turned out to be the mouth of a small and very well hidden cave.

'See!' Rina was triumphant. 'I knew it was here.'

The mouth of the cave was almost concealed behind a collection of loose boulders. Tim scrambled over them, reaching out a hand to help Rina. 'Fossils,' he said. 'Nice ones too.' He bent to examine the large ammonites embedded in the smooth grey rock, fingering them curiously. He moved closer to the cliff face, pulled gently at fragments of outcropping stone. 'Y'know, the strata are really clear here. You can see the fossil layer; it runs right down almost to the beach.'

'Well you'll have to bring your hammer and collecting bag, but I suggest you leave it for another day. As you've already noted, the tide is rising and we don't have much time, so tear yourself away from the Jurassic and come and look at this.'

Obediently, Tim dipped his head and entered the cave. It was taller inside than he'd anticipated. Rina could stand upright, but Tim needed considerably more headroom. Rina had, of course, brought a torch, which she swung around the empty space, showing Tim that it sloped upwards, back into the cliff. 'You see, the water never gets to the far end. Plenty of room.'

'For what?'

Rina shrugged. 'Who knows? But, ah, this is something.'

Tim squatted down to see what she had found.

'Hold this, please,' she told him, handing Tim the torch. She pulled a roll of plastic freezer bags and a ballpoint pen from another pocket in the capacious jacket.

'A Coke can,' Tim said. 'Rina, it probably washed in here.'

'Not likely, it's above the water line.' She poked the end of the pen into the opening of the can and slid it into the bag. 'And this—look, cigarette butts. It isn't likely *they* washed in here, is it?'

'No,' Tim agreed, watching as she bagged those too, 'but Rina, if you look hard enough there'll probably be a selection of used condoms hereabouts as well.'

Rina cocked an eyebrow. 'Not very comfortable for that kind of activity, I wouldn't have thought.'

'Well, maybe not,' he conceded, 'but neither is the back seat of a Mini . . .'

He trailed off and Rina barked a laugh. 'Well, well, we learn something new about our Tim, do we?' She poked about in the loose sand and gravel on the cave floor but there was nothing else and it was Tim who made the last find.

'What's that up there?' Tucking his six-feet-three-inch frame still tighter, he duck-walked to the rear of the cave.

'Do you need a bag?'

'OK, I need a bag.' He took the freezer bag and the pen and flicked the small square of cardboard inside, careful not to touch it. He told himself that this was all a stupid wild-goose chase, a whim of Rina's, set off because she was missing the old days and her alter ego of Lydia Marchant, but he was careful, nonetheless.

'What is it?' she asked.

'A match book,' Tim told her. 'It probably came from the hotel. I can't see the label. It's all a bit dark.'

Rina pocketed their finds. 'We'd better get a wriggle on,' she said. 'Or we'll be getting more than wet feet.'

The tide had risen fast, leaving only a foot or so of beach still dry. Tim was shocked at how fast it had turned. Rina led the way back to the cliff path and began the ascent. Tim gave her a few yards' head start, watching suspiciously as the waves crept closer to his feet. The sky, which had been pleasantly clear and the palest blue when they had left the hotel, had darkened gradually and now, far out to sea, had taken on a steel-grey hue. The wind had freshened again and Tim shivered, suddenly aware at how much warmer the cave had been simply because it had sheltered them from the wind. Dancing back from a more than usually precocious wave, he began to follow Rina back up the cliff, noting as he did the signs of erosion, the scatter of sea weed, the pebbles and larger stones embedded on the softer clays. The tide must rise quite high, he realized. Certainly high enough for a small boat to gain easy access to the beach. And Rina was right: there was absolutely no sign that the water reached the far end of the cave.

Daring himself to glance down, Tim saw that the water now lapped and rushed at the base of the cliff, tearing and eroding even more of the fragile surface. The waves splashed upward, spray falling cold on his already frozen hands and as he risked one more glance out to sea, Tim saw that the steel-grey sky was advancing upon them, swift and dark and threatening.

* * *

Mac sat in Dr Mason's office and sipped the too-strong coffee. He could already feel the caffeine buzz begin. Recently, he had discovered that the little café on the promenade did a decent Italian laced with either almond or vanilla, depending on his mood. So far, Mac had kept this discovery to himself, suspecting that Eden would see it as a somewhat effete vice. There was nothing effete about Dr Mason's coffee. This was medicinal grade, designed for late nights and long shifts and the recipe was, Mac guessed, a hangover from Mason's days as a junior doctor.

'As you saw,' Mason said. 'There are defensive wounds. She tried her best to fight back. Some of the bruising on her arms has only just developed.'

Mac nodded. 'The way I read it is he grabbed her upper arms and grabbed hard, then he got hold of her again, but just the right arm. He shook her, which was when the shoulder fractured, then he hit her, dropped her, finished things off with . . . whatever he used.'

'Seems like a reasonable set of assumptions.' The door opened and Mason's assistant appeared with the photographs Mac had requested. She placed them on the desk and left with a smile for Mac. Pretty, Mac thought, appreciating the dark hair and the vivid blue eyes.

'My guess,' Mason continued, 'is that whatever it was had some kind of base or even plinth.' He pointed at the photographs now laid out between them. 'You see the edge of this wound and then of this one. Clean and straight and there's a distinct corner here that's pierced the skin and tissue far more deeply.' He shook his head. 'I don't know, maybe a heavy ornament with a square base?'

'The place was a mess. So far, though, we've found nothing that fits that sort of profile.'

'You think the killer took a trophy?'

'Wouldn't be the first time.' Mac shrugged. 'We'll take another look in the house but I'm coming to the conclusion he took it with him.'

'It goes without saying he'd have blood on his clothes, probably his shoes.' Mason stood, rinsed his mug in the tiny sink in the corner of his room. 'I'll get the full report to you as soon as.'

Mac nodded. His head reeled from the caffeine hit and his mouth felt oddly dry. 'Thanks,' he said. 'What about the blood found on the stairs?'

Mason nodded, anticipating the question. 'Plenty for comparison,' he said. 'Don't you worry, the bastard left enough of himself behind.'

FIFTEEN

'So, what's up then, our kid?' Karen ruffled George's hair, knowing he hated it but also that he'd hate it if she didn't.

She'd been home for a couple of hours but this was the first chance they'd had to talk, their mother having dominated Karen's time up until now. Carol Parker had fussed as she always did, chattered and nagged about everything and nothing . . .

This boy you're seeing. You're sure he's all right and not . . . you know. They're all OK at first. It's after. You sure you're getting enough to eat? And that job of yours, what is it?

'I've got two jobs, Mam, and I'm at night school three days a week. You remember?

'Yes, of course I do, but what jobs? Karen, you'd tell me if anything was wrong. I'm always so tired these days and the doctor won't give me any more pills he says I should get more exercise, maybe do a yoga class or something, learn to meditate. Meditate! Yoga! What does he know?

'Wouldn't do you any harm though, would it, get you out and meeting people.'

'Why would I want to do that?'

It was significant, George thought, that not once had his mother mentioned the murder three doors down.

Finally, just to get away for long enough to talk, Karen had volunteered to do some shopping and said she'd take George along with her.

'Here,' she said, handing him an insulated cup bearing the convoluted logo of the promenade café. She had treated them both to hot chocolate and blueberry muffins but they had elected to get them to take out, George being prepared to suffer the winds blowing along the promenade if it meant a little more privacy.

He had talked to Paul again and they had decided not to tell yet about Mrs Freer. To wait, see what happened. Paul was scared. George realized his friend just wanted for it all to go away and he was hoping against hope that if he didn't talk about it no one else would and so he'd be safe.

George sipped the sweet hot chocolate and poked at the soft denseness of the muffin.

'So, what's on your mind, our kid?' Karen swung her legs up on to the bench, her back against the arm and her knees raised. Smiling at his sister, George did the same, their feet wedged against each other's, sitting like two bookends. It was an old habit from their hostel days when they had sat either end of the tiny sofas that seemed to come as standard with the accommodation. Facing one another, shutting out the world. On the bench it wasn't exactly a comfortable posture.

He licked the muffin crumbs from his lips and hugged the chocolate cup close and tight to his body, thinking suddenly that the problem with insulated cups was just that. They kept the heat inside and gave nothing back to hug against a cold chest. 'I think I saw *him*,' George said.

Karen didn't need to ask him who. She leaned forward as far as her knees would allow. 'No.' She shook her head. 'You can't have. You know you can't have.'

George looked away, staring anxiously out across the bay. He licked his lips again, then wiped them with the back of his hand as the wind dried the moisture and contracted the skin. 'I know I *can't* have done,' he said. 'But I did.'

Karen shook her blonde head. 'Where? How?'

'I don't know how but he was standing outside the school. I seen him from the bus.'

'How close was he?' Karen demanded. 'George, I was seeing him everywhere for months after. I knew it couldn't be him but I kept us moving all the same just because I kept *thinking* that I saw him. But George, you know that isn't possible. You know that. Don't you?'

George nodded and then shook his head. 'I'm not making a mistake, Kaz, I saw him. I saw him close to, from the bus window; he was stood there on the pavement. He was looking, but I ducked down when we went past. I saw him, Kaz.'

His sister frowned intently, chewing on her lips, her face pale. George could see she no longer doubted him.

'What do we do?' George asked but he knew the answer and his heart sank. He'd finally just started to make friends and even the thought of getting away from Dwayne and his ilk was no compensation. There were Dwaynes everywhere. Dwaynes and Mark Dowlings and they grew up to be people like his dad. 'We're going to have to move again, aren't we?' he said.

Karen nodded. 'Looks that way,' she said.

SIXTEEN

Sunday arrived with spiteful wind and driving rain. By ten o clock, Mac was back at Mrs Freer's house with Andy the probationer and two community support officers he had managed to borrow for a couple of hours. The press contingent had been driven away by the lack of shelter and decidedly inclement weather—and the more immediate and attractive proposition of a stabbing a few miles up the coast. Mrs Freer's house had now been properly secured with metal shutters and padlocks on the doors. Yellow tape, tugged free by the gale blowing down the length of Newell Street, waved and snapped plastic ribbons across the front door and Mac caught at them, tugged them down and stuffed them into the pockets of his raincoat. He hated the look of abandonment suggested by the broken tape.

His three companions shivered despite being wrapped tight against the chill. 'I need a couple of hours,' Mac told them, 'and with a bit of luck you'll be inside for most of that.'

A giggle from one of the community support officers. 'You don't know the locals, do you? Invite us in? They might look guilty.'

Her companion laughed.

'Well, just do your best,' Mac told them. 'Memories have had time to be jogged, so you never know. Andy and

Jane, you take the houses across the street—and best have another chat at the OAP home too. Sally, you take that part of the row from the murder scene back to the crossroads. The people I'm most interested in are the next-door neighbours. They reckon they heard nothing on the night but . . . You know how it works. I'll make my way back down this side as far as the nursing home. Any problems, shout up.'

Mac's interest was in the two boys he had seen the day before but he was reluctant to draw attention to them. He started with the house directly next to Mrs Freer and, unsurprisingly, added nothing to his fund of information as he already knew from previous statements that they worked nights. The next house was inhabited by an elderly couple who invited him in and offered tea. He declined the tea but spent some time getting his ear bent about the young people in the area and how the local shop had been burgled twice in the past five years. 'Drugs, that's what it'll be. Drugs.'

Mac made reassuring noises and went on his way.

The boy with red hair opened the next door down. He stared at Mac, clearly taken aback and not knowing what to say. A strawberry-blonde woman who looked to Mac to be in her late teens or maybe very early twenties came out of a room at the end of the hall.

'Can I help you? We don't buy on the doorstep.'

'I don't sell,' Mac told her. He held out his identification for her to see. 'Inspector McGregor,' he said.

'Oh, you've come about the old lady? I heard. Bloody awful.'

'Who is it?' An older woman emerged through the same door at the end of the hall. Mac decided it must be the kitchen, same as it was in Mrs Freer's house.

'It's all right, Mam, just a policeman asking about that poor old lady.'

The woman, an older, thinner and altogether more fragile version of her daughter, flapped her slender hands nervously. 'Oh, oh no. We don't know anything. Not anything.'

'It's OK, Mum, why don't you make some tea and I'll have a chat with the inspector. I'd like to know what's going on at any rate.'

She led the way through the first door off the hall and Mac followed, anticipating that *he* was about to be the one interrogated. The boy came in after him and perched nervously on the arm of an easy chair. The mother retired to the back room to make the tea. The house was the same layout as Mrs Freer's, Mac noted, though better decorated. Oddly empty, though, considering three people lived there. The living-room floor was uncarpeted, covered only by a couple of large, cheap-looking rugs, and the furnishings were similar to those he had in his own temporary flat. He wondered if they were renting the place furnished.

'Sit down,' the strawberry-blonde said. 'I'm Karen Parker and this is George, my kid brother. I don't think we can tell you anything but I would like to know what the hell is going on.'

'What do you know already?' Mac asked.

'That someone beat the old lady to death with a baseball bat. At least, that's what the rumour mill is saying. And something about her having a gun.' She laughed harshly. 'Pity she didn't. She could have shot the bastard, couldn't she?'

'And then she would have been guilty of murder,' Mac pointed out.

Karen shook her head. 'No, no she wouldn't. Possession of a firearm, maybe, manslaughter possibly. Most likely self-defence. No judge would send her down for murder and she'd still be alive, wouldn't she?'

'You seem to know a lot about the law.'

Karen shrugged.

'Karen's doing university,' George said. It was the first time he had uttered a word. He sounded proud, Mac thought. 'She's doing law.'

She shrugged. 'I'm a part-time student,' she said. 'Working two jobs and still up to me ears in debt but I hope it'll be worth it in the end.'

'I'm sure it will,' Mac said, but he was intrigued. What little he knew about law degrees, he didn't think they put an awful lot of emphasis on those particular areas of criminal law but . . . what did he know?

'And what credence should we give to the rumour mill?' he asked.

She shrugged. 'Mrs Freer's dead. It caused a ripple in the local press, made it on to the national news last night, but unless you lot find something in the next day or so, or whoever did it knocks off someone else, then a ripple is all there'll be. The rumour mill will churn out even more elaborate rumours and she'll still be dead.'

'Maybe,' Mac said. 'But we'll be doing our best to find her killer. I can assure you of that.'

'Any suspects yet?'

Mac laughed. Frantham, he thought, seemed to produce a special brand of feisty woman. This one called to mind a very young version of Rina. 'I can't tell you anything right now,' he said.

'So that'll be a no, then. If you had it would be all over the news.'

'We're following up several leads,' Mac told her and couldn't help but smile at the platitude.

Karen howled with laughter. 'Do you get issued with a phrase book?' she asked. 'Is there a house style for coppers?'

'Oh, increasingly,' he said. 'New words are banned every single year. We get an official list.'

Karen chuckled warmly and Mac could sense that George relaxed, just a fraction. He decided it was time to ask him. 'Yesterday, I saw you standing across the road. I got the feeling you wanted to say something.'

Karen's laughter ceased. She narrowed her gaze and squinted at them both, Mac and her brother, as though trying to bring them into better focus. 'George doesn't know anything,' she said. 'What could he know?'

George shifted uncomfortably. 'I didn't want to say nothing,' he mumbled. 'I was just . . . I just wanted to know what was going on.'

91

'Are you interested in the law too?' Mac asked innocently. George shrugged.

'So, there was nothing you wanted to say. Nothing you might have noticed that might help us.'

George shrugged again and Karen leaned forward in her seat.

'It might be just a little thing,' Mac continued. 'Something a bit odd, like. Something you know isn't quite right.'

'George?' Karen said. 'You got anything to tell the man?'

'Nothing,' George said. 'I'd have been home in bed, wouldn't I?'

Karen exchanged a look with Mac and it was clear that she too thought her little brother was withholding. He wondered if she would do anything about it. She had, he felt, a stronger than normal instinct to protect, not just her brother but her mother too, and she was obviously mature for her years. He found himself wondering what history had created such a strong desire.

'It's a serious business, George,' Mac said. 'An old lady was killed, brutally murdered in her own home. A place she was supposed to be able to feel safe.'

'I told you, I'd have been at home in bed.'

'And the night before that? The night before she died? Were you at home in your bed that night?'

Karen looked sharply at Mac. 'What happened then?' she asked.

'Oh, two boys, they broke in to Mrs Freer's about half past ten that night, used a screwdriver on the back door to lever it open. Not that there was much of a lock.'

'Broke in? Did they steal anything?'

'No,' Mac said. 'They got scared and ran off. Two boys about your age, George. Do you know anything about that? You heard something, perhaps?'

Karen was observing them both so keenly that Mac could almost imagine the pin coming down to fix him to the card. 'What makes you think he knows anything?' she asked, a sharp edge of anxiety creeping into her voice.

'I'm just asking,' Mac said. 'Of course, the two incidents might not be linked, but it is a major coincidence if not. The same elderly lady targeted on two consecutive nights.'

'George?' Karen sounded cautious now and Mac could almost imagine that she was slipping into lawyer mode. For a moment the three of them sat, frozen in expectation of something, anything, that George might say. Mac could hear the boy breathing, tight and tense and scared. A clock ticked somewhere out of sight. Ticked with a slightly uneven rhythm that jarred on the nerves and then the moment was lost, the mood broken as the door banged and Mrs Parker came in, a tea tray shivering in her nervous hands.

Karen sighed and got up to take the tray before the rattle of mugs turned into a crash of breaking china.

'I don't know if you have sugar,' Mrs Parker twittered anxiously. 'I didn't know if you might take milk, but I thought almost everyone takes milk so I put it in. I hope I did right?'

'It's fine, Mrs Parker. Thank you,' Mac said. He sneaked a sideways glance at Karen but she was busying herself with the tea. As she handed him a mug he noticed that her lips were pressed tight as though she willed herself not to speak. She shook her head, a tiny movement, and Mac nodded an equally slight response. *Not in front of our mother*, Karen was telling him and a minute or so later George took advantage of the maternal fussing to slip out of the room.

Mac wanted to call him back. Wanted to threaten to take him to the police station, question him formally, but his instincts told him that Karen would be doing a better job later on and that just now George was far more frightened of someone else than he was of Mac.

* * *

Mac had stayed at the Parkers long enough to drink his tea and to reinforce the impression of Karen's defensiveness of her family.

No one was in next door and no one was admitting to being in the house after that so the next stop was the house Mac had seen the two boys enter the day before.

Mac had already checked his list of names. 'Mrs Robinson?' he asked when someone answered the door.

'Yes.' The woman sounded cautious, a little anxious. Mac guessed she had already seen them in the street and must have realized who he was.

He introduced himself anyway.

'Well, I don't think we can tell you anything,' she said. 'It came as a right shock, I can tell you.'

Mac glimpsed the dark-haired boy hovering in the background. His face still showed the vicious bruising Mac had noted, but the blackest of the marks was fading now, dissolving to a bilious green. He looked over the mother's shoulder and smiled at the boy, aware once again that his smile lacked both conviction and adequacy. He must practise more.

'Hello,' Mac said. 'I've just been chatting to your friend George.'

The boy flinched and the face flushed red beneath the bruises.

Mrs Robertson turned to look at her son. 'He got himself into some stupid fight,' she said. 'I've talked to the school but of course they know nothing about it. Clam up, they do, if anyone should dare to mention the "B" word.'

'The "b" word?'

'Bullying, of course.' She glared hard at Mac. 'You don't think my boy is in the habit of getting into fights, do you?'

'I don't know your boy,' Mac pointed out.

'No, well he's not, and neither is young George. He's seen enough violence, that boy. He's the last person to want to get involved in more.'

'Oh?' Mac tried to look friendly, inviting of confidences. From the look on Nora Robinson's face it wasn't working.

'The father,' she said impatiently. 'Put them through hell, and if it hadn't been for young Karen, the mother would probably be dead and gone by now.'

'Really? And what did Karen do?'

She shook her head impatiently. 'You didn't knock on the door for a gossip,' she said. 'What can I help you with? I've already spoken to two of your lot, you know.'

'I know,' Mac said placatingly, 'but we often find that a follow-up call helps, you know. People remember the little things that shock often blots out.'

She sighed. 'Well, I'm sorry, but we've got nothing to tell. We didn't hear anything that night and we didn't see anything either.'

'And the night before Mrs Freer was killed?'

She looked puzzled. 'What about the night before?'

The boy had retreated to the stairs, sitting a few steps up from the bottom and making a great show of not looking at either his mother or Mac.

'The night before, that would have been late on the Wednesday, two boys broke into Mrs Freer's house. Teenagers, about the same age as your son and George Parker.'

She drew a deep, shocked breath and then released it in a rush of anger. 'Same age as Paul, as George? Mister, do you know how many kids that age there are round here? Do you know how many little toe rags there are? Get yourself along to the Jubilee if you want to catch the little buggers that broke in—and the bastard that killed her. Look over there before you come round here accusing *my* son.'

'I'm not accusing anyone,' Mac said mildly, 'and I can assure you, Mrs Robertson, that we will be looking everywhere.' He paused, looked directly at the boy on the stairs. 'Everywhere,' he repeated, then stepped swiftly back as she shut the door in his face.

* * *

'Anything?' It was half an hour later and his little group stood huddled in the lee of the nursing home wall, beneath the sign that declared this land the property of the Alderman Calvin Trust and threatened to clamp intruders.

It was even colder now and the wind whipped a new batch of freezing rain into greater frenzy.

'Usual mix of abuse and lousy tea.'

'Neighbours still heard nothing. Still say they were watching an action film and had the sound up high.'

'Alderman Calvin House doesn't have windows facing on to the street so how do we expect them to have noticed anything. Oh and they still want to know what we're doing about the kids on bikes over by the sheds.'

Mac sighed and thanked his helpers. 'Best get off,' he said. 'You all OK for lifts back?'

Apparently they were. Mac watched as the three of them escaped with an almost indecent degree of haste and then he too turned for home. He was halfway up Newell Street when a friendly voice shouted his name. Mac turned. Half hidden behind a massive golf umbrella and wearing a raincoat that Columbo would have been proud to claim stood Tim, aka Marvello, alias The Great Stupendo.

Mac crossed the street.

'Rina sent me to fetch you. She figured you might like some lunch.'

Mac laughed, taken aback. 'How did she know I was here?'

'Ah well, Rina knows these things. So, what about it then? Food's good, company is . . . interesting and I've a feeling the ex-Lydia Marchant wants to tell you about her investigations.'

'Investigations?'

Tim shook his head. 'Let her tell you. So, are we getting out of this godawful weather then? Come under the umbrella, there's plenty of room.'

Life was taking on that slightly surreal quality it always did when Rina Martin was involved, Mac thought. He nodded and stepped beneath the shelter of the umbrella Tim had hoisted. 'Thanks,' he said. 'Lunch would be very welcome.'

SEVENTEEN

By one o'clock Mac was installed at Rina's table, sandwiched once again between the Peters sisters, although he still wasn't sure which one was which. The Montmorency twins—much easier to identify—sat opposite with Tim between them, a tall, skinny, austere figure between two flamboyant ones. Rina took her place at the head of the table and handed plates and dishes piled high with vegetables and roast potatoes and rich gravy that Mac could tell just from the scent had never seen even a suggestion of stock cubes or gravy browning. Two kinds of roast meat weighed down large platters set atop warming trays that ran down the centre line of the well laid table. There was enough, Mac thought, to feed an army and, with a sudden flash of insight, wondered how many people like Mrs Freer would benefit this afternoon.

Mac realized that he was famished and was overwhelmingly relieved that conversation was obviously not initially required at Rina's table, just willingly delivered expressions of deep content.

Dessert loosened tongues and, as Rina served apple pie, conversation began in a leisurely kind of way. Stephen Montmorency enquired as to the state of the investigation but did not pursue the matter and Mac got the impression that the Rina Martin household had been given instructions not to bother the copper with questions.

'Custard or cream?' Rina asked.

'Oh, custard please. It looks very good.'

'Stephen is an excellent pastry cook,' Rina said.

'I trained,' Matthew said, tossing back the mane of silver hair. 'Did the whole catering college thing. Our mother felt we should always have a fall-back position. Isn't that right, Stephen?'

His brother nodded. 'A very wise woman, our ma,' he said. '"Stephen," she would say, "you should always have a fall-back position. You never, ever know what's around the corner."'

Mac nodded sagely. He was dying to ask about the so-called twins. Did they really think they were related, or was this an extension of some obscure stage act? He opened his mouth to speak, then caught Rina's eye and closed it again.

'It's always best to be prepared,' Tim agreed. 'The problem is the only fall-back I've got is dressing up in a bloody clown suit.'

'Language, Timothy,' Stephen said sententiously. 'Ladies present, you know.'

'Sorry, ladies,' Tim apologized, inclining his head in the direction of Matthew Montmorency rather than the Peters sisters. 'Seriously though, Stephen, I make a godawful clown. I've really got to give it up.'

'It's honest work,' Stephen reminded him. 'You should never demean honest work.'

Mac tried to visualize Tim in a clown costume and failed miserably.

'How did . . . you all meet?' Mac asked. He'd almost directed the question at the Montmorencys.

'Oh dear.' One of the Peters sisters clapped her hands, delighted. 'Oh dear, it was years ago, wasn't it, Rina?'

'Years indeed. I believe I met the two of you in Southampton. Sixty-two or -three, it would have been. You were still with that Bennet fellow.'

'Clive Bennet.' Eliza Peters sounded dreamy. 'Oh, he was a sweetie. No talent, of course, but a real sweetie.'

'He might not have had the talent,' her sister agreed, 'but he was all heart. All heart. Gave us both a break when we needed it, didn't he?'

'Oh yes.' Her sister clasped her hands together. 'The closing song that season, "All our Yesterdays". It still makes me cry when I sing it. We'd have the audience eating out of our hands, you know, dear. Not a dry eye in the house.'

'"All our *Tomorrows*",' her sister corrected her. 'Eliza dear, you always did get it wrong.'

'Oh, are you sure? No, no, I'm certain . . .' She brightened suddenly. 'We have pictures and recordings if you'd like to see them?'

'Um . . .' Mac began.

'I don't think the inspector has the time just yet,' Rina said, giving gentle emphasis to his title.'

'Oh, but of course not.' Eliza was immediately contrite. 'I'm sure you have so much to do?'

Mac was aware that she'd let the question hang, that she and everyone around the table, with the possible exception of Tim, was desperate to ask him everything, anything about the case. He managed an awkward smile. 'We do have a number of leads,' he said, remembering that he had said something very similar to Karen Parker a short time before and that she had laughed.

Eliza didn't laugh. She nodded approvingly and looked intently into Mac's face. 'Well that's good, isn't it? That you have leads?' She looked around the table, inviting confirmation. 'Well it is, isn't it?'

'I'm sure it is,' Rina soothed. 'Right, shall we all have coffee?'

Mac found himself involved in what seemed to be an established household ritual—the removal of plates and crockery and making of coffee, carrying the fresh pots back into the dining room. He wondered who got the job of washing-up.

Rina handed him a cup and held the door open. 'Shall we adjourn?' she asked. 'Tim, you'd better come along too.'

Obediently they followed her. Mac, glancing back at the others, noted the curious, almost hungry looks cast in their direction as they left: those deprived of secret things.

* * *

Rina flopped down into one of the easy chairs and pointed Mac at the other. Tim deposited his cup on the table and fetched a fireside chair from the bay window. Mac sipped his coffee, wondering what was coming next.

'So,' Rina asked when Tim had settled. 'How is it going?'

Mac smiled. 'You know I can't tell you,' he said. 'I have some thoughts; I have some small leads, but nothing I can talk about. Sorry.'

Rina nodded. 'Have the neighbours been helpful?' she asked innocently.

Mac found himself laughing this time. The sound shocked him. 'Rina, you never give up, do you?'

She shrugged. 'I don't see the point of giving up,' she said. 'You won't have got anything from the next-door neighbours. They wouldn't give anyone the time of day, never mind commit to giving actual information, and the people on the other side, those not actually attached to poor Mrs Freer's house, they work all hours God sends. I believe they want to emigrate to New Zealand or some such. I suppose they're saving.'

She drank her coffee and set the cup down gently on the table. Mac exchanged a glance with Tim and noted the hint of a smile twitching at the corner of his mouth. He waited for the next instalment in Rina's neighbourhood history.

'Then there's the Bennets. The only view they have of the outside world is what they see on the television. They even have their shopping delivered. The single mother next to them, well, she's so wrapped up in herself she notices nothing of the world around her. Jumps out of her skin if you

so much as say good morning. The boy, on the other hand
. . . Eyes everywhere. You gain the impression that he sees
everything and worries about all of it.'

'That would be George Parker,' Mac said.

'I believe that's his name, yes. He has a sister, cast in the
same mould. She has an intelligent look to her.'

Mac realized this was a query directed at him. He nodded thoughtfully. 'I spoke to her,' he confirmed. 'She strikes
me as intelligent, yes.'

'And?'

'Rina, I've nothing to tell and I couldn't tell you if I did.'

'No, but something is troubling you about your morning labours. I could see it on your face.'

'How do you tell?' Tim wondered. 'I think the inspector's natural expression is a troubled one.'

Rina nodded thoughtfully. 'Maybe so,' she said. 'I was
down at Mrs Freer's one day when the school bus arrived. I
saw George Parker get off. There was another boy with him,
the Robinson child. He lives a few doors down, but you'll
be relieved to hear I know nothing more about him. What I
did notice though, was a third boy, about the same age. He
followed them off the bus even though he doesn't live in the
same street. He was taunting the pair of them, teasing, but
not in a nice way. I frowned at him and he walked off.'

Mac caught Tim hiding a smile, but he found himself
half believing that a Rina Martin scowl would be enough to
intimidate almost anyone. He sensed she had brought up the
incident with some specific purpose in mind. 'Do you know
the other boy?'

Rina shook her head. 'Not his name, no. But I've seen
him before. He hangs around with Mark Dowling and his
gang.'

'Mark Dowling?'

'Your local knowledge really *is* lacking,' Tim told him.
'Nasty piece of work. His dad runs a car repair place down
in the tin huts. He's a bit of a wide boy, but by all accounts
he's a good mechanic. The son though, Mark, one of three

boys and none of them any good from what I've seen, but Mark is . . . unpleasant.' The word somehow assumed the character of an expletive.

'I've heard the name,' Mac mused. Something about a burnt-out car? He tried to recall, but it seemed to him that it had been only a passing comment, one overheard and not directed at him. 'Looks like a Dowling,' Eden had said. 'Little toe rag.' It occurred to Mac that in his previous posting the adjective used would have been 'scrote' at the very least, but somehow he could not imagine Eden using more abusive language. Or needing it. Eden could pack as much distaste into the 'toe rag' phrase as could Tim into the word 'unpleasant'.

Someone tapped hesitantly on the door and Tim rose, took possession of the proffered coffee pot and closed the door again.

Rina refilled their cups.

'So,' Mac said, 'tell me about this Mark Dowling.'

He listened to Rina's account of the boy who had truanted from his early teens, shoplifted, took cars that had been brought in for repair at his father's business and broke into his neighbours' houses.

'He got himself caught so often it was almost an embarrassment,' Rina said. 'Always in the local papers, he was. His mother said she'd had enough and took off somewhere. Mark must have been about fifteen at the time. There were rumours that the father was violent, but I wouldn't know about that. Anyway, the courts finally put him away and when he came back home he seemed to have quietened down but the general opinion is that he just learned to keep his head down.'

'It sounds as though the early stuff was attention-seeking as much as anything,' Mac proposed.

Rina snorted. 'Had he been mine, he'd have got attention all right, but it might not have been the kind he was looking for. Anyway, he seems to have gathered this admiring little group around him and whatever he's really up to seems to dip below the radar, as it were.'

Mac nodded, not quite sure how Rina thought this fitted in but making a mental note that he must add Mark Dowling to his list of 'things to discuss with Eden' the following day.

'There have been complaints about kids on motorbikes,' he said.

'By the huts, yes. Oh, most don't do any harm, most stick to that big patch of wasteland Tesco is trying to buy. It's just when they get stupid and cut through by the old folks' home and on to Newell Street that the trouble really starts. No crash helmets and no sense. I don't wonder people complain then.'

Thoughtfully, Mac sipped his cooling coffee. 'Have you ever seen George Parker or his friend with Dowling's gang?'

Rina shook her head. 'No, as I told you, just that one incident with the other boy. Him, I have seen with Dowling.'

'And you think Dowling might be linked to the murder?'

Rina frowned, troubled. She obviously didn't like Mark, but to link anyone with such a violent act was, Mac suspected, a step too far.

'I don't know,' she said finally. 'He's a nasty piece of work, but . . . What I do think, though, is that his little group will have heard whatever gossip there is, which, of course, is not to say you should give credence to it.'

Mac considered himself told.

'There's another thing,' Rina told him. 'Quite a separate thing. You remember telling me about the lights you saw, out by Marlborough Head.'

Mac hadn't given it further thought, but he nodded.

'Well, Tim and I went down there.'

'Down there?'

'There's a little bit of beach and a cave,' Tim supplied.

'Ah.'

'We did some poking around and we came up with these.' Rising from her chair, Rina crossed to a small chest of drawers standing just beside the door. She returned with three plastic freezer bags and deposited them on Mac's knee. 'Evidence,' she said.

'Of what?' Mac examined the bags, peering at their contents through the clear gaps between the blue stripes.

Rina shrugged carelessly. 'Who knows,' she said. 'We thought you could have the fun of finding out.'

* * *

Lunch in the Parker household was a less elaborate affair although Karen had done her best. Their mother had never been much of a cook and her lack of skill had been yet one more bone of contention with their father. Karen had lost track of the number of beatings received over burned dinners. From the time she was capable of handling a kitchen knife and reading a recipe book, Karen had taken on as many of the culinary duties as she could and she had succeeded far better than her mother. Vainly, the younger Karen had tried to improve her mother's skill, but Carol Parker seemed to have lost all faith in her abilities and every small failure simply served to reinforce her sense of helplessness. Later, in school, Karen had discovered the phrase 'self-fulfilling prophecy'. Of this sad concept, Carol, in Karen's eyes, seemed the epitome.

'I made pudding,' Karen said now. 'Want some?'

George nodded eagerly. The only time he could be assured a decent meal was when Karen prepared it or he ate at Paul's house. He was, in self-defence, taking a leaf from Karen's book and learning to cook, but his efforts, though better than his mother's, were still a little hit and miss and getting her to give him money for shopping was a real trial. She felt, somehow, that she ought to be in control of the money and the shopping but in truth was in command of neither. Karen usually made a point of stocking up once a week, getting their mother to accept this as a favour and always careful not to undermine the fragile progress she was making. That she was managing to hold down a job—OK, maybe not a particularly demanding job—was a triumph in its own right and Carol's children did all they could to let her know they were proud of her efforts.

'You want some pudding, Mam?'

Carol blinked. 'Oh, I don't know. What is it?'

'Apple crumble. I've bought some cream to go with it.' Karen was still not totally satisfied with her efforts at pastry making, but crumble was easy.

'Oh, I don't know. I shouldn't. Well, maybe just a little.'

Karen smiled her approval. Another hangover from their father's influence was Carol's obsession with her weight. She was getting better, actually managing to eat a full meal these days, but Karen and George remembered all too vividly those skeletal days just before everything had finally come to a head when she had been terrified of every mouthful.

Karen served the crumble, distributing the lion's share to George and careful not to give her mother too large a portion. She served it in a shallow soup plate, the larger dish making the portion look even slighter, even more manageable. Carol could be so easily scared by anything that looked like too much and her definition of too much was determined by her level of confidence on any given day.

George dug in, listening vaguely to the female conversation as Karen tried to plan a shopping trip. Carol worried about spending on clothes, too, and George noticed that Karen laced the conversation with words like 'good value' and 'really cheap'. He knew too that Karen would end up getting the stuff Carol needed for her, but at least she'd wear it these days, even if his sister still had to lie about the price paid.

'We'll wash up,' Karen said. 'You go and have a rest.'

George felt his full stomach turn over, knowing that Karen was getting their mother out of the way so that she could begin the interrogation. He knew he couldn't get away from it either. Karen had ways and means of worming inside his head and she had a bloodhound instinct should he try to tell her a lie. He dropped his spoon into his now empty bowl with a resigned sigh and the acknowledgement that, actually, he really wanted to tell and that any resistance on his part would be in part for show and in part because he knew it was going to be hard to find the words. Since Paul had told him what had gone on with the old woman he'd been sort of hoping that Karen would force the information from him. It had weighed so heavy that, along with the fear that he had seen his father standing outside his school, George felt like his brain had been loaded down with lead.

Karen waited until their mother was safely out of the way and the washing-up begun before she started in on George. She was well aware of the way occupied hands seemed to free up the tongue and she set George to drying, something Carol never bothered with as a general rule. George wielded the striped tea towel with elaborate care, setting the dishes on the counter as he dealt with each one. Karen eyed him cautiously, selecting her moment.

'So,' she said finally. 'Tell me.'

George stalled. 'Tell you what?'

'Whatever it was you didn't tell the policeman the other day, like who it was broke into the old woman's house.'

She kept her voice carefully neutral, not wanting to scare him off, but inside she was screaming at him, wanting to know what the hell he had been thinking. What possible excuse he could have had. Karen had no doubt at all that George and his friend had been the ones responsible for that; his behaviour when the policeman had visited had just been too suspicious. Karen was horrified, but she recognized that George was horrified too and, well, he was her little brother. Karen would do what she'd always done for her family: she would put things right, whatever.

'What makes you think I got anything to say?' George mumbled.

'Oh, come off it, George. So, what happened then? You do it for a dare? You get pissed or what?' She turned sharply, a further worry surfacing. 'If I find out you or that friend of yours took drugs, I swear, I'll shop the pair of you.'

'We never done drugs,' he said. He seemed relieved to have something to deny.

'So what was it then? George, I can't believe you did such a stupid thing willingly or sober so . . .'

'It were this girl,' he said reluctantly. 'Sharon Bates. She said Paul didn't have the nerve for nothing, that he was—'

'Better a wimp than a fool,' Karen said sharply. Then, seeing George's expression change, she cursed herself for interrupting at the wrong moment. 'OK, sorry, little bro. You just tell me and I promise I'll keep it shut 'til you've finished.'

George reached over and took another plate from the stack, set it down and began to dry it. At this rate, Karen thought, he'd still be drying come tea time.

'We were all over in the tin huts,' he said. 'Mam had fallen asleep and Paul came to the back door. His mum and dad had gone out. We were all over there, about eight of us, and Sharon had this bottle. She said it was cider but it tasted funny.' He glanced anxiously at his sister. Karen kept her face carefully neutral. 'I only had a swig or two,' he said. 'But Paul . . . well he had a load. He said he was all right but he weren't and I knew we had to get back before his mam and dad came in so I was trying to get him away and then Shaz said we were scared of everything and everyone else started to pick on me and Paul and . . .' George's hands stopped moving and he closed his eyes.

'And what, George?'

'And Sharon said about the old lady. About how it would be easy to . . . to . . . just to break in. Prove we weren't scared.'

Karen stood very still. So much she wanted to say. So angry with him that she knew once the words were released she'd have the devil's own job to call them back. She took a deep, slow breath. 'And so?'

'I managed to get Paul to come away with me and he were falling over all over the place. I thought I could get him back home and it would all be OK, but then he fell down again and he found this bit of metal.' George sighed. 'You know what it's like over there, all sorts of stuff gets dumped and well, anyway, that were it. Paul said he could open the door with it. He said it would be easy and we wouldn't steal nothing, nothing that mattered, just something to prove we'd been there and he weren't scared.'

Why, Karen wondered, was it so important to prove anything to the morons they'd been drinking with over in the sheds? She had a fair idea who the girl was and didn't exactly have a high opinion of her, but then she remembered what she'd been like at George's age. An outsider, partly because circumstance had forced her to grow up fast and partly because she could never dare to invite anyone home. Young Karen would, she remembered, have done a lot of stupid things in her efforts to fit in—had fitting in ever been an option—and she knew that both George and Paul were having a hard time of it in their different ways.

Still, that didn't excuse what they'd done. 'Did you ever think how scared she might have been? George, I can't get my head around this, I really can't. I thought you'd got more . . .' She broke off, biting back the words she really wanted to say. 'Go on,' she said. 'Tell me the rest.'

'We got the door open. I told Paul we should go. Right then. It would be reported to the police, you know, that someone had broken her door. We didn't need to do no more, but Paul, he pushed the door open and she were standing there, in the kitchen.' He swallowed convulsively. 'She had a gun, Kaz; it were pointed straight at us. We just ran and I got Paul back in his house and we were just shaking like . . .' He turned to look directly at his sister. 'I ain't never been so scared since Dad. You know?'

She nodded, shook the water from her hands and wiped them on her jeans then went over to him. 'Come here, you daft bugger.'

He accepted the quick, sisterly hug but then pulled away. 'There's more, Kaz, and it's really bad.'

Karen felt her heart skip. 'What?' she said softly. 'George, you know you can tell me anything.'

'It weren't me,' he said. 'It were Paul. Mark Dowling forced him to tell. He heard rumours, see. Shaz teased Paul about being a wimp and Paul said we'd done it. Done what she said and he must have told her about the gun because she told Mark Dowling and Paul tried to say it was all a joke but Mark got him and he almost broke his arm, gave him two black eyes and Paul told him.'

'And then?' Karen felt she knew the answer but she hoped against hope that she was wrong.

'Mark Dowling made him go with him to the old woman's house and Paul . . . Paul was there when he killed her.'

EIGHTEEN

Eight in the morning on a wet Monday, wind blowing off the sea and bringing with it the salt tang of cold sea spray.

Mac walked briskly along the promenade, glad that the weekend was over but not quite as depressed by it as he usually was. That, he figured, was because he had worked for a good part of it. And, of course, he'd had company, a rarity in itself.

After leaving Rina's the previous afternoon, he had taken a walk down towards the tin huts. It had been dusk, too late for him to gain anything but a general impression of the place. To his surprise he had discovered a creative mix of newer, purpose-built units, large Portakabins and what looked like giant arches with corrugated roofs, which, he supposed, were remnants of the Nissen huts left over from the war. Apparently there had been a small airfield here, Tim had told him, but he didn't know what function it had served. There had also been accommodation of some sort—Rina thought it might have been a POW camp—where the small industrial units were now.

Peering into the gathering dusk, Mac had tried to get a feel for the layout of the place. The huts themselves were the buildings furthest back from the town, probably about a mile and a half from the sea front. The newer buildings reached forward towards the town and Mac could make out the embankment from where the railway line swung back towards the promenade. The little coffee shop where he had found his Italian coffee had once served as the main station building, though, oddly, the Railway pub was nowhere near the now defunct line.

Well, Mac thought, *that's Frantham-on-Sea. No regard for logic.*

Returning to his cheerless flat, he had spent the evening checking through a week's worth of accommodation pages trying to find himself a place to live once his short tenancy expired. The date was now fast approaching. He had a couple of numbers to try later but, frankly, had found the whole experience a little deflating. Anything decent seemed allocated as a holiday let. In fact, judging by the state of his own flat, anything not so decent seemed assigned that way too.

Andy was just unlocking the doors when Mac arrived at the station.

'Morning.'

'Morning, Boss, have a good what was left of your weekend? The bigger boss said to come into his office when he arrived. The coffee's on.'

Mac nodded thanks, not that he actually liked Eden's coffee. Thick enough to stand a spoon and strong enough to dissolve same, it devoured milk and refused to change colour even for artificial creamer. In Mac's experience, it took three sugars just to tame it enough to be drinkable. Still, it did guarantee to keep you awake; a morning cup lasting until mid-afternoon before the caffeine crash came.

Mac paused at the desk and checked the day book. A couple of entries had been added regarding the Saturday night but they were the expected range of drunk in charge, disorderly or passed out on the pub steps. Plus a lost dog and a stolen car that turned out to have been borrowed by the teenage daughter and not stolen after all. Mac wondered how long she was likely to be grounded for—and, indeed, if kids actually did get grounded these days.

Sergeant Baker wandered out of Eden's office with a steaming mug in his hand. 'Thought I heard you,' he said. 'Andy, lad, get yourself in here too. Anyone wants us, they can ring the bell on the desk.'

It was, Mac reflected, a stark contrast to any other place he had ever worked. They were technically in the middle of a murder enquiry here; anywhere else would have been a hive of activity and awash with additional staff. Here, in Frantham, they hadn't even set up an incident room and his 'additional help' had been Andy pulling a bit of overtime along with the two community support officers.

For a moment, Mac felt his irritation rise at what might have looked like neglect of duty, but in truth that really was not the case. He couldn't fault the forensic side of the investigation. Couldn't argue, either, with the efficiency with which the initial enquiry had been carried out or with the additional officers who had arrived and busied themselves within that first, precious, golden hour when evidence is fresh and shock might be relied upon to lower guards and loosen tongues. The truth was, until all the forensics reports were in and the initial information collated, there was little else that could be done.

Mac knew it was all a question of priorities but he could not help but compare this to the last time he had been involved in a violent death—the manpower dedicated to *her* death, to the search for *her* killer, the level of public interest in the enquiry, the way the media had kept it in the news for weeks.

Mac had been a policeman long enough to know that there was no such thing as equal, especially when it came to murder. Some deaths, like some lives, just generated more column inches, shouted louder than did others and, Mac reflected sadly, Mrs Freer had no one to keep her face in the papers and her pain on the television screen.

Could he be the one to keep it there? Shuddering, recalling the days, the weeks when he'd had no choice in the matter and no control over the type or level of exposure, Mac knew he could not.

Dragging his thoughts back to the present, Mac grabbed his mug from the shelf just inside Eden's office and held it out to be filled.

'Sit your bum down,' Eden said. 'Hotch up a bit, Andy, give the inspector some elbow room. Now, what do we know?'

Ten minutes were spent in bringing everyone up to speed. Mrs Freer, events over the weekend, news from up the coast of a drug bust and a stabbing outside a nightclub. 'Not life-threatening, thankfully. Fight over some girl, it looks like. I've managed to get a recent picture of the old lady,' he added. 'Her previous carer had one taken with her last summer. She came forward with it over the weekend, thought it might be helpful. The local papers have picked it up and the news will carry it at lunchtime. You know how it helps if the public can put a face to the victim.'

So maybe that would equal the score just a little, Mac thought. 'The wasteland at the back of the house. How well was it searched? From what I saw the focus was on the road and gardens.'

Eden nodded. 'Manpower,' he said. 'Or, to be PC, should I say, "availability of personnel". I had the search extended to the ditch just at the back of her place and that bit of a path the kids use on their bikes. I'm hoping to hustle up some bodies later in the week. Particular reason for asking?'

Mac shrugged. 'I was over there yesterday,' he said. 'It occurred to me the weapon might have come from the waste ground rather than the house. A half brick would have fit the wound profile.'

'Anything forensically to back that up?'

Mac shook his head. 'No, nothing in the wound,' he admitted. 'It was just a random thought.'

Eden nodded. 'It needs searching,' he admitted, 'but the size of team required to do it is considerable and not at present forthcoming. Cordoning the area is not only impossible but impracticable. The world and his wife have access. I'm hoping if we put the word out we'll rustle up some local volunteers. Your friend Rina might help out there?'

Mac nodded. 'I'll get on to it,' he promised. 'Might be worth putting the word out at the local pub too, and even on the Jubilee, try to get them onside.'

He paused for the general murmur of agreement then asked, 'What do we know about the Parkers? I'd lay money on the boy being involved in some way. The Robinson boy, too, though according to his mother butter wouldn't melt. Someone had beaten seven shades out of him and I'll lay another bet it didn't happen at school.'

'It could have done,' Sergeant Baker pointed out. 'Boys that age do get into fights. Any reason why not?'

Mac shook his head.

'I do,' Andy said unexpectedly.

'Oh, and what would that be?' Frank Baker demanded.

'Because I went to school, didn't I? I mean, I went to the same local comp and they have staff standing by the school bus, watching the lines. If he'd been beaten up at school then even if the staff didn't catch up with it in class, chances are they would have done when he got on the bus.'

'How much notice do they actually take?' Mac asked. 'I mean, if a kid wanted to hide something . . .'

Andy was shaking his head. 'Four members of staff plus others. Teachers, classroom assistants, prefects, all on a rota. They have to check all the bus passes. The passes have photos on and, believe me, they're worse than passport control. The bus drivers used to do it but it was too slow and they reckoned it wasn't their job. Anyway,' he finished, 'it wouldn't have happened at school without someone noticing. *I'd* bet on that.'

'Regular little gambling den we've got going,' Eden commented.

Andy grinned. 'I know the Parkers and the Robinsons,' he added. 'Karen Parker was only a year behind me in college. *Everybody* fancied her. Everybody.'

'Give you the brush off, did she, lad?' Frank Baker wanted to know.

'She gave everyone the brush off. I reckon she just wasn't into men, if you know what I mean.'

An explosion of laughter from Sergeant Baker. 'She maybe didn't meet any men at that college of yours,' he said.

'Or it could be she'd seen enough to put her off,' Eden added. He got up and crossed to one of the large metal file cabinets lined up on one side of his office. Mac watched in fascination. A file, actually in the cabinet? One that was not part of the strata on Eden's desk?

Eden sat down with a thump. 'Get me some more coffee, will you, Andy? Anyone else?'

Mac shook his head. He'd be buzzing for hours as it was. 'She has a record?' The surprise showed in his voice.

'Karen Parker? No, not her. The father. He's how come they ended up here. Thanks, Andy. The local refuge lets us know when one of their families gets housed, just in case whoever they're running from tracks them down. I had a chat with Karen when they first moved here, and called her now and then afterwards, just to make sure she knew she could ask for help if she needed it. She's a good kid, kept the family together. They moved nine times in two years before they finally fetched up here. My liaison at the local hostel told me they were terrified the dad would find them, but I figure they must have realized if they'd gone any further south they'd be in the sea, or in France.'

'So, what do we know about the father?' Mac asked.

'Nasty piece of work, as you may have gathered. No mastermind but a habitual criminal, finally ended up inside with five years for armed robbery. The wife waited for him, though by all accounts he was already treating her like dirt. He served his time, came out to join a terrified wife and two kids that barely knew him. Karen was thirteen at the time and George must have been seven, and by all accounts it all went very wrong very fast. Two years on and Carol Parker gets taken into hospital for the umpteenth time . . .' He paused, rifled through the file and handed photographs to Mac. Mac recognized the hair rather than the face. The features were too bloated and bruised to be properly recognizable.

'That time he broke her jaw and her cheekbone. Oh, and three ribs, and she was still refusing to press charges. Scared out of her wits. Karen was fifteen by then and she took young George and camped out in the local police station, refused to move until someone got them the help they needed. Parker senior had beaten on the kids too, and Karen was ready to testify even if her mother wouldn't—or couldn't. Anyway, by the time they went to arrest the dad, he'd flown.'

'She struck me as a very mature young woman,' Mac said. 'The boy though, he was twitchy, nervous. Like I said, I had the impression he wanted to tell me something but didn't have the nerve.'

'Best give it another try,' Eden said.

Mac nodded thoughtfully. 'I was planning on it.' He glanced at the clock on Eden's wall. Nine fifteen, the kids would already have gone off to school.

The phone in the outer office began to ring.

NINETEEN

The trip in on the school bus had been tense and uncomfortable. It was impossible to talk about anything that mattered. Looks cast their way, curious and shocked, queried the bruises on Paul's face but no one asked. George and Paul were always on the farthest bank of mainstream popularity anyway, but those few enquiries that might ordinarily have been made were diverted by the fact that Dwayne had positioned himself in the seat on the opposite side of the aisle and spent the entire journey taunting both Paul and George, hinting that he knew exactly how Paul had come by his injuries. The kids close enough to hear listened warily, but no one commented. No one wanted to become the focus of his attention and then, by implication, attract the further attention of Dwayne's gang. Most didn't even dare think far enough to include Mark Dowling in the equation. Mark was the bogeyman, the unthinkable.

Paul kept his head down as they got off the bus. Staff watched as they filed into school, pointed and whispered to one another as they saw his face. One stopped him, laying a pale, manicured hand on his shoulder. 'What happened to you?'

'Got into a fight, Miss.'

'That isn't like you, Paul. Does your form tutor know?'

He shrugged. 'Dunno, Miss, me mam phoned in on Friday. I was off.'

George shuffled awkwardly as Paul mumbled his reply. Dwayne, already in the corridor, had turned, inane grin in place as he mimed someone with their arm twisted behind their back.

George looked away, afraid someone would notice. Someone would guess. They would guess that part and then know everything.

'Well, get along both of you or you'll be late,' the teacher said finally, seemingly blind to the irony that she was the one responsible for their tardiness. Silent and tense they made their way to their classroom. Their form teacher, Miss Crick, eyed them both thoughtfully, her gaze resting longest on Paul's face. She said nothing but entered their 'present' mark into the electronic register that linked to the central computer system.

'Everyone have their ID cards?' she said. The standard morning question. Today, unusually, everyone did. ID cards, scanned through readers, allowed library books to be borrowed, lunch to be paid for, attendance in class to be registered as they filed through the electronic doors and swiped their cards. Not to have a card was a serious offence and involved a trip to the principal's office to beg for a temporary replacement. Dwayne was a regular in that particular queue.

Then the bell for first lesson rang and they were heading out again, Paul separated from George by the press of the crowd and, George felt, because Paul had contrived for it to be like that. George blinked angrily at tears that forced their way to the corners of his eyes; he suddenly felt so terribly alone.

* * *

Andy put the call through to Eden's phone. 'Anonymous tip,' he whispered to Mac and Sergeant Baker as he re-entered the room.

Mac raised an eyebrow and turned his attention to the one-sided conversation going on at Eden's desk. Finally, Eden laid down the receiver.

'Anonymous phone call to our colleagues in Exeter,' he said. 'A woman, calling from a phone box in Dorchester, naming one Mark Dowling as the culprit.'

'Dowling,' Mac said, the name that had been unfamiliar a few days before now all too common. 'Any details?'

Eden shook his head. 'Just the name. She stayed on the phone just long enough to give them that.'

Mac glanced at the others and knew they were thinking the same thing. 'There's absolutely no reason we should think . . .'

'That our informant is Karen Parker? No, none at all, but . . .'

'So,' Mac got to his feet, 'where do I find Mark Dowling?' he asked. 'Time for a talk.'

* * *

Rina had dragged Tim off to the local library. 'The fresh air,' she told him, 'will do you good.'

'In a library? Library air is full of dust and microbes, Rina. Books that haven't been opened so long we probably don't even have immunity to the microbes any more. Full of Victorian microbes.'

'The fresh air on the walk there will do you good. It's bracing out there this morning, and anyway we aren't going to look at books, we're going to look at the newspaper archive and we might make use of their internet connection too.'

'Rina, you've got internet here.'

'I've got dial-up here. The library has broadband. Get your coat.'

Still grumbling, Tim did as he was told. 'What are we looking for anyway?'

'Smugglers, of course. Didn't you listen when I told you about the cigarettes, the people?'

'I listened,' Tim said. 'I just don't see what it has to do with us?'

Rina shrugged. 'Look upon it as your civic duty,' she said.

'I can't.'

'And why not?'

'Because,' Tim told her grandly, 'Frantham is only a town. To have a civic duty you have to be a citizen and for that one must live in a city.' He looked sideways at her, received Rina's best brand of withering look and fell silent. Well, he'd thought it rather clever. Maybe she was right and he should get out more.

The walk to the library was only short. The walk to anywhere in Frantham was pretty much the same. Tim entered the red brick Victorian edifice in Rina's wake and looked about with interest, noting the high galleries that ran around three sides and housed what looked to be an extensive reference collection and a music section. The gallery was supported on high Roman-style arches in red brick and white stone that reminded him vaguely of the Natural History Museum in London.

'Never been here either, have you?' Rina asked him.

Downstairs was a more utilitarian affair. A pair of librarians sat behind a Formica desk that supported a computer attached to a barcode scanner and a stack of box files. Behind them, file cabinets acted as a divider between them and the suite of computers Tim glimpsed beyond. Rina, of course, knew them both and Tim endured the inevitable five minutes of chat before they moved on. It wasn't actually Rina's need to stop and exchange pleasantries that irritated him, Tim realized, so much as his profound inability to make that kind of small talk; that lack left him feeling awkward and self-conscious. He nodded politely at what he hoped were the right moments and then, gratefully, followed Rina once again right to the back of the building, past the newly refurbished computer suite to where, she told him, the newspapers and the microfiches were stored.

'Can't I go and play with the computers?' Tim asked.

Rina sighed indulgently. 'Soon, Tim,' she said. 'We'll see what we can find here first, then you can go and play on the internet or whatever.'

Tim gave in with reasonable grace. After all, he had nothing better to do with his day. 'OK, so how far back do we want to go?'

It was actually more interesting than he had anticipated, though that was largely because he kept getting sidetracked and reading articles that were not totally relevant to the search. He was surprised that Rina had been right about the smuggling in the area. Frantham had its own weekly paper, the *Frantham Echo*, mostly taken up by advertising but also carrying a round-up of the local news and also some original reporting. Smuggling in Frantham had been a major story both times it had been discovered, and the second report had put this in the context of historical occurrences going back several hundred years. Rina's little cave and others like it dotted along the coast had certainly seen some action.

Tim cross-referenced the abridged articles taken from other papers and, following Rina's guidance, printed the sections they wanted. A couple of hours in, they had a stack of cuttings and notes to add to Rina's file, and Tim was bored.

'Can I go and play now, Mummy?'

Rina slapped him with her cuttings folder. 'Go on then, but I doubt you'll find anything fresh. I think we've gleaned all we can.'

Tim wandered back into the library and sat down at the nearest terminal, following instructions for logging on. One of the Exeter papers had an extensive website, but it told Tim little more than he had already discovered—at least, so far as he could remember. The articles had tended to run together in his mind after a while, though he knew from experience that later on, when his brain had time to figure it out, the articles he read would collate themselves almost of their own accord. That, Tim knew, was the way his mind worked.

Idly, Tim began to enter other things into the search. His own name—yes, he did have a website, though it was badly in need of updating. Rina Martin, of course, both as Lydia Marchant and in other less famous roles, provoked a clutch of entries, and the Peters sisters, he was pleased to discover, were still remembered with great affection by fans of music hall.

On a whim, he entered Mac's name. Detective Inspector Sebastian McGregor. He hadn't expected anything and was surprised to come up with a whole raft of hits. Reports in national as well as local papers and even a couple of entries on TV news sites.

Curious, Tim opened one of them up and read it quickly. 'Bloody hell.' He read on, then returned to the back room.

'Rina? Rina, I think you should take a look at this. Our pet policeman has a past.'

Rina shrugged. 'Of course he does, dear. We all do.'

'Well yes, but I mean a *past*, past. No wonder he looks so bloody harassed.'

Rina came back with him to the computer and together they read about Sebastian McGregor. He was, it seemed, something of a hero. Twice over. He had saved a motorist from a burning car, faced down an armed man in a hostage situation, had an impeccable record, or so the papers said. Then it had all fallen apart, big time.

A child had been abducted by a friend of her family. He had a record for violence and sexual abuse but her family had not known that until afterwards. The reports were unanimous, that no one was quite sure what happened in the intervening time but that three days later, DI McGregor had come face to face with the man and the child on a deserted beach. A handover had been arranged, so someone claimed. Another claimed that McGregor had tracked him down. A third that it was a tip-off from a member of the public. Tim was astonished at the vagueness of it all.

There were arguments too about Mac's actions on that night. Had he called for backup? Had he decided to go it alone? The fact that other officers arrived only minutes after the terrible events indicated that he had in fact called for help, but the statements made by the police were vague and there was nothing from Mac himself.

The one thing that was indisputable was that the child had died.

Tim and Rina studied the picture of Cara Evans. Six years old, pretty, with light brown hair, smiling out of the picture. She wore a party hat and hugged a doll and she looked happy and vibrant and so very much alive.

'He killed her on the beach,' Rina said softly. 'The man that took her. Cut her throat. You know, Tim, I remember this. It was all over the news because it was so utterly horrible.'

'And our policeman was there.' Tim was oddly moved. 'But he couldn't do anything to stop it happening. My God, Rina. How must he feel?'

'We don't mention this,' Rina told him. 'Mac has travelled a long way to get away from this; we don't tell him that we know.'

TWENTY

It was mid-morning before George managed to get Paul alone for long enough to tell him what he had confessed to Karen. Morning break was only fifteen minutes, just long enough to grab a drink, and it was under the pretext of going to the vending machine that George managed to get his friend out of the classroom.

Finding a relatively empty stretch of corridor, George stopped, forcing Paul to halt beside him. 'Listen,' he said. 'Karen knows. I know I said . . . But you can't keep anything from our Karen and I'm glad I told her. She said she'll help.'

Paul grew so pale beneath his bruises that George honestly thought he was going to faint. He leaned back against the wall, closing his eyes. His breathing became frighteningly fast and shallow.

'Paul, I'm sorry . . . Actually no, I'm not. We can't do this on our own.'

'He'll kill me,' Paul whispered. 'He really will. I'm dead.'

'He won't know. The police will come for him now. It'll be OK.'

Paul opened his eyes and stared at his friend. 'You mad?' he said. 'What's your Karen going to do? Phone them up and say "I know who killed the old woman. It was Mark

Dowling. You know, psycho Mark what beats the shit out of you soon as look."?'

George didn't know what to say.

'How they going to prove it? You think we'll get home and he'll be gone, just 'cos your sister says so?'

George shook his head but it occurred to him that, naively, that's exactly what he was thinking. That's what had happened with their dad. Karen said she'd sort it after the ambulance took their mum away and she'd sent George off to the shops. Their dad had disappeared when the ambulance arrived but George knew he'd be back as soon as the police cleared off. He always did and he'd been worried about leaving Karen there alone, but she'd insisted. 'Go,' she'd said. 'Here's a list of stuff we need.'

And when he'd come back, their dad wasn't there. Karen was still cleaning up the mess, scrubbing blood off the kitchen floor. But their dad wasn't there and Karen said he was gone for good.

She'd been wrong though, hadn't she? George had seen him.

And if she'd been wrong that time, maybe she was wrong about this. Maybe Paul had been right all along. Say nothing, do nothing. Hope it all went away.

'Look,' he said. 'It'll be OK. It's got to be.'

Paul pushed away from the wall and began to walk away.

'Paul!'

'Just leave me alone. Just leave me alone!'

George stared after his friend, hurt beyond words and terrified that he really had done the wrong thing. 'Paul!'

The bell rang for the end of break and the corridors began to fill. Gnawing at his lower lip, George headed for class, wondering what the hell he should do now.

* * *

Mac had half expected to be going to the Jubilee to see Mark Dowling, but instead Andy drove them both to a neat, detached house out on the main road close to the tin huts.

'Dowling senior's OK,' Andy said by way of explanation. 'He worked hard to get this place. The oldest son, Terry, works with his dad, but my dad reckons he's a lazy sod and not that good either when it comes to cars. Then there's another brother, Alan. He left a couple of years back. I don't know where he went to but he was like an insipid version of Mark. Fancied himself as a hard man but never did quite hack it. Rumour has it he and Mark didn't see eye to eye and Alan thought it was safer to leave.'

'You know the family well?'

Andy shook his head. 'Not really. I remember Alan from school and Mark too. Alan actually stayed on and took some exams. Can't remember what. Mark left first chance he got and he wasn't there much anyway. When I was a kid living on Newell Street, our mam would only let us play up the posh end and we were allowed to go down to the promenade and on to the beach but woe betide if she found out we'd gone down the lower end. I had a friend lived in the housing association houses and he was allowed to come up to us but I was never allowed to go to his. His mother had a right go at mine, one time. Reckoned she was a right snob.'

'And was she?'

Andy laughed. 'Well, yeah, a bit. But she was always worried about Dowling's lot. She said that some kids were born bullies and that he was one of them.'

Mac looked up at the Dowling house. Edwardian, he guessed, red brick with a gravel drive and surrounded by a tall laurel hedge. It sat oddly in the landscape. The brick had mellowed a little with the years but still struck a strident chord. Mac was growing fond of the look and feel and pallor of the local stone.

'You worried about this?' he asked. 'Bearding the lion in his den?'

'No,' Andy scoffed. 'Course not.' Then, when Mac allowed the silence to grow, he shrugged. 'Well, maybe a bit. When you've spent half your life avoiding someone it feels a bit odd deliberately confronting them.'

Mac nodded. 'But you think he's capable of having done it?'

'Oh yes,' Andy said softly. 'Damn right I do.'

The front door was opened by a middle-aged woman. Her dark brown hair struck a harsh note against the white of her skin, as did the overly bright red of her lipstick. She had once been pretty, Mac guessed. Her bone structure was good and her blue eyes a very intense forget-me-not. Age had not been kind. Lines that he did not think were due to laughter cobwebbed out from her eyes and channelled deeply beside the bright slash of a mouth.

'Mrs Dowling?'

'Yes?' She scrutinized the identification, then shrugged. 'You want Mark, he's upstairs,' she said. 'Second door on the left of the landing.' Then she left them, disappearing into what appeared to be a sitting room off to the right of the large hall.

Mac raised an eyebrow. 'OK,' he said slowly. 'Well, up we go.'

Mac led, aware of the nervousness exuded by his younger companion. It wrapped them both in a miasma of uncertainty and Mac felt the illogical desire to hurry ahead, escape from its penetrating influence.

Music filled the upper floor, greeting them on the landing and leading the way to the second door designated as Mark's room, which turned out to be a surprisingly long way down the corridor and towards the rear of the house. *A deceptive property, as the estate agents would say*, Mac thought. From the front it had the appearance of something squat and square, when in fact it possessed a surprising depth.

Standing outside the room, Mac could feel the bass beat coming up through his feet. Knocking and hoping to be heard seemed a lost hope. He opened the door and the two of them stepped inside.

'Who the fuck are you?' Mark Dowling, sprawled across an unmade bed, had to shout over the top of the music. Mac crossed to the stereo and turned it off.

'Your mother said we should come straight up,' he said. 'I told her we wanted a word.' He flashed his ID, but was aware that Dowling wasn't looking. He was staring over Mac's shoulder at Andy. Mac shifted position so that he could keep both younger men in view. Andy, mouth pinched and tight, had coloured up, the redness of his face and neck now challenging the brilliance of his hair.

Dowling was smiling now. 'Oh, I know who this is,' he crowed. 'You. A bloody copper? That desperate, are they?'

'Mr Dowling.' Mac drew his attention away from the blushing probationer. 'Where were you last Thursday night?'

Dowling scowled. 'How the hell would I know?'

'Last Thursday, into Friday morning. There was a murder, Mr Dowling, and your name came up with reference to our enquiries.'

Mark Dowling laughed and tossed back the thick black hair that had fallen across his face. It needed a wash, Mac noted, and it looked as though the length of it was due more to lack of a good cut than a desire to be unconventional.

'What's that got to do with me?' He got up off the bed and crossed to where Mac stood, ignoring Andy now, though Mac was sure he'd noticed how the probationer took an unconscious step away as he passed by. He was as tall as Mac, but not as well built. He had a wiry, agile frame, and a feline, dangerous quality to the way he moved. He stank. Sweat, beer, a faint sweetness that might have been cannabis. Mac breathed shallowly.

Dowling was naked apart from a pair of designer underpants and the heat coming off his body transmitted his scent across the few inches between them. Dowling either had no regard for personal space or he had every regard for the usefulness of ignoring it. Mac didn't move.

'I said, what's that to do with me?'

'We're following up on information received. So, where were you last Thursday night and into Friday morning?'

Dowling shifted position, scrutinizing Mac closely; he moved in even closer. Inconsequently, an image from one of the *Alien* movies popped into Mac's mind. Ripley being sniffed by the alien queen.

'I was with a girl,' Mark Dowling said.

'I'll need her name. She'll confirm this, will she?'

Dowling laughed as though Mac had cracked a really impressive joke. 'You can bet your life she will,' he said.

* * *

Paul had said nothing during either of their two after-break lessons and when the lunch bell rang he was out of the class faster than George could gather his things. Desperately worried, George piled his stuff into his bag and took off after him, struggling down the corridor against the crowd now headed for the dining hall. He almost lost him by the rear entrance that led out on to the playing field, caught a glimpse as he rounded the side of the building, heading back towards the small side gate. The gate would be closed at this time of day, George knew. It was locked except first thing in the morning and at home time when it was opened up for those students who lived on that side of the town. But George also knew it was climbable and he realized suddenly what his friend was planning to do.

'Paul!' He ran after him, turning once to glance back towards the school, wondering what were their chances of being seen. Empty classrooms faced out over the field, as did the kitchens and the kitchen store, but no one there would be looking out of the window at this, their busiest time of the day.

'Paul, wait.'

'Get lost,' Paul shouted back. 'Ain't you done enough?'

Panting, George caught up with him at the little gate. 'Maybe,' he agreed. 'Maybe I did, but I was trying to help. You gotta believe that. You can't run away from it.'

'Just watch me,' Paul told him.

'It don't work, running away. Paul, I should know. Look at me and me dad. We run away halfway across the country and he still found me.'

Paul turned and looked at him and George remembered that he hadn't told his friend this. He'd been too shocked at Paul's news about the murder. Too aware that his own problem must seem small in comparison.

'What d'you mean?'

George sighed. 'I saw him. I'm sure I did. Last Friday when you weren't here.'

Paul said nothing but it had at least given him pause and George was grateful for that. 'They'll know we've gone,' he said. 'Soon as next lesson starts. The register will show it up.'

'We?' Paul said. 'I never said I wanted you to come with me.'

'You think I'm going to be left behind? You got any money? Anything?'

Paul shrugged.

'Thought so. Well, I do. I've got me bank card with me. Karen makes me put money in the bank and makes me keep me card with me. She says you never know.'

Paul shrugged again and began to clamber over the gate but he no longer objected to George following. George sensed that he was secretly relieved not to be alone. But this was still a daft thing to be doing.

'We could go back now,' he said hopefully. 'No one would know.'

'And catch the bus home?' Paul was scathing. 'He'd be waiting for us—you know he would. Waiting for me anyway.'

George sighed but could think of no words to confound his friend's argument. He'd set things in motion now. Told Karen. Karen would have told the police and, of course, Paul was right, Mark Dowling would still be out on the streets, not locked away on the grounds of anyone's say so, and he'd have guessed that Paul had been the one to tell on him. Mark would be waiting. Paul was right. He couldn't go home and while he couldn't, neither could George. He should have left well alone.

George dropped down on the other side of the gate and trotted off after his friend, catching him at the end of the road.

'So, where do we go now? We need to keep out of sight till home time.' The school had a serious policy about truanting and even the local shop keepers had been given the number to ring should they see kids in uniform roaming about during school hours. Those that had a legitimate reason to leave had to apply for a letter from the principal and be sure to carry it with them.

'We'll find somewhere,' he said. He stopped and pulled his coat on over his uniform.

George did the same. It was cold out and he shivered, wished he'd brought gloves. He slung his backpack across his shoulders and shoved his hands deep into the pockets of his coat, hoping that wherever they found to hide it would at least be somewhere inside.

* * *

'So, what now?' Andy said as they returned to the car.

'We check out his alibi—which, of course, will be confirmed—then we chase up known associates and interview them. We put the pressure on and keep it there and hope forensics come up with something useful.'

'Think we have enough to apply for a search warrant?'

Mac shrugged. 'I think we should let Inspector Eden take care of that. He's more likely to know who to approach; I'm still sorting out who's who.' *And I've got a lot of that to do before he retires*, Mac added to himself. 'But I'm hopeful, let's say. If the blood found at the scene is a match, we're ninety per cent there.'

Andy started the car but made no move to put it into gear.

'Got a problem?'

'Yeah. I do. I behaved like a big girl's blouse, in there, didn't I?'

'Not that I noticed,' Mac told him. Out of the corner of his eye he saw Andy sneak a sideways glance and open his mouth as though he'd like to say more.

'Look,' Mac said. 'No sense beating yourself up about it. You did fine and you'll do better next time. We've all got our Mark Dowlings. We all have to learn to face them down. Now, where does this so-called girlfriend live?'

'OK, right.' Andy nodded emphatically, snicked the car into gear and eased slowly back on to the main road. 'Trisha Howard. I was at school with her too. Never figured her for Dowling's sort.'

'Oh? And why's that then?'

'Because she always had more than half a brain,' Andy told him. 'Just goes to show.'

TWENTY-ONE

Trisha Howard wasn't home. The next-door neighbour informed Mac that no one would be in until later—and what did the police want anyway? The Howards weren't trouble makers. Mac was getting used to this kind of treatment on the Jubilee Estate.

'Just want to ask her a few questions,' Andy said. He smiled at the woman. 'It's Mrs Norman, isn't it? You remember me; I used to go to school with your Alison.'

The woman scrutinized him closely. 'Andy Nevins,' she said. 'Never figured you for a life of crime.' She laughed at her own joke. 'I thought your mother wanted you to go off to university.'

Andy shrugged. 'I thought about it,' he said. 'But I'd had enough of school. Mam always fancied I'd be a lawyer or some such but I didn't think I'd got the brains, to be honest.'

A burst of laughter from Mrs Norman. 'So you became a copper instead. Not so many brains.'

Not thought that one through, Andy, Mac thought. But he said nothing, deciding that the woman, having got the better of the local police, might open up about Trisha Howard.

'Our Alison went to university,' she said.

'I heard. Doing OK, is she?'

'Oh, she's doing very well. First of our lot to get a degree, she will be. So, what did you want with young Trisha?'

'Just a few questions,' Mac said. 'Her name was mentioned in connection with our enquiries.'

'Oh?' She took a step towards him.

She's almost salivating, Mac thought. 'Nothing serious,' he said. 'But she might be able to confirm something for us. What time is she likely to be home?'

'About five,' the woman said. 'I always told my Alison, keep away from that girl. She's a bad lot.'

'I thought she and Alison got on OK at school,' Andy said mischievously.

Mrs Norman scowled. 'She had to get along with her, didn't she, seein' as how she lived next door. Anyway, she wasn't so bad then. It's since she took up with that other lot.'

'Other lot?'

'Oh, you know. She's been hanging round with that Dowling boy. Now there's one that was never any good. Not even as a little kid.' Her eyes narrowed. 'It's about him, isn't it? What's he been up to now? Is that girl involved? As if she hasn't put her mother through enough. I always told my Alison—'

'So, about five then,' Mac said. 'Thanks for your help.'

Andy grinned broadly. 'Say hello to Ali, won't you?' he said and followed Mac back to the car. 'It'll be round the whole estate before Trisha gets home,' he said. 'Mrs Norman will be waiting on the doorstep for her. Always was a right gossip. Y'know, we should send uniform to do the follow-up call. I mean, not me. I mean, proper uniform.'

'And you're not proper uniform?'

'You know what I mean, Guv. So, where next?'

Mac realized the younger man had recovered from his encounter with Mark Dowling.

* * *

The school noticed the absence of Paul and George at the start of the next lesson but nothing was done until the end of that period when the teacher dropped into the office on the way to her next class.

'Paul Robinson,' she said. 'I saw him come in this morning; his face was a right mess. Is he all right, do you know? Only he wasn't in class.'

The secretary checked the computer log. 'He was in all the morning classes,' she said, 'but he didn't buy lunch.'

'Gone to see the school nurse?'

'No, nothing this morning except a verruca.'

The teacher frowned. 'What about George Parker?' she asked. 'He's Paul's best friend, that's why I thought . . . about the nurse . . . George might have gone with him.'

She checked. 'He didn't get lunch either. Was he missing from your class as well? Right.' She picked up the phone and dialled through to the principal's room. Fifteen minutes later, Miss Crick had been summoned and they were checking the cameras, scanning through the time code just after the start of lunch.

'There, look.' Miss Crick pointed. 'What the hell are they playing at? This isn't like Paul and it certainly isn't like George. He never steps out of line.'

'Yes, well he has now. Time to call the parents, I think. Do we have work numbers? Right, good. And we don't know what happened with the boy's face?'

Miss Crick shook her head. 'The mother phoned him in sick on Friday, said she'd had to take him to casualty with a suspected broken arm. Paul had told her he'd been in a fight, which isn't like him at all. She was convinced he was being bullied, but I told her we weren't aware of anything in school.'

'The arm, the injuries to his face, *did* they happen in school time?'

'No, even the mother had to admit that. She said Paul went out on the Thursday evening. Friday morning, she discovered the injuries and took him off to hospital. She doesn't know what happened and he's not telling.'

'And now he and George have run off.' The principal, Mrs Hedgeware, drummed her fingers on the table top. 'Who dealt with her on Friday? Just you?'

Miss Crick nodded. 'She asked to be put through to me. It was lunchtime by then but I'm not sure what time. I had to come into the office and change Paul's record to an explained absence. That should be logged and I spent about fifteen minutes on the phone with her. Very insistent, she was, that her son had been bullied. It took an age to establish that the supposed bullying hadn't actually taken place here. I'm afraid that's all I know. Paul looked very hang-dog this morning. I was going to grab him for a chat after last period. They were due to be with me then.'

Miss Hedgeware nodded. 'OK,' she said. 'So, we know when they went, we call the parents, and I think we should inform the local police. I wouldn't bother, normally, not this fast, but considering Paul's trouble last week, I think it might be wise. My guess is they'll sneak back before home time and try to get on to the bus as normal.'

'I hope so,' Miss Crick fretted. 'I really do.'

* * *

At three thirty Miss Crick, Mrs Hedgeware and assorted other staff took up their positions close to the school entrance. Mrs Robinson was on her way but George's mother had been impossible to contact. The police had sent a uniformed officer and he had been posted by the rear gate, just in case the boys should return that way. Miss Crick was of the opinion that they would try and join the crush of kids waiting for the buses just inside the main drive. It would be fairly easy to slip unseen through the gates and simply mingle with the crowd. She waited by the gate, chatting idly to some of the sixth formers whose turn it was to help with crowd control and looking out for the shock of red hair that marked George. She was irritated by the attitude of the police. *One officer. What good would that do?*

'That man's here again,' one of the sixth formers said.

'Man?' Miss Crick asked.

'Oh.' Jo, a bright girl in her final year, shrugged. 'He was hanging about last week. We thought he might be a parent but no one met him.'

'You reported this?'

Jo shrugged again. 'Sorry. Forgot all about him over the weekend.'

'He was here on Friday?'

'Yeah, and someone said they'd noticed him earlier in the week. Think it was Chris, Chris Johnson, he was on the duty roster for then but he'll have already gone tonight.' She looked at her companions for confirmation, received tentative nods. 'Sorry, Miss, I didn't really think about it.'

Miss Crick glanced around, scanning the crowd for signs of the two missing boys. 'You know what George Parker and his friend look like?' Jo nodded. 'Well, keep a look out. I'm going to talk to our curious friend.'

The man was staring hard at the queues of kids waiting for the bus. He stood on the opposite pavement, hands thrust deep in the pockets of his leather coat. Grey trousers, sharply creased and polished shoes. *Not cheap*, Miss Crick thought. The man was tall, perhaps six feet, and his sandy hair was close cropped. Clean shaven, he nevertheless showed a degree of shadow about the jaw and upper lip, as though he was thinking about trying for a beard but not yet committed. A faded scar marked his jaw and ran down on to his neck.

'Excuse me,' she said. 'Are you waiting for someone?'

His eyes were the palest of blues and utterly expressionless. *Not dead*, she thought, *just without . . . any emotion.*

'Excuse me, but are you waiting for someone?' she repeated.'

'What's it to you?'

She was taken aback. The voice did not fit with the clothes. 'This is a school,' she said.

'It never is.'

She frowned. 'You don't have to be rude.'

'And I don't have to tell you my business.'

He had turned away from her again, and was once more scanning the queues of kids boarding the line of buses.

'Are you waiting for someone?' she persisted.

The man glanced angrily at her, blue eyes hard now. 'If I am, it's my business.' He moved away from her. Not sure what she should do and wishing that the police officer had been posted on the front gates and not the rear, she returned to where the sixth formers were standing.

'I've not seen them,' Jo reported.

'Do you have a camera on your phone?'

Jo looked surprised. 'Yeah, sure. Why.'

'That man. Do you think you can get his picture? But do it so he doesn't notice.'

Jo nodded, grinned at Miss Crick. 'What's he done, Miss?'

'Nothing. I just don't like the look of him.' *Or the feel*, she added to herself. The man had unnerved her. Rudeness she could deal with, was almost used to. This was something else. It filled her with a sense of unease, and it raised the hairs on her neck.

Jo took the phone from her pocket and discreetly took a couple of pictures. 'You want me to try for another one from over there, closer to the gate?'

Miss Crick shook her head. 'No, he might see. I don't think that's a good idea. Jo, how awkward would it be to download them to one of our computers?'

'No probs; it's got Bluetooth, Miss. Want me to do it now?' She was clearly thrilled to be part of something mysterious and just a little bit risky.

'Please. Could you do it now and print them out?'

She scanned the area again. The buses were leaving now and the crowds thinning. The man turned to walk away. She went to the gates to try and see where he might go, but the buses blocked her view of him. When she could look next the man had gone.

* * *

When Dwayne hopped off the bus at Frantham, Mark was waiting for him and Dwayne could see he was not in the best of moods.

'Where's Robinson? Don't he get off the bus at this stop?'

'Er, next stop,' Dwayne said warily. 'But he ain't on the bus.'

Mark squinted at him and then looked back at the vehicle, pulling away from the stop. 'Not on the frigging bus? Why not?'

'I dunno. He weren't in class this afternoon. They were looking for him after school. Him and George Parker. They called the cops.'

'They *what*?' He grabbed Dwayne by the shoulder and shook him. His fingers dug deep into the boy's shoulder.

'Gerroff. You're hurting.'

'So what. What do you mean they called the police?'

'I told you, I don't frigging know. They went off somewhere at lunchtime. Never came back. Paul's mam came up the school and there was a copper waiting by the back gate.'

Mark released him and Dwayne staggered backwards. Aggrieved, he rubbed the painful shoulder, knowing it would bruise. 'What's up anyway?'

Mark Dowling didn't answer him. He turned on his heel and strode away. Gratefully, Dwayne slunk off towards home, head down as though the weight of the world prepared to bury him.

TWENTY-TWO

More of Eden's coffee. Mac felt he needed it after an unproductive afternoon of chasing Mark Dowling contacts. The only good thing to have come out of it was his feeling that all of their enquiries would get back to Dowling. He was convinced they would rattle him sufficiently.

'So, this warrant. Any chance?'

'Oh, I think that might be easy enough. No one likes thugs who beat up on old ladies, never mind kill them. Leave it to me.'

Sergeant Baker knocked at the open door. 'Just had a phone call from our colleagues in Dorchester,' he said. 'Two kids have gone missing from the local comp and you'll never guess who they are.'

* * *

The obvious things done—checking the boys' homes to see if they'd returned there, driving around Frantham to see if they could spot the pair on the streets—Mac and Andy made their way to the school.

'Both kids were scared,' Mac said. 'I could see that when I talked to them. But what scared them so much they had to do a runner?'

'If our anonymous caller was Karen Parker . . .' Andy began.

'And if George was the one who gave her the information, then yes, they might have guessed that things would hot up with Mr Dowling.'

'So, they thought they'd get the hell out.'

Mac nodded. Eden was going to contact Mrs Parker and also try to get hold of Karen. 'Where would two thirteen-year-olds get off to? Did they have money? Or, more to the point, did *George* have access to money? According to Paul's mum, he might have had a bit of change on him, but that would have been all.'

'Let's hope not,' Andy said. 'Can't run far without cash.'

Mac nodded. He thought about Mark Dowling and the way he had intimidated Andy and, if he was honest, caused a distinct sense of unease in Mac himself. Paul and George would be terrified.

'So, what did Mark Dowling beat out of young Paul?' he wondered aloud.

Andy shrugged. 'Karen will know,' he said.

* * *

Mrs Robinson was frantic. She blamed George, she blamed the police, she blamed the school for not controlling its bullies. She blamed the state of the world.

'Mrs Robinson,' Mac said quietly, interrupting her tirade. 'Did Paul ever mention Mark Dowling?'

Mrs Robertson sat down with a thump. 'Dowling? No, I told Paul to keep clear of that little lout. You don't think . . . ? Oh. Oh my God, you don't think . . .'

'Mrs Robinson, it's inevitable that your son should come into contact with him—or, if not him, then with the kids who associate with him. From what I hear, Dowling attracts a lot of interest from the local youngsters. Did Paul ever mention him?'

'Or ever change the subject when you did?'

Mac glanced at Andy in surprise and then nodded. Of course, far more likely to be that way around.

Mrs Robinson had grown pale under her pancake of foundation. 'I don't know,' she whispered. 'I really don't know. I mean, he wasn't a subject that came up in our house unless I was telling Paul to keep away. And he's a good kid, Inspector. Never really stepped out of line. Neither did George. I mean, I know what I said just now about him leading Paul astray, but George is a good kid too. And he had such a rotten time before they came to Frantham. I tried. I tried . . .' She was in tears now; the anger that had carried her through until now had dissipated and been replaced by frantic worry.

'Where did they go? Why did they go? What did that animal do to my Paul?'

Mac drew Andy to one side, leaving Mrs Hedgeware to try and comfort. 'You know her,' he said. 'And you seem to be hitting the right notes. Talk her through anything that's happened in the last week or so. Anything off-key. See if she knows how to contact George's mother, or better still, Karen. The school doesn't have their work contacts, but she might. I'm going to take a look at the CCTV footage.'

Andy nodded and went back to Mrs Robinson. Mac went with Miss Crick to look over the tapes.

'We lock the back gate during the school day,' she told him. 'But as you can see, it's hardly an obstacle.'

Mac nodded. 'Did any of the staff mention that their behaviour was off? Unusual in any way?'

She sighed, shook her head. 'Everyone wondered about Paul's face,' she said. 'He'd got two right shiners. But you know that. He seemed very reluctant to talk and, frankly, I don't think anyone had the time to press it. I would have done at the end of the day but . . . well, I never got the chance.' She shrugged helplessly. 'The thing is, George and Paul are usually quiet. They don't draw attention; they don't stand out. I like the pair of them and I could tell you what their grades are in every class they have, but the fact is—and it's only just hit me today—I don't really *know* either of them. They're quiet, average, nice boys.'

Mac nodded. The woman was clearly pained by this but he didn't know what he could say that would offer comfort. 'That's probably what my teachers would have said,' he told her. 'I don't think I was ever particularly memorable.'

She grimaced and Mac guessed that this offering had not been what she wanted to hear. 'And definitely no sign of them at the gates tonight,' he mused, more to himself than to her.

'No, nothing. There was something, though. But it's probably totally unconnected.'

Mac raised an eyebrow. 'What would that be?'

'Oh, this man. He was standing on the other side of the road, watching the kids getting on to the buses. He didn't do anything, but it was just a bit odd. Some of the students said he'd been there last week too.'

'Did you talk to him?'

'I tried. He was downright rude.'

'Can you describe him to me?'

'Oh,' she said, 'I can do better than that.' She sounded pleased finally to have something positive to offer. 'I got one of the students to take his picture on their mobile. Oh,' she added anxiously, 'I made sure he didn't see her. Of course I did.' She went over to the printer and fished out two A4 sheets from the tray. 'This is him,' she said.

TWENTY-THREE

There were no lights on in the house. Karen swung the front door open and shouted. 'Hello? Anyone home?' Puzzled, she flicked on the lights and slammed the front door, calling out again before looking in the kitchen and then going up to George's room. It would not be the first time he'd retreated to his room as soon as he'd come in and just stayed there.

'George, you in there?' She knocked then pushed the bedroom door open and switched on the main light. He sometimes played his computer games in the dark, but this time there was definitely no one there.

'Bet he's at Paul's,' Karen muttered to herself. Their mother would not be home yet; Mondays she worked a later shift and caught the last bus, getting in just after ten. Leaving the front door on the latch, Karen went in search of her brother.

It was clear from the alacrity with which Colin Robinson opened the door that something was wrong. 'Oh,' he said. 'I thought . . .'

Karen stared at him in puzzlement. 'Is George here? There's no one home.'

It was his turn to be puzzled. 'You don't know?' he said. 'I assumed . . .'

Seems to be the night for broken sentences, she thought. 'Knew what? Has something happened to George? To Paul?'

Colin Robinson stared helplessly. 'You'd better come inside,' he said.

'I can't; I've left the door unlocked. Mr Robinson, what's going on? What's happened?'

He shook his head and it occurred to Karen that she'd never actually seen him without his wife before and that usually it was Nora Robinson who did most of the talking. Without his mouthpiece he seemed unmanned. Helpless.

'What's been going on?' Karen persisted. 'Where are the boys?'

'We don't know.' The reply spluttered out. 'I assumed the police must have called and told you, or told your mam at least.'

'What do you mean you don't know?' She felt like shaking him. Make the words fall out. 'Mr Robinson?'

'They're missing,' he said and she could see that this man was struggling with the tears now he'd had to say the words. 'They went missing at lunchtime, climbed the gate. Nora's at the school, she's not come back yet. She reckoned I ought to stay just in case . . . Said someone ought to be here.'

Karen took this in, then made her decision. 'Make me a coffee,' she ordered. 'I'll shut up the house and I'll be back, then you've got to tell me everything. Before our mam gets home.'

Colin Robinson looked momentarily taken aback but then he nodded gratefully. 'I'll leave the door ajar,' he said. 'I'll get the kettle on.'

Mark Dowling, Karen thought as she went back to secure the door. *Bloody Mark Dowling*. The police must have gone to see him and he must have threatened the boys. But no, that couldn't be it; she'd only made the call that morning and the boys would have been safely in school by then. She collected her keys and fastened the door, made her way back to the Robinsons'. No, that wasn't it; couldn't be. George must have told Paul that he'd spilled everything to her and Paul must have freaked out. George wouldn't just leave his friend. That just wasn't in his nature, though, thinking about what the pair of them had got up to the week before, Karen half wished it was. Paul would never have had the nerve to break in anywhere on his own, any more than George would.

She pushed open the Robinsons' front door and called out to alert Colin Robinson that she was back. He appeared at the kitchen door.

'Um, do you want to go through or . . . ?'

'Kitchen's fine.' She managed to smile at him. She sat down and took the proffered coffee, refused the sugar, trying to keep her expression calm and simply concerned while her mind screamed that she and George had both played this one all wrong.

'So what happened?' she asked gently. 'Did anybody see them go?'

* * *

Half an hour later Karen had left the Robinsons' house. She stopped off at home to pick up her coat and a torch and then went out again, walking with determined steps across the wasteland and back towards the main road.

'Lunchtime,' Colin Robinson had told her. The cameras had recorded the boys climbing the small gate and then running off down the road. The school had noticed they were missing by a quarter to two and raised the alarm.

Karen paused, shone the torch on her watch, glad now that she'd bought it. She'd picked it up at a sale in an army surplus shop a while ago and now the weight of it in her hand and the powerful beam was very reassuring. It was almost seven. George and Paul had been missing for almost five hours.

Paul would have had no money with him, but Karen was pretty sure that George would have his ATM card. She'd always nagged him about having access to at least enough cash to get himself home, get himself a meal. Until now

Karen's advice had been unnecessary; now she wondered if it had, after all, been for the best. She wasn't certain how much cash George had in his account, but reckoned it was at least fifty or so. How far could two boys run on fifty quid?

Not far in real terms, she supposed, but far enough.

'Does Paul have a mobile?' Karen had asked.

'Yeah, but it's still in his room. I checked.'

So, she thought, no luck there. She had thought about getting George a cheap one last Christmas, but knew neither he nor their mother would be able to afford to keep putting credit on it and that it would be another financial strain she would have to take on. She wished fervently she had done so now though. Mobile phones could all be traced these days— she was pretty sure of that. She had read somewhere that, even switched off, most emitted a signal of some sort.

Angrily, she shook her head. No good asking 'what if?', is it? Probably no good doing what she intended to do now either, but that was beside the point.

The back of Mark Dowling's house was visible now, rising beyond the six feet of privet hedge.

Karen skirted the boundary and pushed her way through brambles out on to the main road. She brushed herself down and then marched up to the imposing front door. A light burned in one front window but neither of the Dowling cars was there. It was Mark himself who opened the door.

'Well, well. Look who it is,' he said. 'It's Georgie Porgie's big sister. What the hell do you want?'

Good question, Karen thought. Just what did she want? All fired up, she'd come here wanting to confront this bastard and now she was here she hadn't the slightest notion of what good it would do.

Annoyed with herself as much as she was provoked by Dowling, she took a step forward, placed her hand in the middle of his chest and pushed him back inside.

It was the last thing he expected. No one laid hands on Mark Dowling. Off balance, he staggered back.

'Hey! Right, you want to play like that?'

Regaining his balance, he lunged at her. Karen brought the flashlight down hard upon his outstretched arm, then, before he could react, she had swept it upward, her full strength behind it. It caught Dowling square on the jaw. Stunned, he went down. Karen, merciless now, followed through with a vicious kick. She caught his nose with her heel. The crack as it broke was both unnaturally loud and deeply satisfying.

'You're a bastard, Dowling,' Karen spat as he lay writhing on the tiled floor of the Edwardian hall. 'You may have scared two kids witless, but you don't scare me and I promise you this, I'll make bloody sure you go down for what you did to that old woman and for what you did to my brother's friend.'

Dowling made as if to struggle to his feet but she raised the torch again and he thought better of it. From the pocket of her coat she produced her mobile phone. Eyes fixed on Dowling, daring him to move, she took his picture.

'Always good to have a souvenir,' she said.

Dowling staggered to his feet, but she was ready for him. The long-stemmed torch caught him a glancing blow on the temple this time and sent him reeling across the hall.

'I'll bloody get you. I know where to find you, bitch; you'll wish you'd not been born.'

Karen's look was pitying. 'Mark,' she said softly, 'someone already tried that. They didn't manage it either and, believe me, beside him, you're just a sad little amateur.'

She left, slamming the door behind her, hurried back towards the waste ground and only then did she ask herself what the hell she thought she'd been doing. It was so utterly irrational.

Karen glanced at her watch again and then shone the torch on her coat and shoes. Some blood, but not a massive amount. Abruptly, she turned on her heel and went back to the Dowling house. Mark Dowling, a towel pressed over his bloody nose, opened the door again. Karen really hadn't thought he'd be that stupid.

His eyes widened, but she gave him no time to react this time. She left him where he lay on the hall floor, wiped the doorbell with the end of her scarf and headed towards home.

That, Karen figured, was a much better, much more rational way to finish things.

* * *

Back at the house she shed her coat carefully, emptying the pockets and then rolling it so the blood was inside. On her way home she had made two phone calls to her mother's mobile. Neither had been answered. She then washed her hands, checked her shoes and went back to the Robinsons' and knocked on the front door.

'Any news? I've been trying to get hold of Mum but she must have left her phone in her locker when she got changed.'

'Nothing. Nora's on her way home. Did you try her work number?'

Karen shook her head. 'No point. Reception's closed. There's just the cleaning staff and they won't answer the phones. You think Mrs Robinson will be long?'

'A half-hour I would think. I'll give you a ring if you like, when she comes in.'

'Thanks. I appreciate it. Mum's going to go frantic.'

She trotted back to her own house and checked her watch again. Half an hour. That was fine.

She collected the torch from where she'd placed it on the draining board, washed it under a running tap, scrubbing at it with anti-bacterial cleaner. Then she popped her raincoat into the machine on the quick-wash setting, half load. Karen never bought anything that might encourage dry-cleaning bills.

She dismantled the torch, cleaned the batteries and wiped everything down with a clean cloth, then placed the dismantled sections into a carrier bag. Moments later, fresh coat and gloves on, she was cutting across the wasteland once again, but this time towards the undercliff.

Karen was almost shocked at how calm she felt. If George was right and he really had seen their father then she'd obviously not done the proper job she thought she had that other time. This time, there would be no errors. No one, but no one, was going to threaten her family ever again—and she had absolutely no conscience about ridding the world of Mark Dowling.

'Justice,' she said softly. 'Just common law.'

Her watch told her that fifteen minutes had passed. One by one she took the parts of the torch and threw them far out over the cliff. The carrier bag she folded neatly and shoved into her pocket to join one already there. Karen was a green citizen; she always reused her bags. She could post it into the supermarket recycling box the next day. Her gloves went into one of the large bins at the back of the hotel.

Back home, she checked the phone for missed calls. No, the last number recall was exactly the same as it had been when she left. The Robinsons had not yet phoned.

Don't you just love technology? Karen thought.

She was upstairs hanging the damp but well cleaned raincoat on a hanger in her room when the phone rang. She rushed downstairs.

'Hello? Oh, Mrs Robinson. Any news? Yes please, I'll be round in a minute. Thanks so much.'

She lowered the receiver and took a last careful look around. Then, checking that her damp trainers were drying out beneath the radiator, she put on her slippers and went back round to see the Robinsons.

TWENTY-FOUR

George and Paul had spent a cold afternoon hiding out in the local park about half a mile from their school. A thicket of trees close to the children's playground provided them with cover but not the best of shelter and they shivered in the fierce wind that blew across the open grassed area and between the swings before it was finally muffled by the trees.

At least the cold put people off coming to the playground with their kids, George thought to himself, but it was cold comfort. Bitterly, icily cold comfort.

Three fifteen came finally and at least gave them permission to move and be out and about. The only danger now was from any kids that might know them. George was thankful for the fact that both he and Paul merged so much into the background that only their classmates were likely to be looking out for them and most of those bused it in to school from Frantham and other settlements nearby.

They made their way back into the town centre, trying to look purposeful, as if they were actually going somewhere. George quickly realized that no one was really paying them any attention anyway.

They kept warm by wandering in and out of the bigger shops. They talked very little. Paul seemed sunk in the deepest and most morose of thoughts and after a while George gave up all attempts at conversation.

By five o'clock George was really suffering from the lack of lunch and what threatened now to be the lack of dinner.

'I'm starving,' he said. 'Look, we'd better get something to eat.'

'What with?'

'I told you, I've got money in the bank. I just need to find a hole in the wall. Come on.'

Reluctantly, Paul plodded after his friend. He stood watching listlessly as George fed his card into the slot and slowly keyed in his PIN. He'd only used it a couple of times and he panicked momentarily, wondering if he'd got it right, then a moment longer as he wondered if the police knew about his card and if they'd blocked his bank account or something.

'Look,' he said finally, retrieving his card and two crisp ten-pound notes. 'I told you.'

Paul seemed to rally a little. 'How much you got?' he asked.

'About another forty. I've been saving. Look, let's get some grub, then we can have a think about what we're going to do next.'

Paul sank once more into despairing mode and George sighed impatiently. 'Come on,' he said. 'There's a chip shop back that way. Got seats inside. Let's sit down for a bit.'

'What if someone sees?'

'So, they see. We're going to be eating fish and chips just like a load of other people. What's the big deal?'

'What about CCTV?'

'God sakes, Paul, we've been captured on camera I don't know how many times since we got here. Everybody is. But no one's going to be looking that hard for us, at least not yet. We've only been gone since lunch.' He sighed. 'Look, maybe you better call home, let them know you're OK. You got your phone?'

Paul shook his head. 'Left it home, didn't I?'

'Then we'll find a phone box somewhere.'

Paul shook his head.

'Come on then, let's at least get something to eat. My belly's hurting.'

With a show of reluctance, Paul ambled after George and they found the chip shop George had noticed earlier.

'Eat in, please,' George said. 'Fish and chips twice, thanks.'

'You want mushy peas?'

Manners cost nothing, Karen always told him. He could hear her saying it now.

George shook his head and then nodded. 'Yes thanks, and two Cokes.'

He paid and then led the way to a small table at the back from where they could watch the door. Paul slumped down and George arranged cutlery while they waited for the food to be brought. Karen was right about that too, he thought. It was always better, somehow, when you had something to do with your hands.

'Enjoy your meals.' The woman smiled at them both.

'Thanks,' George said, absurdly glad he'd remembered his manners. He sprinkled salt and then vinegar, tucked in, ignoring Paul completely, noting a few reluctant minutes later that his friend finally began to eat and that soon he was filling his face with as much enthusiasm as George.

George put his worries aside and focussed on his food. He was always hungry. Kaz said it was because he was growing, but George reckoned it was because he could remember going without food so often when their dad came home. Food became another weapon to be used and denied whenever it pleased him.

Kaz said once he was like a stray dog that had finally been taken in. He just couldn't believe that there would always be food and he felt he had to stock up every time it was offered, just in case.

Their dad, George reckoned, had a hell of a lot to answer for. It was probably just as well he was growing or he'd end up fat.

He wiped his plate clean with the last of his chips and was pleased to see that Paul had demolished most of his meal too and, though he'd slowed down a bit, was showing no sign of giving in. He didn't look as pinched and pale either, though the bruising still looked stark and painful.

'You want another Coke?'

Paul nodded and George went to the counter, feeling in his pocket for some change.

'What happened to your friend?' the woman behind the counter asked.

'Oh, he was in an accident,' George told her. 'He's a lot better now.'

The woman looked quizzically at him but made no further comment. George glanced out into the street. It was fully dark now and the streetlights had come on, the crowds thinned down almost to nothing.

He'd made no further mention of his father to Paul; tried not to make it obvious as he scanned every face as they passed, just to make sure. He wondered if he'd been waiting at the school gates again, and if anyone had noticed him.

Karen had been so sure, George thought as he took their drinks back to the table. But it seemed that in the complicated world of George Parker, nothing was ever certain.

* * *

There was only so long that they could string out their stay in the little café and when the woman came from the counter and started clearing their plates, George figured it was time to be off. They wandered aimlessly, back up the main street, unconsciously headed towards the school.

'So, what do we do?'

'I can't go home.'

'And we can't wander round here all night. We'll freeze for one thing.'

Paul shrugged. 'I dunno.'

'Look,' George decided he had to take control. 'The only place we know round here is school and we can't hide out there. I say we go back to Frantham, hide out in the tin huts.'

'You nuts? He'll find us there.'

'No, no he won't. He'll be like everyone else, expecting us to have run off, not going back home. You got a better idea?'

'You've got some cash,' Paul said slowly. 'We could go somewhere.'

'And how long you reckon that's going to last? We've got to eat as well.' He sighed heavily, wishing himself back home. In the warm. With his TV and his computer games. More than that, he wished himself back before any of this had happened. 'Look,' he said, 'I'll get the rest of the money. We'll go to the bus station. We passed a sign for it a bit back. We let ourselves be seen on the cameras so everyone will think we must've caught a bus, and then we go back to Frantham.'

'How? I mean, that's the one place we can't get a bus to.'

'We walk,' George said. 'It's a straight road. It ain't that far.'

Paul scowled but George could tell he couldn't fault the plan and he couldn't better it. 'OK.' Paul shrugged. 'OK, I suppose that's what we'll do.'

George felt a surge of anger rise from the pit of his stomach and wedge itself in his chest. 'This isn't my problem,' he wanted to say. 'It weren't my idea to skip out of school.' But he swallowed the words before they reached his tongue. Paul was his friend, and anyway, part of this *was* his problem. He couldn't just walk away.

He was generous enough to realize that he, George, had already experienced some really bad stuff and had come through it. He had some idea of what he could survive. For Paul this was the worst of the worst and he had nothing in his life with which to either compare or from which to gain courage.

'Come on,' George said. 'We'd better get off. We've got a long way to go.'

TWENTY-FIVE

Just after eight, Mac made a call on the Robinsons' house.

Nora Robinson sat with her husband at the kitchen table, a half-drunk mug of coffee in front of her. Her husband's appeared to be untouched. A third mug sat between them, a trace of lipstick on the rim.

'Karen's been in and out all evening,' she said. 'The poor girl's worried sick. She's only just been able to contact her mum.'

'And how are you?' Mac asked quietly.

'Oh, you know.'

'Any more news?' Colin was staring hungrily at Mac. 'I just can't understand it. It isn't like either of the lads to do this.'

'We've got a possible sighting,' Mac said. 'It came in just as I was driving back.'

'Oh?' The eagerness with which they both turned to him caused Mac acute guilt that it wasn't more. 'You know the school provided us with pictures?'

Nora nodded.

'Well the local beat officers and community support have been doing the rounds with them. A woman in a chip shop in the middle of town is sure they came in for a meal about half past five. They had fish and chips and mushy peas and, she says, they just about ate the pattern off the plates.'

'Little sods.' A burst of laughter came from Colin. 'She's sure, is she?'

'Ninety per cent. George is fairly distinctive with that red hair. She says she took special notice because he was so well mannered, but the clincher is she noticed the bruises on Paul's face. She says she asked George what happened to his friend and he said he'd been in an accident.'

Mac smiled his tight, awkward smile. 'At least you know they've had something to eat.'

Nora Robinson nodded slowly. 'But nothing since that?'

'Not yet, no. But the pictures are out there now and there's CCTV close to the café where they ate. And, now we've got a rough time, it should be possible to pick them up again. It will just take a bit of time.'

'Karen said George would have his bank card with him,' Colin Robinson said. 'I knew Paul would only have a bit of change for the drinks machine.' He seemed relieved, as though Mac's news meant that his son would soon be walking through the door. Nora still seemed harassed and doubtful. No less anxious.

'But why did they go off like that? I can't understand it.'

Mac had his ideas, but now was not the time to posit them. He needed to talk to Karen first. 'The important thing is that they seem to be OK at the moment. We've got a lot of eyes looking for them, Nora. We'll bring them home.'

She nodded, unconvinced. 'It's got to be something to do with what happened to Paul,' she said. 'Doesn't it?'

Mac rose, ready to go. 'I'm going to have a word with Karen,' he said. 'I'll let you know the moment we have anything more.'

He let himself out; glancing back from the front door he could see them both, still sitting at the kitchen table, each buried in their own thoughts. It was odd, Mac thought; they were married, had a child together, lived together, but they both seemed so very much alone.

* * *

157

Karen opened the door as he stepped up to it. 'I saw you go to the Robinsons',' she said. 'I almost came round, but Mam's on her way and it would be just bad luck if she arrived when I wasn't here. Any news? You want some coffee? I think I've drunk a week's worth here and round at the Robinsons'.'

Mac smiled. 'Thanks,' he said. 'That would be welcome.' He told her about the sighting and she laughed as Colin had done. 'Good old George,' she said softly. 'Always bloody starving. This woman, she said they looked OK?'

'She liked George's manners,' Mac said. 'She said that he looked fine but that Paul seemed a bit out of it. She'd actually wondered if he was on something until he started to eat. Then she reckoned he looked more normal. But yes, they looked all right.'

'Thank God for that,' she said with a fervour that surprised him.

'You know why they ran?'

Karen poured boiling water on the instant coffee and added milk. 'Sugar?'

He nodded. 'Do you know why they ran, Karen?'

She hesitated. 'It sort of depends,' she said. 'Depends if it was George or Paul doing the running. I've been thinking about it and it could be either way.'

Mac frowned. This was a new angle. 'I admit,' he said, 'I've been working on the assumption that Paul was running scared of whoever beat him up. I'm assuming you know who that might be?'

She smiled. 'And why would I know?'

'Because even though he wouldn't tell his parents, he'd be likely to confess all to his best friend, and from what I've seen of his best friend and said friend's sister . . .'

Karen smiled, shook her head. 'Mark Dowling,' she said. 'Paul got on the wrong side of that little bastard.'

'And George? What was George afraid of?'

Karen chewed her lower lip. It was the first sign of indecision Mac had observed in her. 'He thought he saw our dad,' she said finally. 'Outside the school gates last week. He was really freaked out. I'd told him we'd run far enough, that he'd never find us here, and I think he'd actually started to believe that.'

Mac frowned, another piece of the puzzle slipping into place. 'Outside the school, close to where the buses wait?'

'Yeah, I think so. Why?'

Mac dug into his pocket for the photograph they had printed for him at the school. He'd folded it to put in his pocket and a crease now ran, scar like, cutting the man's face in two.

He watched as the colour drained from the girl's face, then pulled out a chair from beneath the kitchen table and sat her down. 'It's him, then?'

She nodded. 'He's put on a bit of weight.' She took the picture from Mac, laid it out on the table and studied it intently. 'That scar's new, on the side of his face, down on to his neck. But yes, that's him. Oh my God, poor George.'

'Karen, did you make a phone call earlier today? To the police in Exeter?'

She looked puzzled. 'What, about our dad?'

'No, about Mark Dowling, accusing him of Mrs Freer's murder?'

The front door opened. 'That'll be Mam.' She got up, headed towards the kitchen door.

Carol Parker had a sense of timing, Mac thought. 'Karen, did you make that call?'

She turned to Mac. 'Please,' she said. 'Can we talk about that later on? I know it's important but . . .'

Carol Parker burst into the kitchen and dropped her bag on to the floor. 'What happened to our Georgie? Oh, Karen, where's he gone? Where's he gone?' Then she stopped dead in her tracks and fell silent, staring at the picture which still lay on the kitchen table. Her scream took Mac utterly by surprise. Loud and piercing and repeated, on and on and on.

Karen grabbed her mother, forced her down into a chair and Mac grabbed the picture, fumbling it into his pocket. No need to ask, he thought abstractedly, if she recognized who it was. Karen was fighting with her mother now, as Carol ripped at her hair and tore at her face in a frenzy of grief and fear that had Mac retreating, helpless, into a corner.

'What do I do?' he shouted over the noise. Carol was wailing now, the screams less piercing but no less distressed. 'I'll call a doctor.' He went out into the hall, then into the living room so that at least he could hear. He spoke to Eden, explained what was happening. Karen appeared at his side. She went to the sofa, pulled the cushions free and dug deep into the lining.

'Sedatives,' she explained. 'We keep them for emergencies. George knows but Mam doesn't; she'd take the lot.' She extracted two from the bubble pack, handed the rest to Mac. 'Put them back, will you?' Then she retreated to the kitchen.

Mac looked at the pack he was holding. The prescription was an old one, the date almost a year ago. 'Two tablets, as needed,' the label said. From a bubble pack of sixteen, eight tablets were now gone. A second pack was untouched inside the crushed box. He recognized a trade name. His own doctor had prescribed them for him when he'd finally crashed. Couldn't think, couldn't function, couldn't even sleep. He'd taken them for a week or so, Mac recalled, and the world had retreated to a pleasantly hazy distance for a while and—though he'd still been unable to think and decidedly unable to function—sleep, albeit with the most vivid of dreams, had at last come without the need for a half bottle of whatever was available that night.

Not sure what else to do, he hid the pack and replaced the sofa cushions, joined Karen in the kitchen where screaming and panic had now subsided into choking sobs as Carol tried her best to swallow tablets and the water Karen was holding for her.

The doorbell rang, and Mac opened it to the doctor who'd attended Mrs Freer that first morning when the carer had found her.

'Inspector Eden called me,' he said. 'I'm just up the road.'

Mac nodded. 'Thanks,' he said. The doctor passed him and went through to the kitchen. Mac looked on as Karen explained what she had given her mother and gave a medical history with a precision and calm that left Mac astounded again by the quiet control of this very young woman.

'We've got to go,' Carol was saying over and over again. 'Got to go.' Hysteria returned as the doctor suggested she lie down upstairs. 'No, we've got to go. He'll come back. We've got to go.'

Mac could see from her eyes that the drugs were kicking in. 'We've got to get her out of here,' Karen said. 'She's terrified he'll come back.'

'I'll try to arrange a safe house,' Mac said. 'Or a hostel?' He looked expectantly at the doctor but it was Karen who replied. 'They give priority to women in immediate danger,' she said. 'Mam's not. Not that immediate, anyway.' She sighed. 'Maybe a hotel, just for tonight?'

Mac felt in his pockets, knowing even as he did so that he was going to regret this impulse. 'Here,' he said. 'I'm renting a flat looking out on to the promenade. Take the keys, grab what you need.'

The doctor nodded. 'I'll get my car,' he said. 'Drive them up there.'

'Thanks.'

'But what about you? Is there somewhere for you to sleep as well?'

Mac thought about the lumpy sofa. Too short and too uncomfortable to do anything more than sit for a brief while. 'You'll have to share with your mam, I'm afraid. You'll find clean sheets in the top of the wardrobe. Frankly, I don't think I'll be getting much chance for sleep anyway, but if I do, I'll crash on the sofa.' He smiled in what he hoped was an encouraging fashion.

'Thanks,' Karen said again. She looked so relieved that Mac's misgivings faded, just a little.

Glancing at the kitchen clock he saw that it was already almost ten but when he ran through in his head all of the tasks that lay ahead of him that night, sleep, even on the lumpy sofa, looked to be a long way away.

TWENTY-SIX

By half past ten, Karen and her mother were installed in Mac's flat and he had informed the Robinsons of this additional problem.

'If George should happen to turn up here,' Mac said, 'I don't need to tell you to hang on to him and call me.'

Eleven o'clock saw the arrival of a drizzly rain. Mac reported to Eden, marking how old and tired his senior colleague looked, though, to be fair, even young Andy Nevins was flagging.

'You think Karen was a definite for making that phone call?' Eden asked him.

'She would have admitted it if her mam hadn't turned up,' Mac said. 'I'm sure of that. I'll talk to her about it later.'

'Question is,' Eden mused, 'does she have any proof of that or is it pure speculation based on what Dowling did to her little brother's friend? And, of course, it depends what else the rumour mill's been putting about. You seemed to think she had her ears open.'

'I think there's more to it than that,' Mac said. 'I'm just about convinced the two boys broke into the old woman's house. If Mark Dowling got wind of what scared them off . . .'

'Then the opportunity to get himself a nice little revolver would be just too much to pass up.' Eden nodded. 'It figures,' he said. 'I've got a warrant to search his home. Came through an hour ago. I suggest five o'clock might be a reasonable enough hour. He'll like as not be back from a night on the town and he's not likely to be awake enough to do a runner.'

'What if he's at his so-called girlfriend's?'

'Then we'll have officers posted there, just to be sure. I've managed to wangle a few extra bodies from our friends in Dorchester. I suggest we all try to grab a couple of hours' shut eye.'

Mac nodded. He got up and stretched. His body ached, through tension as much as tiredness as the old focus returned. He was, he realized with a slight but pleasant shock, starting to feel like a policeman again, instead of some great pretender.

'See you here at four, then,' he said.

* * *

Mac stopped off at the flat to collect some of his things but had decided not to stay. It didn't seem appropriate.

'Mam's asleep. Fast off,' Karen said.

'Good.'

'You stopping then?'

He shook his head. 'Going to bunk down at a friend's,' he said. 'You've got my mobile number?'

'Yes. I've got it.'

'Look.' Mac stood in the middle of his living room, his overnight bag clutched in his arms. He lowered it to the floor. 'Look, I know it's late but . . .'

'But you've got to ask about the phone call.' She nodded. 'Yeah, that was me, but you already sussed that. You want to know why? Because Mark Dowling beat seven shades out of Paul, made him tell about the gun and then beat on him some more just because that's the way he is. Then he made Paul go with him when he killed that poor old woman.'

Mac was stunned. He'd suspected most of this, but to hear it out loud and delivered so starkly came as a shock. 'Paul was there? Jesus wept.'

'Poor little bugger was scared out of his wits. He told George but made him promise to keep it secret. Course, I got it out of George. He's not used to keeping stuff from me. I thought, stupidly I suppose, that if I put Dowling in the frame, Paul's problems would be over. I mean, I knew it would have to come out that he was there and, as you've probably guessed, that it was him and George who broke in the night before.'

'Why did they do that?'

Karen shrugged, resigned. 'Got pissed on Sharon Bates's dad's booze, and couldn't resist the dare. Or face being made to look like a pair of wimps if they chickened out. Oh, they both knew it was wrong; George has been going through hell over it. I'd have made him tell, but it seemed more important to get someone to take notice of Mark Dowling.'

'Karen, you should have just come to us, told what you knew. When did you know?'

'Sunday night. I got it out of him. You're right though; I should have brought him in but he was horrified at the idea of dropping Paul in it. Paul's convinced he's an accessory to murder.'

'Well, in a way he is. But any decent lawyer would plead mitigation.'

She nodded. 'I know. It's just I'm used to protecting my own the best way I know how. I guess I don't always get it right. George must have let on to Paul that he'd told me and he must have been terrified. People—if you can count Dowling as a person, though I can't call him an animal; that would be downright insulting—the Dowlings of this world thrive on knowing they have everyone running scared. Even if that's just a thirteen-year-old kid. The Dowlings of this world need their entourage and that entourage has to be too shit-scared to step out of line. It's like Machiavelli said: "Men shrink less from offending those who inspire love than those who inspire fear."'

'Machiavelli?' Mac laughed. 'OK, Machiavelli. Though to be frank, I suspect that comparing him with Dowling probably insults the Prince more than it insulted the animals. Look, Karen, I'll need you to make a formal statement. I'll arrange it for tomorrow. If need be we'll sort out someone to come and sit with your mum while you do it. Meantime, try and get some sleep.'

She nodded. 'Yeah. I'm knackered. Look, thanks again. I really don't know what to say about this . . .' She gestured, taking in the scruffy little flat.

'Get some sleep,' Mac repeated and quietly let himself out, pausing on the stairs to listen as she locked the door and slid the bolt.

Then he went out into the night, his bag oddly heavy though there was very little inside it. He paused on the promenade and called Eden at home, waking him from sleep and then waking him more fully as he revealed that they had a witness to Mrs Freer's murder.

For a few minutes they discussed the possibility of bringing the raid forward, but it was already midnight and by the time everything was rearranged maybe only an hour or so would be saved in time.

'I'll arrange for a patrol to keep obs,' Eden said.

As Mac closed his phone and slipped it back into his coat, he glanced over at the headland where he had seen the lights. Nothing tonight. The sky was black and small clouds were scudding, not yet heavy with rain but busily gathering their moisture for later in the new day.

He turned and walked down on to Newell Street and paused outside Peverill Lodge, recalling that he had done the same just a few nights before. A light burned in Rina's inner sanctum. This time Mac knocked quietly on the door.

* * *

Rina sat him down at the kitchen table and Tim made tea. The rest of the house, it seemed, was asleep, but the two had been watching a late film together.

Mac filled in sparse details about his day, about the Parkers, Paul, Mark Dowling. He knew Rina could be trusted to say nothing and he needed to unload. She seemed unsurprised by any of it.

'There's a small spare room,' Rina said. 'We use it for storage so it's a bit cramped, but you can get to the bed. I'll find some fresh sheets.'

It sounded like heaven to Mac. Tim set his tea down in front of him and he sipped the scalding liquid gratefully.

'So,' Rina said, 'how much of a threat is this Parker fellow?'

'Hard to say, I suppose, but I've seen pictures of what he did to Carol Parker and I saw her reaction to his picture. She was terrified.'

'Why wasn't he put inside? It's common assault.'

'Because,' Tim said, 'she wouldn't press charges. Am I right, Mac?'

Mac nodded. 'Now, of course, the police can decide to press charges whether the victim is willing or not. But that wasn't true a few years ago. Karen was willing, apparently, but Edward Parker took off into the wide blue yonder before anyone could bring him in.'

Mac's phone began to ring, the tone uncomfortably shrill in the calm of Rina's kitchen. Wearily, Mac answered it. *What now?*

'You're kidding me? You're not kidding me. Right, OK, I'm on my way. No, be as quick for me to walk down. Fifteen minutes. Right.'

He closed the phone and stared at it, disbelieving.

'What is it?' Rina asked.

'It's Mark Dowling,' Mac said softly. 'His parents arrived back from seeing friends and found him dead on the hall floor. Someone killed him.'

'Should I applaud?'

'Rina,' Tim said. 'It's still murder.'

'And your point is?'

Tim shrugged. 'You want a lift down? The car's parked out the back.'

166

Mac had forgotten that Tim owned a car. 'Thanks,' he said.

Mark Dowling dead? Mac just hadn't seen that one coming.

TWENTY-SEVEN

George, used to the journey by bus only taking three quarters of an hour to get to or from the school, had not realized just how far it was by foot. Or how lonely.

They had carried out their plan and gone first to the bus station, but had been disappointed that no one seemed to be taking any notice of them. George thought that was inevitable, given that there was hardly anyone there. A sole driver sitting in his cab, reading the paper. A couple of people in the draughty-looking waiting room. They duly wandered round a bit and then George decided they should begin their trek back to Frantham.

Once away from the comfort of the streetlights, the night closed in around them. Barely any moon, little starlight despite the clearing skies. It was better once their eyes had grown accustomed to the dark, but it was still seriously spooky, their footsteps unnaturally loud on the tarmac and the night rustlings in the grass frighteningly alien.

Mice and foxes and stuff, George told himself. *That's all. Nothing scary.* He thrust his chilly hands deep into inadequate pockets, wriggled his backpack into a more comfortable position and plodded on.

Paul trailed behind him, lost in thought. Or, at least, George assumed he was. Paul seemed to be in shock. He had cheered up considerably once he'd eaten, though he'd still been morose even then. Now, with the fish and chips a long time ago and George's stomach telling him it could happily eat the same all over again, Paul seemed to have lapsed even deeper into that state of emptiness which, frankly, worried George to death.

It annoyed him too. He wanted company just now, someone to talk to, to pass the time with. A human voice to block out the skittering, creeping, twig-snapping noises that accompanied his every step.

An owl hooted and George nearly jumped out of his skin, despite recognizing it for what it was. A vixen called and a dog fox answered. George stared in the direction of the sound. Any other time and this contact with nature might have seemed exciting. Tonight, it just added to his sense of unease.

There had been little traffic and, thankfully, as most drivers were on full beam this late at night, they'd had plenty of warning and time to get off the road. That they might be seen by someone scared George even more than all the night-time stuff going on in the undergrowth. Who'd be out at this time of night? Somehow, George couldn't think of any good reason, any valid reason, and therefore anyone who was out driving this time of night was likely to be someone who George wouldn't want to meet.

It was two o'clock according to George's watch when they saw the sign that told them they were entering Frantham. George sighed in deep relief. 'Look,' he said to Paul. 'We just have to get round this bend, then we can cut off the road and hide out in the tin huts.'

Paul shrugged.

'Look, snap out of it, will ya? I'm tired too, and I'm scared too, and I don't know what to do either, but we got to get inside and get some sleep or something.'

Paul's look was withering. George could make that out even in the dark. Then he sighed. 'I'm sorry,' Paul offered. 'I'm sorry. I'm just . . .'

'I know,' George told him. 'But we'll figure it out. Just not tonight.' All he wanted to do tonight was sleep and he was pretty sure he would be able to sleep anywhere that was out of the biting wind and away from the increasingly cloud-laden sky.

Walking side by side now, they rounded the bend and then stopped dead. Recovering himself, George pulled his friend into the shadow of the high hedge. 'What the hell's going on? That's Mark Dowling's place, ain't it?'

Beside him he felt Paul nod. Then he heard him swear, softly but emphatically.

The brilliant neon blue of police lights illuminated the road. Car headlights were on. Figures passed by, silhouetted against their brightness.

Stealthily, George crept forward. There was, if he remembered right, a gate close by, with a stile that gave access to the public footpath across the old airfield. They were on the opposite side to their destination of the tin huts, but George was reluctant to cross the road when so many lights were pointed directly their way.

'Come on,' he whispered. 'Over here. Keep your head down.' Staying low against the fence, they got over the stile, back tracked a little in the shadow of the hedge, then George made a run for the old buildings he remembered seeing from the road on the odd times he'd travelled on the top deck of the bus.

Paul followed, his breathing hard and ragged. George wanted to tell him to calm down, that they'd hear him right across the road making that much noise, but then he realized that his own breath wheezed in his lungs, caught whistling in a throat that seemed closed tight against the flow of air.

The flat land, unbroken by hedge or tree, allowed for better visibility and a broken window gave them access into the building. This, George thought, must have been the conning tower—no, a conning tower was on a submarine. This would be the place where the flight controllers sat. It smelled damp and stale, as though the air inside had remained static and unmoved despite the years and the winter gales.

He tried to get his bearings, eager to find somewhere from where they might be able to see the road.

'Up here, mind the steps, they might not be good. Keep your feet near the wall.'

Gingerly, they climbed upward. George wondered how long it was since this place had been used. Vaguely, he remembered it had been built in the war and then used by a flying club until the money had run out. Reaching the top of the stairs, he tested the wooden floor. To his relief it creaked but felt sound and he was right, there were windows up here that looked towards the road.

George heard Paul stumble and then sit down hard. Glancing back, he could make out his friend's shape, slumped against the wall. He found a broken pane and, wrapping the end of his coat sleeve round his hand, managed to remove a few slivers of the cracked glass, enough to peer through into the outside world.

'I can see,' he said.

'What's happening?'

'Looks like three—no four—police cars and one of them vans, you know, they've got something scientific written on the sides.'

Paul grunted.

'You know what this means,' George said. 'Karen was right. They've come to arrest him. We can go home.'

He crept over to his friend and shook him hard. 'We can go home, Paul.'

In the dark he felt rather than saw his friend shake his head. 'Not till I know for sure,' Paul said. 'Not till someone can tell me they locked him up and threw away the key.'

George's heart sank but he knew there would be no point arguing with Paul tonight. He sighed and went back to his place by the window, grateful that at least it was not quite so cold in here, and they were out of the rain that had just begun and which he could feel as drops splashed through the broken window. Patiently, George settled down to wait for the night to pass and morning to bring some kind of solution. Minutes later he heard Paul snoring softly from across the room.

* * *

Mac followed the path laid out by the first officer on scene. The parents had rushed in, he told Mac, seen their son and tried to revive him. Getting the position of the body established had not been the only challenge; they had turned him over, tried to make him wake up and then spread trace and bloody footprints all over the scene.

Mac could see the tracks of a woman's shoe, high heeled and slipping in the blood as she hurried across to the hall phone.

'God, what a mess,' Eden said. 'And I don't just mean the state of the body.'

Mac nodded. The parents had done what parents do. They may not have liked their son, but he still was their son. They had reacted to the shock and the pain by doing what anyone would have done when they saw a loved one covered in blood and motionless on the floor: they had tried to help.

They had also messed up the crime scene, big style.

The crime-scene coordinator motioned them across to the foot of the stairs. 'You get the best view from here,' he said. 'So far as we can make out he was lying close to the door when they arrived. Face down on the floor with his head closest and legs stretched out towards the phone table.

'Time of death?'

'Based on liver temp, probably between seven and eight this evening, but as you can feel, the place is like a hot house, and that could throw our figures off.'

Mac nodded. 'They moved the body?'

'Turned him over, flipping him to the right. The father tried to give him CPR, but, well . . . It was a bit late by then.

172

The mother says she shook him, tried to get him to wake up. When she phoned the ambulance she said her son had collapsed and was bleeding. It wasn't until the crew got here that anyone realized how long he'd been gone.'

'Cause of death?' Eden asked. The jowls seemed particularly pronounced tonight, Mac thought, and the bags under his eyes had expanded to the size of steamer trunks.

'Your old-fashioned blunt-force trauma, so far as we can tell. Which blow killed him is a moot point, of course, but there's one odd detail.'

'Oh? And what's that?'

'His nose was broken. And you know how much noses bleed, even worse than head wounds at times. Well, there's a blood trail leading to the kitchen and that blue towel there—you see it? It's half beneath the body now, but . . . anyway, it's a match to the towels in the kitchen and Mrs Dowling confirms that's where it came from.'

'So,' Mac began, trying to figure it out, 'either he had a nose bleed and went into the kitchen for a towel then came back and opened the door to his killer, or his killer allowed him to clean himself up before hitting him again?' He looked expectantly from Eden to the coordinator, expecting a response. A contradiction.

'That's about what we've come up with. If there's a third way, as it were, I'm buggered if I can think what it might be.'

* * *

Karen, though tired beyond words, could not manage to sleep. She watched the television, sound turned right down, moving pictures refusing to make an iota of sense as she thought about her father and George and her mother and what they would have to do now.

She was reluctant to move on again. She had her jobs and her course and a boyfriend who, while not entirely serious as relationships went, made her feel good about herself.

Made her feel womanly, feminine, desired. And that was something she would be sorry to give up.

Just briefly her mind rested upon the earlier incident with Mark Dowling. And to Karen, that was all it had been: an incident born of necessity. Earlier, talking to Mac, she had quoted Machiavelli, and now another of his dictums came to mind. Irritated, she wished she had thought of it earlier and then there would have been no stupid hesitation in her dealing with Mark Dowling.

'If an injury has to be done to your enemy,' the Prince had said, 'then let it be done with such severity that you should have no fear of his revenge.'

Karen nodded, satisfied. She had thought she had dealt with their father that same way all those years ago, but she had been just a fifteen-year-old child then, fallible and afraid.

'I won't make that mistake again,' Karen said softly. 'Oh no, never again.'

TWENTY-EIGHT

The morning briefing on the Tuesday was a more formal and more crowded affair than Mac had been accustomed to in Frantham. Extra bodies packed into the reception area—a larger space than either Eden's lair or the general office. A mobile incident room was on its way from Exeter and expected by mid-morning. Until then, the usual display of crime-scene photos, approximate timelines and notes on the victim would have to wait.

'Mark Dowling,' Eden intoned. 'Let's say he's well known to us, shall we? Usual mix of joyriding and petty theft, but it looks as though he might have excelled himself this time.'

He produced a set of photographs from a manila folder on the front desk. 'Mrs Marjorie Freer,' he said. 'As she was a year ago. The picture was taken by her carer at the time.' He lifted a second picture. 'Mrs Freer after her killer had finished with her.'

Mac watched the reaction of those gathered in the cramped space.

'What's the connection?' someone asked.

'DI McGregor will fill in the details, but from information received, we believe that Dowling may have been responsible for the old woman's death.'

'Reliable information?'

Eden deferred to Mac, who stepped forward. 'We believe so,' he said, and proceeded to give them the facts, keeping it brief and concise, watching as notes were taken, attention focussed. Pictures of the two boys were handed round. Questions asked.

'No, never been in trouble,' Mac said. 'Not until the break-in, and we're assuming peer pressure. Maybe even coercion, but obviously we need to find these two.'

A few more questions and the meeting began to break up. Mac found himself thinking that the local cafés would be making a fair bit of extra profit that morning.

The phone rang. Andy took the call and after a brief conversation handed over to Eden. Mac heard him mutter the name of one of the larger local papers. Eden rolled his eyes and took the phone.

It's beginning, Mac thought. Two killings in sleepy little Frantham-on-Sea, within a couple of weeks. Media interest this time would not be restricted to a few locals standing on the street corner, and the pressure would be on for everything to be tidied up and out of the way before the tourist season began.

Eden put down the phone. It began to ring again. 'Andy, tell anyone interested that there'll be a press call at noon.'

'OK. Where?'

Eden shrugged. 'That's for the officer in charge to decide, isn't it?'

'You're not in charge?' Mac asked.

'Thankfully, no. Let's go and get us a coffee, shall we? No, not one of mine; that little caff you like so much should be open by now.'

Mac raised an eyebrow.

'Oh, lad, not much gets past me.'

Lad? Mac thought. It was a very long time since that description fitted. 'So, who *is* in charge?' he asked.

Eden shook his head. 'Don't know yet. They'll assign someone from along the coast. Probably arrive with the incident room. I've been told I'm too close to retirement and you're too new to be bothered with a double murder.'

'New? I'm hardly new.'

'Well, you are round here.' Eden let the doors swing closed behind them. 'Folk can get a bit territorial, you know. It takes time . . .'

Mac was shaking his head. 'They think I'll fall apart,' he said flatly. 'Like I did last time.'

Eden paused, clasped his arm. 'Let it go,' he said quietly. 'Time will prove you right and them wrong. Meantime there'll be plenty of work to go around.'

They walked in silence along the promenade and entered the little café. It was filling up fast and most of the customers were fellow officers. Eden found a table close to the window and plonked himself down. 'I'll have whatever you're having,' he said. 'You know what gets to me the most?' he added. 'Course you do, it's eating you up inside just as much as it is me. I mean, look at this lot, and reinforcements on the way too. An incident room, Lord help us. An OIC from Exeter. And all for what? A little bastard who probably deserved what he got.'

'We can't sanction execution,' Mac said. 'It's still murder. And we don't know for certain yet that Dowling . . .'

Eden's hand flapped irritably in Mac's direction. 'Oh, I know, we don't speak ill of the dead no matter what. But you know what, that's just so much crap. I always thought I'd be sorry to leave the job, but you know something? I'll be glad to go. More than glad. It can't come soon enough.'

Mac queued for coffee, exchanged the odd neutral comment with his new-found colleagues. Carefully, he deposited their drinks on the narrow table.

'So,' he said. 'Who did for Mark Dowling?'

Eden shrugged. 'Not likely to have been young Paul. I doubt he'd have had the time to make it back home even if he'd had the nerve.'

'George Parker?'

'Seriously?'

'No, not seriously. Not with that level of damage done anyway.'

'The sister? She did try and turn him in.'

Mac nodded. 'I find it hard to accept,' he said. 'And the timing would be difficult. The Robinsons reckon she was around all evening. Of course, we have to look at her as a possible, but what's the motive?'

'He's a threat to her little brother?'

'A threat she tried to deal with legally. All right, so she withheld information but it's a long stretch from that to murder.'

'True.'

'So who else? The list of those with a Mark Dowling problem is likely to be long.'

Mac sipped his coffee thoughtfully. The almond undertones were warming, sweet. Observing Eden's face, he didn't think his colleague shared his enthusiasm. 'Dislike is one thing, murder quite another, and from the look of the crime scene, whoever killed him wanted to be very sure that he was dead. It's odd,' he went on, 'but when I was at the first scene, at Mrs Freer's, I was struck by both the frenzy of it and just how personal it was. Mark Dowling, on the other hand . . . I don't know; it was different. There was not even a hint of other motive. No destruction, no search, no threat. Whoever it was seems to have gone there with the sole purpose of murdering Dowling. That's it. They took their weapon with them to the house and they took it away again after they'd finished.'

'Which begs the question, why not shoot the bugger and be done with it? And I don't mean having to buy an illegal gun. Half the population round here either has a shot gun or could get access to one.'

'So, maybe they belong to the half that doesn't. It does speak of a certain confidence though. Dowling might easily have fought back. He wasn't big but he was wiry, strong. I wouldn't have wanted to go up against him.'

'No, I'd agree,' Eden said. 'But it also suggests something else. Dowling opened the door, let his killer in. Either he knew them or he didn't see them as any sort of threat. Didn't view anything they were *carrying* as any sort of threat. Which is not such a useful insight as it might have been,' Eden continued. 'When you think that everyone in this place has at least a passing acquaintance with everybody else.'

Mac chuckled. 'Long list of suspects then.' He drained his coffee. 'I suppose we'd better make a start.'

* * *

The crime-scene investigators had released the main scene by the time Mac and Eden returned. The body had been moved, blood spatter mapped and charted, everything bagged and tagged and taken away to a clean clinical laboratory, ready to be sifted and examined and interpreted.

Mac took in the empty hall, seeing in his mind's eye the body of Mark Dowling as it had been when he arrived. Then he tried to imagine how it had been before the boy's parents got to it.

The towel, he thought. That was a real anomaly. He wondered too how much blood the murderer had carried from the scene. Nothing had been marked on the gravel path, but the rain would have washed so much away and anyway, in Mac's experience, blunt-force trauma—in other words, hitting someone with a heavy, non-sharp object—didn't generally cover the killer in their victim's blood. There was no sudden arterial spurt. Blood would be flicked from the object used, spatter patterns had been marked on the walls and floor, but the killer would not necessarily have been covered in it.

Mac made his way up the stairs to Dowling's room. Three white-clad figures were taking it apart. The scent of Mark Dowling still clung to the furnishings.

'Anything?'

One figure detached itself from a wardrobe and came over to him, collecting a blue box on the way. Mac recognized the dark-haired, blue-eyed woman he'd met at Mrs Freer's autopsy.

179

'Hello again.'

'Miriam Hastings,' she said. 'Hi. Look.' She set the box down and Mac squatted beside her on the landing. 'Evidence of drug use, but no drugs as yet. Money. Five hundred and odd change. A rather vicious-looking knife—and this. I remembered the post-mortem report and I think this might well be what you want the most.'

Mac took the evidence bag and peered through the transparent plastic. Square base, heavy, a bust of a smiling man that Mac didn't recognize, though he wore a Tam o' Shanter hat. Mac hefted it gently, feeling the weight. 'I think this might be it,' he said.

'It looks like it's been cleaned,' she told him. 'But if you look at the base, the texture's roughened there and sticky, as though there was felt or something attached and it's been torn off. I'll bet we get something off it.'

Mac nodded. 'Thanks.'

* * *

Karen had half expected Mac to return that morning. From the window above the promenade she had seen the increased activity and noticed the strangers in uniform chatting to the local police. So, they had found him then.

Idly she flicked through the pictures on her phone until she came to the one she had taken the previous evening. Mark stared up at her, his hand reaching, his nose pouring with blood and a look of sheer fury in his eyes.

Karen knew it was stupid keeping this. She'd have to lose it—and not just the picture but the phone as well. Even deleted images could be recovered. Karen knew that.

She analysed her feelings, or rather her lack of them. She still experienced a kind of cold fury when she thought about her father and, towards her mother she felt a sort of passive concern mingled with the knowledge that she despised Carol for the weakness she had exhibited for all those years. She loved George. Quite intently, in fact. George was her kid brother and he had nerve, tenacity. George would grow into a good man and Karen was proud of that. Her urge to protect him was almost inhumanly strong.

She heard her mother stumbling around in the bedroom and she exited the image library on her phone. Carol would have forgotten where they were and probably why too, and Karen knew she had better go to her, make her understand, calm the hysterics and probably administer more of the sedative. Hopefully, she'd manage to get some food down her mother before she collapsed once more into drugged sleep.

Karen sighed, acknowledging that her emotional responses were probably way off kilter. Acknowledging too that she probably wouldn't have it any other way.

TWENTY-NINE

George had slept finally but fitfully, and woke up to find daylight flooding the room, filtered through a decade or so of dirt on the cracked and stained windows.

Paul had rolled on to his side. That his head was now resting on a maths text book wrapped in his scarf was the only clue George had that he'd woken up at all during the night. He was still snoring.

George needed to pee. He crept downstairs and found a toilet beyond what looked like a storeroom. It hadn't been used in a long time and there was no water in the cistern but it still felt more civilized than pissing in a corner somewhere. Now that he was downstairs, he risked a quick reconnaissance of their hideout, slipping outside so he could get the lie of the land. He could make out overgrown runways and the remnants of a wind sock hanging from a post on what he assumed must be the furthest perimeter. The rain had stopped but the grass was soaking underfoot and weeds were industriously repossessing the paving slabs and undermining the tarmac. George took a deep breath of the fresh, cold, rain-drenched air. The sun was breaking through the grey and, absurdly, a sudden feeling of optimism—almost sheer joy—rushed up from the soles of his damp feet and surged through him.

A kestrel hovered, then swooped; George watched as it rose again and took off towards the line of trees that blocked his view of the further horizon.

This was a good place, George decided. A place to visit again once all their problems had been solved. He'd seen a cheap pair of binoculars for sale in the little second-hand shop up in the old town. He still had money left. Maybe he could buy them, come back and watch the kestrel. Once this was all over, he could bring Paul back too . . .

George sighed, the momentary exuberance draining out of him and back into the sodden grass. Who was he kidding? Once this crisis was over they'd be moving on again. Far away from his dad and from his friends and from all the things that he'd begun to call his own this past couple of years.

George didn't want to go. He wanted to be left in peace, just left alone. To have a normal life and normal friends and hobbies and . . . and just stuff. Was that too much to ask?

Wearily he climbed the stairs again and shook Paul awake. He handed him a can of Coke left from the previous day's lunch. He reminded him that this was all they had and not to drink it all. Paul blinked at him sleepily, then opened the can and took a swig before handing it over.

'We got any food?'

George shrugged. 'Packet of crisps and a chocolate bar.' He delved in his bag, fishing out the rather crushed packet and the broken bar, divided the chocolate and left Paul with all the crisps. Then he went back to his position by the window.

'What can you see?'

'Still two police cars at Dowling's place but there's something happening on the wasteland near the tin huts. People, lots of people.'

Curious, Paul came over and took his place. 'What they looking for?'

He sat back on his heels and tucked into the broken crisps. George put his eye to the gap in the pane. He'd seen pictures like this on the news. Rows of people, some in uniform, some in overalls, some in ordinary clothes, moving across the open land between the industrial units and the houses. Paul was right: they were searching for something. For a murder weapon? Maybe Mark Dowling had confessed and they were looking for whatever he'd used on the old lady.

'What did he use to kill her?' George asked suddenly. Paul stopped chewing and George realized belatedly that his question had not been tactfully phrased. Too late now. 'Did you see?'

Paul nodded slowly. 'This kind of statue thing. She had it in her hand when . . . you know. Mark took it off of her and hit her with it.' His voice was flat. Emotionless. He put the pack of crisps down and moved back away from the window.

'Well that's good,' George said. 'You can tell them. Tell them what to look for. Tell them what you seen.'

Paul shook his head, wrapped his arms around raised knees. 'I ain't telling no one,' he said. 'I ain't going nowhere.'

George gnawed at his lower lip. He sensed it would do no good to remind Paul that they couldn't stay here indefinitely. That they had one can of Coke and a half-eaten bag of crisps to sustain them and not much hope of gathering further supplies. That their parents would be going frantic. That they'd most likely be grounded for the rest of their lives.

Paul had closed his eyes again, seeking sleep, wanting to shut out the world. George was familiar with this behaviour. He'd seen his mam resort to it often enough in that past life they'd been trying to escape. He knew it brought, at best, only the most temporary relief.

'Paul,' he began, 'we should get off home now. Tell your mam and dad. Tell Karen. They'll go with us to the police—and they must have Mark Dowling. We saw them last night. The police, at his house.'

Paul said nothing; he kept his eyes tight closed and his knees up close to his chest. Arms wrapped unnaturally tight as though he was literally holding himself together.

George didn't know what to do. Briefly, he thought of leaving his friend and going for help, but he wasn't sure how

Paul would react to what would seem like a betrayal. He'd probably run off again and George wasn't sure how well he'd cope on his own.

No, he'd have to convince Paul to leave too. He turned back to face the window, watching the ant-like beings trekking in their ragged lines and praying that sooner or later the search would come their way.

* * *

'What are we looking for? Tim asked.

'They didn't say, but they're not expecting any of us to find it anyway.' Rina gestured expansively at the small army of volunteers creeping their way along the main road.

'Oh? What makes you say that?'

'Because, my dear, the experts—in their overalls and with their big sticks and their radios—are all searching over there. This is just a community exercise. A way of getting people involved without them getting in the way.'

Tim prodded a clod of earth with the end of the walking stick he had borrowed from Rina. 'But they use volunteers all the time,' he argued. 'Someone goes missing, the community turns out and walks up and down prodding things.'

'If someone goes missing, yes. But I'm guessing what they're looking for here is a murder weapon. Mark Dowling must have been killed with *something*. They're assuming that the killer threw that something away, probably on the waste ground.'

'And? That differs from a body how?'

Rina sighed. 'Tim darling, people finding bodies usually scream and run away. They don't bend down to pick bits up. You can rely upon members of the public not to go on prodding when they find someone dead; you can't rely on them not to grab the object and wave it excitedly in the air when they find a murder weapon.'

'Unless it's a gun,' Tim said. 'Most people are a bit iffy about guns.'

'True,' she conceded.

'Or a bloody knife. Or a hand grenade or a mine or a—'

'Tim, I get the point.'

'And as we don't know what we're looking for anyway, how's anyone going to know that it's the murder weapon to get excited about?' When Rina said nothing he asked, 'Why do you have walking sticks anyway? You must have a dozen in that stand in the hall but you've never used any of them.'

'I'm preparing for eventual old age,' Rina growled.

'And if you think this is a waste of effort, which you obviously do, then why are we here?'

'Because, Tim,' Rina said heavily, 'when things are going on, I like to know *what* is going on, and the best way of doing that is to get involved.'

* * *

The word went out that tea was available at the portable catering station that had arrived with the mobile incident room and that their section of the search team was welcome to imbibe.

Tim sipped his tea thoughtfully, gazing out, not over the waste ground and the rows of searchers, but instead towards the old airfield and the remnants of a building just glimpsed over the high hedge.

'What was that place?' he asked.

Rina followed his gaze. 'There's a public footpath that runs around the perimeter and then hooks back round to the coastal path,' she said. 'Local tradition has it that the airfield was built in the Second World War, but I've heard tell it was earlier. There used to be a big estate. Grand house, the works. Owned by the DeBarrs.'

'Oh, like the hotel at Marlborough Head?' Tim grimaced, recalling the kids' party he had so recently endured.

'Yes, but the DeBarrs don't own that now either. In fact the last of them is old Nick who runs the filling station just down from the hotel. You know the one?'

Tim nodded, then brushed back the heavy lock of black hair that fell into his eyes.

'Anyway, as I was saying, they owned the airfield before the war, sold it off to the MOD, and after the war it was sold again. Some sort of private consortium. Folded about fifteen years ago after several changes of owner. Shame really.'

Tim wandered over to where the hedge gave way to a five-bar gate beside which a green sign indicated the footpath Rina had mentioned. He stared long and hard at the dilapidated old building, complete with modest control tower that still dominated the flattened landscape and a sudden thought occurred to him. One, he suddenly realized, that had been forming since the previous evening when Mac had told them about the missing boys.

'If I was a thirteen-year-old boy and I needed a place to hide for a while, where would I go?' he said.

Rina's bright blue eyes demanded an explanation. 'You think they've come back to Frantham?'

'I do. Better to hide out in a place you know and in a place you know no one bothers with than to try to find a new place in a strange country.'

Rina snorted. 'Dorchester is hardly foreign fields,' she said. 'They both go to school there.'

'They catch the bus here. Bus drops them at school gates. Picks them up from same. Drops them home.'

'All right,' she conceded. 'You have a point. But over there, in the tower?' She frowned, wriggled her shoulders irritably. 'They'd see us coming a mile off.'

'True, so we have to be seen to go somewhere else. If they are there, they'll be watching to see what's going on, which means they're looking this way. How about if we pick up the cliff path and come back in through the other way?'

'It'll take an age,' Rina objected. 'Tim, at times you're far too subtle.' Hitching up her skirts she mounted the stile and jumped down on the other side. 'Better to try the direct approach. They see us and make a run for it, we'll spot them and if, as I suspect, there's no one there, then we won't have wasted half a day on a nature ramble.'

'How much do you want to bet?' Tim challenged. 'Look, hang on.' He took their cups back to the catering van and bought two bottles of pop and some chocolate and biscuits, then he ran to catch up with Rina. 'Best to come bearing gifts.'

Rina rolled her eyes.

* * *

George was never quite sure what it was that made him just sit still and watch as these two strangers headed in the direction of their hiding place. At first it was disbelief: they couldn't be coming here. The amount of dust that had settled on the ground floor told him that no one *ever* came here. Then it was curiosity: a short old woman and a tall man whose long strides had him loping ahead of her. Every three paces or so he stopped to wait for her to catch up. George thought it looked like someone with a large, over-energetic but patient dog out for a walk.

As they drew closer he began to panic, then panic was replaced by resignation. If he'd wanted to run, he should have got a move on long before. He looked across the room to where Paul lay sleeping once again, then got up and tiptoed over to his friend. Paul didn't stir, even when he touched his hand.

George went to the stairs and descended halfway, listening. Maybe they'd pass by. If they did, should he run after them, pretend he was just out bird-watching or something? He could at least ask what was going on.

He heard voices, a man and a woman. They sounded OK, he thought. Happy, chatty, like they were making fun of each other but in a friendly way. Hesitantly, George descended the rest of the way.

He heard the sound of feet on broken glass as they came close to the door and the scuffing of gravel. Then the door swung wide and the woman entered first.

'George Parker, I presume,' the woman said. She extended a gloved hand in his direction and, bemused but operating on auto-pilot, George shook it. His eyes, however, were fixed on what the man was carrying.

'Here you go,' the man said. 'Your friend upstairs, is he?' He handed George the drink and then dug in his pocket for the biscuits and chocolate. 'All they had in the catering van,' he explained. 'I understand they'll be doing bacon batches and such like later on.'

Bacon rolls. George felt himself grow faint at the thought. The fish and chips of the night before seemed an eternity ago.

'He's not right,' George said. 'Paul, he's been acting funny and he just keeps wanting to sleep.'

Rina clasped him lightly on the shoulder and headed for the stairs. George and Tim followed her. She knelt beside the other boy and shook him gently, calling his name. Paul opened his eyes and then yelped in panic.

'It's all right,' Rina told him. 'No one will hurt you. Your mum and dad are worried sick, but it's all going to be all right now.'

He shook his head, dark eyes cold with fear. 'He'll get me,' Paul said. 'He said. He said he'd kill me and he'd hurt me mam too. He said . . .'

Rina was shaking her grey head. 'If you mean Mark Dowling,' she said, 'he's in no position either to issue threats or to carry them through.'

'You see!' George was triumphant. 'I told you they arrested him, didn't I? That's right, isn't it? We saw the police cars round his house.'

He watched as this woman called Rina, who he recognized vaguely because she'd visited Mrs Freer, and this strange tall man, exchanged a glance.

'It was a bit late for that,' Rina said. 'Someone killed him, I'm afraid. That's what the police were doing there.'

* * *

George supposed he should feel shocked at the news but somehow he just couldn't. Relief flooded him, just like the moment of pure exultation had earlier that morning, only the relief seemed just a bit more permanent. The man called Tim had laid out the pop and biscuits and chocolate and even Paul was enlivened enough by the news that he ate and drank. Some of the colour had returned to his cheeks. The threat—that awful, overwhelming, immediate threat—had been lifted and George could tell that Paul wasn't even thinking about the rest of the stuff. About the breaking and entering and the gun and then going back with Mark Dowling and watching the old woman die.

He hoped so much that Paul would have at least a bit of time before the rest of that stuff all descended on him and he had to be afraid of it again. He needed a break, some time out, a little bit of a reprieve.

Rina answered George's questions as best she could and then she reminded them both that people were seriously worried about them, that they had parents who'd been going frantic all night. Tim produced his mobile phone and called someone called Mac who Rina explained was a policeman.

George almost stopped listening after that. What Rina had said about parents reminded him of his dad and that he was back and that he had troubles of his own that he'd now have to deal with.

'OK,' Tim said. 'Mac's been called away somewhere but DI Eden and someone called Andy are on their way. You know who that is, Rina?'

She nodded. 'You'll be fine with them,' she told George.

'But anyway.' Tim withdrew a small card from the pocket of his coat and then wrote a name on the back and placed it in Paul's hand. 'Tell them you want to talk to this man. D.I. McGregor. You can trust him, George, Paul. He knows what's happened and he'll do everything he can to help you both through this. You understand?'

George nodded and leaned over to look at the card. Paul was twisting it in his hands as though not sure what to do with it. George saw the name and little advert on the other side to the scribbled name. 'You're a magician?'

'I sure am.' Tim grinned. A second card had suddenly appeared in his hand though George had not seen him move. It was dog-eared and just a little bit creased. He handed it to George. 'Marvello at your service,' he said, with a little bow and a wolfish smile.

George did his best to smile back but the weight of worry was bearing down upon him again. He slid the card into the pocket of his coat. 'Thanks,' he said, wishing that magic tricks and escapology extended to situations like this.

THIRTY

Mac had been called from the scene by his opposite number, an Inspector Kendal from Dorchester HQ. Kendal told him that they had an address for Edward Parker, George's father.

'That was quick.'

Kendal laughed. 'We try. No, we've known about him for a while now. Moved down here from Manchester four months ago; our colleagues up there gave us the tip-off. Mr Parker has some interesting associates.'

He gave Mac the address of Parker's flat and told him he'd meet him there.

Edward Parker's flat looked surprisingly expensive, Mac thought as he pulled up outside the modern and purpose-built block. It was part of one of those mews complex things that seemed to be so popular these days and which, frankly, Mac hated passionately. To him they were the architectural equivalent of fast-food restaurants; identical countrywide and making absolutely no concession to local character.

He nodded to the man in the rather good grey suit leaning against a rather battered Ford Mondeo. 'DI Kendal?'

'Nice to meet you.' They shook hands and Kendal indicated the suit. 'Court this morning. Got to look the part.'

Mac laughed. 'It's a bit posh, this,' he said. 'Must have come into money. Renting, is he?'

'Nope, he bought it. Cash. Reckons it was a private loan. From a friend.'

'A friend?'

Kendal nodded. 'I'll fill you in properly back at the station. Let's just say that Parker's friends accept payment in kind and charge a considerable amount of interest.'

The flat was on the third floor. Entry to the building was controlled by an intercom and buzzer. To Mac's mild surprise, Kendal announced himself and was buzzed through without comment. 'He knows you then?' Mac said as they got into the lift.

Kendal nodded. 'We've had our conversations. Thing is, Parker reckons he's well out of our reach. We've nothing on him yet, and his friends are as slippery as a net full of eels.'

'What are we talking here? Organized crime? Drugs?'

Kendal shrugged. 'Drugs, yes, but that's not the main game. Identity theft, computer scams. Techie stuff.'

'Sounds a bit smart for Edward Parker.'

'I don't think he's employed for his brains. Thing is, we're not sure just who is employing him or exactly what for. These past months, apart from two visits to Manchester and another to, we think, London, he's been a model citizen. Shopped at the local supermarket, joined the video store, worked out at the gym. And it might be pure coincidence that his little trips have coincided with two dead and one left in a vegetative state.'

The lift doors opened. 'I've been told to share what we've got with you. We didn't know the family were here when Parker arrived. If we had, we'd have disclosed, but the funny thing is, this is the first slip up he's made, trying to make contact with the boy. I can't think his so-called friends would be impressed.'

'Unless,' Mac said, 'they found his family for him and brought him here because of it.'

Kendal shrugged and led the way along the plush landing. He pressed the bell and Edward Parker opened the door.

A few minutes later, Mac sat in the leather wing chair to which Parker had directed him and observed the man. He was clean shaven, with cared-for skin which drew attention to the scar on his lower jaw. It travelled down on to his neck. Thinning hair was cut short but stylishly. Clothes that Mac guessed he'd never afford on *his* salary. He glanced around the flat at the thick carpet, the rather tasteless but expensive leather suite, and mentally compared it to the house Parker's family inhabited.

The only thing the two dwellings had in common, Mac noted, was the lack of personal stuff. No pictures, no photographs. There was a car magazine on the coffee table but an absence of books or even music. A sizeable television dominated the corner of the room and the sofa had been angled, the better for the viewer to recline, but the handful of scattered DVDs on the floor were the only indicator of personality or interest.

'I hear the boy's done a runner.'

'He has. Mr Parker, you were waiting outside the school. When challenged you were abusive.'

'Some woman asking questions,' he said. 'None of her damn business, was it?'

'She's a teacher, Mr Parker. If she sees a stranger loitering outside of her school, then it becomes her business.'

He shrugged. 'I wanted to see my boy.'

'And if he didn't want to see you?'

Parker barked a laugh. 'Course he would. What boy wouldn't want to see his dad? It's those other two, poisoned his mind against me.'

'Your wife and daughter?'

'What wife? She was never a wife. Useless bit of . . . And as for that other one.' He touched the scar on his face. 'Little bitch. She gave me this.'

'Karen?'

'Dead right.' Parker sat forward in his chair and pulled the crisp white shirt out from his trousers. Displayed for

Mac's perusal a second scar that ran from just below his ribs and disappeared behind the waistband of his trousers. 'This one too. I want her brought in for it. Arrested, you got that?'

This was taking a bizarre turn. 'Mr Parker, when is your daughter supposed to have assaulted you?'

'Four year or more ago. Time I got out of hospital, she and that other one had long gone, taken my boy with them. Poisoned his mind against me.'

'I rather think you assaulting his mother might have done that,' Mac said slowly. 'Four years ago. That would be the last time you put her in hospital, wouldn't it?'

Parker got to his feet and glowered over Mac. 'She press charges, did she? She take me to court over it? No, because the bitch deserved all she bloody got.'

'Sit down, Mr Parker,' Mac said. Kendal had risen to his feet, reached for his phone.

'I want to see my boy and I want her punished.'

'You'll leave your family alone, Mr Parker,' Mac said.

'You threatening me?' That bark of a laugh again. 'Bloody funny that is.'

'I'm warning you. Keep away.'

'Or what? You'll make me, will you? You and whose army? I don't need your help to find them any road.'

'And are you threatening a police officer?' Kendal asked quietly.

Parker turned ice-blue eyes upon him. 'No, like the man said, just delivering a warning.'

Mac's phone rang, breaking the tension. He flinched as the shrill note cut through him, but he hoped no one noticed. 'McGregor.' He listened to the news that George and Paul had been found, safe and well. He schooled his expression not to change, not to let Parker senior know, though the delay, Mac realized, would be small enough. He was glad that he'd acted upon Karen's fear and moved them from the house, but didn't figure that his flat would be safe for long. He stood up.

'Goodbye, Mr Parker,' he said. 'We can see ourselves out.'

* * *

195

'Nasty bugger,' Kendal declared once they were outside. 'Sooner we get something concrete on him the better.'

'Just concrete would do,' Mac smiled wryly as Kendal laughed at the bad joke. 'His son's turned up,' he said. 'And the other boy.'

'Both OK?'

Mac nodded.

'Well that's a small relief. What do you reckon to what he said?'

'That was news to you too?'

Kendal nodded. 'Have you met the daughter? What do you make of her?'

Mac considered. 'Mature, capable, very sensible. Do I think he could be telling the truth about what she did? Maybe. I really wouldn't want to say.'

'Deserved all he got if you ask me. I'll have a go at tracking down the hospital records.'

'Thanks,' Mac said. 'Look, this is probably not related but . . .' He explained about the lights, the cave and what Rina had found there.

Kendal laughed. 'Sounds like you've got yourself a resident Miss Marple,' he said. 'The coastguard has reported odd activity all along this stretch of coast. Nothing conclusive. Look, tell you what, get Miss Marple's evidence to me and I'll put it through to forensics. Not that we could use it, of course; there's the chain of evidence problem for a start. But I think it would be worthwhile taking a look at that cave.'

Mac nodded. He stopped off at Kendal's car and collected the reports Kendal had copied for him, then took his leave. Mac glanced up at the third-floor flat before getting into his car. Edward Parker, glass in hand, was looking down at him.

THIRTY-ONE

It was five o'clock on the Tuesday afternoon when Mac drove back to Frantham. He'd been told that the boys were at the police station, having been reunited with their families, fed and watered, and checked out by the doctor. Paul had come in with his parents and George had Karen there to protect his interest.

'They want to talk to you,' Eden told him. 'They don't want to confess their all to anyone else. Seems your friend Rina put them up to it.'

'Rina? What's she got to do with it?'

'Oh.' Eden hadn't realized Mac didn't know. 'She and that lodger of hers, Timothy Brandon, they were out with the search teams.'

'Right,' Mac said. 'I'll be ten minutes.' *Definitely a Miss Marple clone*, he thought. *Or should that be Lydia Marchant?*

Passing the Dowling house he noted that most of the searchers had now departed, their numbers replaced by television cameras and local reporters all busy staking their claim to a scrap of verge, fenced in behind a cordon of traffic cones and tape. The road had been closed for much of the day, traffic facing a ten-mile diversion through half a dozen villages and back on to the coast road. The road was partly

opened now, with uniformed officers checking the cars that
wanted access. Andy, on point duty, saw Mac and waved
him through. The press, bored with the lack of action and
alerted to Mac's known status, craned forward to see just who
he was. Mac was grateful for the cordon, flimsy as it was.
Cameras captured his image for the morning news and the
locals, knowing him from the Freer murder, acknowledged
him, gaining themselves a little kudos in the process.

Mac parked up behind the police station, squeezing his
car between a Range Rover and a scientific support unit van.
Usually there was his car, the patrol car and Eden's motor-
bike installed in the tiny yard and it felt full even then. He
opened his door as far as he could and tried to make himself
as thin as possible. How, he wondered, was everyone going
to manage to get out? There wasn't room to swing a moggie,
let alone turn a car.

Sergeant Baker handed him a cup of Eden's coffee as he
came in through the rear door. 'Saw you drive into the yard,'
he said. 'The boss said you'd need this.'

'Thanks, I do.' When had he last slept?

'Upstairs,' Frank said. 'Everyone's waiting on you.'

The interview rooms had not been much used since
Mac had been at Frantham. In fact, the smaller of the two
was used for storage and was packed with box files. The two
boys, along with their guardians, Eden and an officer Mac
did not know, were waiting in the one remaining, sitting
silent around a Formica-topped table that looked like a relic
from a 1950s café.

Karen spared him a small, tight smile. The unknown
officer was disclosed as DI Newman, the new officer in
charge.

Mac sat down in the only vacant chair. 'Hi, George.
Paul, we met when I came to your house. Do you remember?'

Paul nodded sullenly.

'I've discussed things with DI Newman,' Eden said quietly, his tone somewhat chilly, Mac thought. 'He's agreed
with me there's no need to interview the boys separately at

this stage. They're not about to try and pull the wool, are you, boys?'

George shook his head. Paul swallowed hard and just stared at Mac. The tape was started and those present listed. It sounded like a three ring circus, Mac thought. 'Now,' he said gently. 'Suppose we begin with Sharon Bates's cider.'

* * *

It took time to coax their story from them and Mac wished more than once that Paul's parents weren't there. Paul would have found it easier without their shocked silences and horrified exclamations. Karen held George's hand tight, as though scared he'd try to run away again, but she stayed calm and quiet. But then, Mac thought, she already knew all this, had already absorbed much of the shock.

George helped Paul through the early part of their story but by the time he had reached his account of the beating he had received from Mark Dowling, he was effectively on his own. Mrs Robinson began to cry. She didn't stop. Her weeping became an audible backdrop to her son's words but he was speaking more fluently, more determinedly now, and Mac did not want to break the flow by asking her to leave. All he could hear was the sobbing, Paul's words. There was no other sound.

'I thought he'd break me arm,' Paul said. 'He'd grabbed me and twisted it up behind me back and then he started thumping me in the ribs and I couldn't breathe and he hit me in the mouth and across the face and me lip was bleeding and me eyes were swelling up. I tried to tell him I'd been lying about the gun. That I never saw no gun. That I'd just lost me nerve, but he just said that liars deserved a beating anyway. He weren't going to stop, no matter what I said.

'Then he made me go with him to that old lady's house. He said if I didn't go he'd beat up George and me mam, only worse, so they wouldn't be able to tell on him. So I went with him.'

'You believed him?' DI Newman asked; Mac wanted to tell him to shut up and listen.

'Yeah, I did.' Paul's face was white, his breathing shallow. He was back there, on that night, scared half to death. 'He took a hammer from the tin huts where his dad works. I told you, that was where we were. And he smashed the panel in her door. We got in and she was just standing there, in the front room, leaning on her frame and with this statue thing in her hand and Mark said . . . Mark said, "Where's the gun?" and she said she ain't got no gun. The police took it away. But he didn't want to know. He grabbed that statue thing from her and he hit her with it and she fell down and then he started on wrecking the place and I tried to go to her, but he had a knife in his hand and he told me to stay where I was and then he told me to go upstairs and look and I tried to get out the front door but he came and grabbed me and hit me again.'

That explains the blood on the stairs, Mac thought. 'And what happened then, Paul?'

Paul sighed. 'He dragged me up the stairs and he started wrecking the stuff in the little room and then he pushed me into her bedroom and told me to look there. I didn't know what for. I didn't ask. I started to look through drawers and stuff and then I heard him go back down and I just stopped there, in that room, then when I heard him in the hall again I thought I'd better go back down.'

'And when you went downstairs?'

Paul flushed bright red and then the colour drained again. Now, Mac noted, his skin was grey, his lips pale. 'He made me look. He grabbed my arm and he dragged me into the room and he made me look. She was lying there, on the floor near the bed and her head was all bashed in. She was . . . He said that's what he'd do to me mam if I said anything—and to George and George's mam too.'

Finally, the tears began to flow. He tried to wipe them away but now they'd been released he just could not stem the flow. Eden signalled the end of the interview and then stopped the tape. Mrs Robinson's sobs seemed louder still in the silence. Her son wept silently, sitting quite still, and when Karen reached out and placed his hand as well as George's between her own, he did not pull away.

Instinct to protect, Mac thought. *Some might say what better reason to kill?*

THIRTY-TWO

Mac had finally slept. Rina's tiny spare room was cramped but the bed was comfortable and breakfast something to celebrate, just himself and Tim and Rina at the kitchen table with a full English and a large pot of tea.

Rina had told him how they'd found the boys but had made little comment upon Mac's quietness and reluctance to talk. Tim didn't seem quite awake enough for conversation. Mac was grateful of that. His mind was buzzing and not with pleasant thoughts. Yesterday, at the end of the interrogation, he had suddenly and irrationally *known* that Karen had taken Mark Dowling out of the picture.

He asked himself if the thought would even have crossed his mind if he'd not spoken to Edward Parker that afternoon and heard his accusations. *Was she capable of it?* Kendal had asked, and now more than ever Mac wondered if the answer was yes.

The day's work brought the post-mortem report on Mark Dowling. It had been rushed through late the previous night. Mac studied it but it told him little he did not already know. Someone had hit Dowling a total of seven times. The killing blow had been to the head or possibly to the back of the neck, just where it met the skull. Either would have done it, so which came first was a moot point. Mac thought about it, reading between the lines of the report. His killer could have hit twice in quick succession. One blow while he was standing and the second as he fell. That would make sense. Not, Mac concluded, that it really mattered. The outcome was the same.

The weapon was a pipe or a bat or something similar. It was ridged, at least on some part. Small, parallel indentations showed in two of the wounds.

Mac put the report aside and checked to see what else had come in overnight. He was surprised to find details of Edward Parker's stay in hospital, which had been faxed through to him by Kendal.

A police report had been filed. The assumption had been that Parker was the victim of a violent mugging and he'd not disabused anyone of the notion. He'd been stabbed in an alley at the side of his favourite pub. No one had connected him with the Edward Parker wanted for domestic abuse simply because for five days no one even knew his name and also because no one was looking very hard for Edward Parker, abuser. He was assumed to have long gone.

By the time the connection had been made, Parker had disappeared from there as well, together with a hospital wheelchair, implying that he must have had some help.

'These friends of his, I suppose,' Mac muttered to himself.

Two knife wounds, both potentially life-threatening. One was a slash to the face and neck. He'd lost a lot of blood, but his attacker had failed to connect with the major vessels, the knife deflecting off the jaw. The second was a deep stab wound to the side and from that he should have died. Luck saved him. Another drinker taking a short cut back to his Sunday lunch. He'd run back inside, raised the alarm and the barman had administered first aid, keeping pressure on the wound until the ambulance arrived.

Mac leaned back in his chair and stared hard at both reports as though staring could bring him answers. She'd have been fifteen then, abused for a good portion of her life, witness to abuse that Mac could not even begin to imagine.

That gave her a reason, but, Mac asked himself, did it give her the *right*?

* * *

Paul had gone with his parents to stay with relatives for a few days and George missed him. He was bored. His mum had woken up for a while and had some tea and toast but then flopped on the sofa in a half doze, staring at the daytime television.

Karen had gone back to the house to get some more of their stuff and George hoped she'd remember his PlayStation. George hoped she'd be OK. He told her she should ask Mac to go with her but she'd just smiled and told him she'd be fine. She'd keep her eyes open.

George sat on the windowsill, staring out on to the promenade and watching people go about their daily tasks. It was too early in the season for there to be tourists and the locals were all bundled up against the steady drizzle that had started at dawn and gave no sign of letting up.

George glanced across at his mother, wondering if he should make her a cup of tea. At least it would be something to do. He went across to the sink and filled the kettle, flipped open the cupboard doors, curious to see what policemen ate. This one, it seemed, not a lot.

Sighing, George slammed tea bags into the pot and then wandered back to the window, waiting for the water to boil. George froze. Out there on the promenade, leaning against the sea wall, stood Edward Parker—and he was staring up at George. Then, absurdly, as though it were the most natural thing in the world, he smiled and waved.

George backed away. He was seeing things. He should tell his mother, call the police. Phone Karen on her mobile.

He moved back to the window, half convinced that the man would have gone, or transmuted into some harmless stranger who just happened to bear a passing resemblance to his dad. But no, Parker senior was still there and now he was crossing the promenade and heading towards the front door.

George, eyes wide with fear, looked again at his mother. She was oblivious to it all, mouthing the answer to the questions on the quiz she was watching. George could not let his father come inside. He couldn't even let him bang on the door. She'd hear. She'd know. She'd freak out.

Squaring his shoulders, he sneaked behind the sofa, paused to grab his coat from the peg near the door, and slipped out. He met his father on the stairs.

'Georgie boy!'

'Shhh. Please, Dad.'

Parker's grin broadened. 'Your mother there, is she? Your bitch of a sister?'

Shocked, George shook his head. 'She went out,' he stammered.

'Yeah, I suppose she must have. I don't hear any sirens, see any little hell cat with a knife.'

'Knife?' George was confused now.

'Oh, you don't know?' Edward Parker turned and headed back down the stairs and out on to the promenade. Hesitant, George followed him.

'I don't know what you're on about.'

'Maybe we should go and find her?' Parker threw back over his shoulder. He started to walk down the promenade.

'No!' George shouted after him. 'I told you, she went out.' Worried about his dad getting to Karen, it didn't occur to George that his father was headed in quite the wrong way anyway. The opposite direction from their house.

Not sure what to do, afraid that if he retreated to the flat his dad would follow, George trailed after him, trying to keep a decent distance behind. They reached the end of the promenade. Turn one way now and you were on the stone-built jetty that jutted into the bay. The other way took a big loop round towards the Railway pub or up to the hotel at

Marlborough Head. George wondered desperately what his father was planning to do.

Edward paused, waited for George to catch up, then beckoned him on. 'What's up, Georgie boy? I ain't going to hurt you.'

'You said that before,' George told him. His dad's eyes hardened but he forced a laugh.

'Well I'm sorry I scared you, old son,' he said. 'But sometimes your mam would provoke me so far I just didn't know what I was doing. I'd lose it with her and I know that probably frightened you, but it's past history now. You and me, we're going to start again. Be a team like. Father and son. Like it's supposed to be.'

George stood stock still. He couldn't be serious. Could he? He shook his head. 'I ain't going nowhere with you.' He turned on his heel and started to run. He only managed three paces before strong arms swept him off his feet. George yelled but then a hand was clamped tight and moments later George was bundled into a car, squashed on the back seat between his dad and the man who'd grabbed him.

George whimpered in fright. He couldn't help himself.

'Nothing to be scared of, Georgie boy,' his father said. 'Nothing at all.'

* * *

'Where's George?' Karen demanded as she came back into the flat. Her mother looked up momentarily from the television then turned back to her chat show.

Karen switched the television off. 'Mum, where's George?' She marched through to the bedroom. Knocked on the bathroom door. It swung open to her touch. There were only so many places in the flat that a boy could hide. Where the hell was he? She checked the coat hooks, but his coat was gone. 'Mum, didn't you even see him go?'

Momentary bewilderment on Carol's face was followed by blankness. She shook her head. 'Isn't he here?'

'Oh, for God's sake, Mum!'

She grabbed the phone; delved in her bag for the number Mac had given her. 'George is gone,' she said. 'No, I don't know where. I don't know how long. I went to the house to get some things and left him with Mum. I got back and he'd gone and she'd not even noticed. OK, I'll wait here. Please hurry.'

She lowered the phone and tried not to give into the dread gnawing at her belly. It was their dad, she just knew it. She just knew.

* * *

George found himself in a tiny room papered with large cabbage roses. More roses, red this time, climbed a trellis print on a pair of ageing curtains. A window gave a view out on to the sea. The window was locked. He angled his neck, trying to see what was below, but he couldn't even glimpse the ground and, considering the several flights of stairs it had taken to get up here, he figured he must be three floors above the ground.

George had a vague idea where he was. They'd taken the road past the hotel, winding up on to the headland, and then joined the coast road. He'd managed to look at his watch. It had been ten fifteen when they'd passed the hotel and only fifteen minutes after that they'd turned into a long cart track of a drive. The car had been put in a garage before they got out and they entered the house by a side door. George had then been taken upstairs and locked in. He'd rarely had reason to be out this way but he remembered that from Marlborough Head you could see a cluster of buildings, whitewashed and imposing, on a craggy outcrop of land jutting out into the sea as Marlborough did. The house was tall, unusually so for one as exposed to the elements, and George felt certain that was where he was now imprisoned.

All he had to do now was let someone know. Easy.

He surveyed his tiny kingdom. A single bed, made up with clean sheets. He could smell the fabric conditioner. A chest of drawers, empty. A bedside table with a single drawer and a cupboard, also empty. George had used the cupboard to climb up on to the high sill of the locked window. He rested his feet on it now and perched uncomfortably on the sill.

He couldn't see much of anything, and even less of anything helpful.

His dad had taken his coat from him before leaving the room and made him empty his pockets. Where, George wondered, was the carefully concealed Swiss Army knife when you most needed it?

He sighed. A right mess he'd made of things, yet again. He couldn't quite figure out what his father wanted. He didn't for one minute think that his father really, actually wanted him. He'd always despised George and had never bothered to hide the fact. 'You're just a waste of skin,' he'd say and mean every word of it. 'Your mam must have put it around while I was inside. No way I fathered a ginger idiot.'

And what was all this stuff about Karen? This stuff about a knife?

George thought back to the day they'd run away from their father. The ambulance had come, taken their mum away and instead of following her on the bus or cadging a lift in the police car like they usually did, Karen had said they'd wait and go later on.

The police woman had been a bit quizzical, but he'd heard her fellow officer say that the kids must be used to it by now. Probably sick of it all. Good that Karen wanted to put her dad away. They'd arrange for a responsible adult to come to the station to sit with her while she made a statement.

'Don't change your mind,' he told her sternly.

'Oh, don't worry,' Karen had said. 'You'll be seeing us.'

Then she'd told George to go to the shops and given him a list of stuff to get. He tried to recall how long he'd been gone and guessed it must have been about an hour. He'd not been scared. Not been worried about meeting their dad. They knew his habits, knew he'd be getting pissed in one of two local pubs and George could easily avoid both.

When he'd come back, Karen had still been cleaning up. She told him to pack a bag, just with his favourite stuff, then she'd phoned for a taxi and they'd gone to the police station, sat in the reception area and waited. George had fallen asleep stretched across the chairs. They never had gone back to collect the rest of their gear.

He tried hard to remember anything else that had happened that day, but it was four years ago and so much had happened since. So much moving around and turmoil and anxiety that it all got a bit confused—and anyway, he didn't spend much time these days trying to recall a time he'd rather blank from his memory. If it was possible to take a pill that would selectively wipe out bits of your past, then George would probably have done so.

He remembered he'd been offered counselling in one of the hostels they'd stayed in. The chance to talk things through and tell this woman called Philly what had happened. George's mum had. She'd spent hours with this Philly woman, crying and wailing and talking about how bad it had been but George just said 'no thanks'. Why would he want to keep remembering all that? George wanted to move on, to have a future, not to keep rehashing a lousy past.

Thinking about it, he couldn't remember what Karen had done.

Footsteps coming up the uncarpeted stairs told him his dad was probably on the way back up. George tensed, but stayed put. The door opened. His dad and the man from the promenade came into the room. George had not had a proper chance to look at the other man until now. He was younger than his dad and tall with blond hair that was kind of spiky at the front. He was smartly dressed in dark trousers and a blazer with shiny buttons. George stared at him and the man stared back.

'Get down,' his dad said. George obeyed.

Edward Parker handed him a mobile phone. 'Call your sister. Tell her you're with me.'

George took the phone and stood nervously passing it from hand to hand. 'I don't know the number,' he whispered.

'What do you mean you don't know the number?'

'She's not going to be at home,' George was desperate to explain. 'She'll be at the flat by now and I don't know the number for the flat and I don't know her mobile either; she just got a new one and I wrote the number on the list on the wall in the hall near the phone but I don't know it.'

Edward Parker stared hard at his son and took a step closer. 'You what?' The hand came back and George cowered. He was back then. Nine years old and scared to death, knowing how much his dad's fist hurt.

'I ain't lying to you. I wouldn't lie to you not ever.'

'You better not be. What's this load of junk?' He dropped the business card Tim had given George on to the bed.

'He's a friend,' George stammered. 'He does magic.'

Parker senior laughed loudly. 'Magic,' he said. 'Bloody magic.' He stepped closer once again, a thought striking him. 'He seeing your mam?'

George was genuinely taken aback. 'No. Course not. Mam ain't seen no one. You got her too scared.'

His father's eyes narrowed and George prepared himself for a blow that never arrived. His dad pushed past the other man and left. In the doorway, the blond man turned. 'Don't get him riled,' he said. 'He enjoys it. Don't forget that.'

'What's he want?' George begged. 'I don't understand what he wants.'

The man paused, considered George for a moment, then seemed to make up his mind. 'He wants your sister,' he said. 'He reckons it's payback time.'

'Payback time?'

'Tried to kill him, didn't she? Nearly managed it too. That's not nice. Not nice at all.'

THIRTY-THREE

Karen was in a state. Mac made her sit down and breathe slowly before she tried to tell him what had happened. Carol Parker watched. She seemed unable to function even enough to ask questions. Mac wondered if she was even aware her son had left and how many of the little pills Karen had given her.

'How long were you gone?'

'I don't know. About an hour, a bit more. I told him to stay put.'

'You don't think he might have just gone to the shops? Maybe you needed something.'

She shook her head. 'I made a list before I left. He knew I'd be going shopping as soon as I got back.'

'Maybe he got worried, came looking for you?'

'Then I'd have passed him on the way, wouldn't I? I went straight home and came straight back.'

'He boiled the kettle,' Carol Parker said. They both stared at her. Mac got up and felt the kettle. Still hot.

'Mrs Parker, do you know when he went? Where?'

She blinked, her mind searching for the words. 'I was watching that chat show thing. All those adulterers.' She lapsed back into her reverie.

Mac shrugged. 'Mean anything?'

'Not really, no. I don't watch daytime TV. Mac, he's got George, I just know he has.'

'But how? There's no sign of anyone being here and George wouldn't let anyone in, especially not . . .' He glanced anxiously at Carol, not wanting to spark another bout of hysteria. 'OK,' he said. 'We've got a basic time frame. You got back at ten thirty?'

'About then.'

'So I'll get someone to talk to the shopkeepers, get their CCTV tapes, see if he's on them.'

'That will take an age.'

Mac shrugged. 'Karen, it's the best I can do. At least we've got extra help on hand.' He glanced at his watch. 'I've got to get back. I'll get someone on to the CCTV.'

Karen nodded but she looked mutinous. 'So a dead thug takes priority over an abducted thirteen-year-old,' she said.

Mac sighed. 'Karen, that's not fair. You know I'll do all I can.'

When she didn't respond he left, irritated and anxious in equal measure.

* * *

From the window, Karen watched him go. She was furious with herself and now angry with Mac and frustrated with her mother. Was every bloody thing her responsibility? Could no one else be trusted to do anything right?

For some time the two women sat in silence, Karen with her thoughts, her slow-burning anger; her mother, she assumed, with that blank space where thoughts should be. Then Carol switched the television back on and Karen flinched at the sound of it. It was lunchtime. News time. She turned to watch as a picture of Mark Dowling flashed up on the screen followed by one of Mrs Freer. Listened to the vague speculation, dressed up in authoritative words that the two incidents might be connected.

Mac's face swam into view as he made an official state-ment. Several leads, too early to tell, but yes, it was natural to make assumptions about two murders so close in time and location, especially in such a quiet place as Frantham-on-Sea. The two boys? Yes, both safe and well. They'd been interviewed as a matter of routine and it was being treated as a domestic incident. The important thing was that the kids were now safe.

'Safe!' Karen spat at the television. 'You say they're safe? You bastard.' So this was what was so important he had to rush away. A television slot that anyone could have filled. It would have been fine if he'd used the opportunity to say, 'Look, George Parker has been abducted. His father has him. The father he's been running away from these last four years, has got him now, and I want you all to go out and look. Find Edward Parker, find George.'

Karen blinked the tears of frustration and hatred from her eyes. She had thought that Mac was different. That he cared. That he'd really cared.

Now, it was up to her again, just like it always was. The problem was this time she didn't know what to do or where to start. The decisions she'd made before had either been obvious or she felt she'd been led to make them by some kind of intuition. Now even that had failed her.

Karen sat down on the sofa next to her mother, wishing that her mam could take all the trouble away like she used to when her dad had been in prison. When Karen had just been an ordinary little girl.

She began to cry. Her mother moved, her attention attracted by the strange sound issuing from deep inside her child.

'Karen?'

Karen felt her mother's arms slip around her shoulders and for a brief instant she wanted to shake them off, resist. But she couldn't do it any more, couldn't do this on her own. She laid her cheek against her mother's shoulder and sobbed, feeling her mother's tears as they fell softly on to her hair.

THIRTY-FOUR

'Phone call for you, Tim,' Bethany twittered. 'They asked for "that Marvello chap". Maybe it's a job?'

'That would be a change.' He picked up the receiver of the hall phone. 'Tim Brandon speaking, aka Marvello.' He fell silent, shocked by the tone of the voice on the other end. 'Who is this? What?' He felt his legs go weak. This wasn't happening; it wasn't real. 'Look,' he interrupted. 'How did you get my card?' Of course, he remembered: he'd given one to Paul and one to George. George had been impressed. 'Look,' he said again, 'I'm not even sure where she is. I'd have to go and get her and why the hell should she believe me anyway?'

He listened as the man gave him an address, told him he'd better make bloody sure that Karen took notice—and no police. Someone would be watching. He'd be calling back in an hour and Karen had better be there by then.

Tim lowered the phone slowly and then stepped back from it as though worried it might bite. What the hell should he do now? He did what anyone else in the Martin household would have done. He stood in the hall and yelled.

'Rina! Rina, we've got a problem. A big problem.'

* * *

Karen snatched the door open, thinking, hoping that it must be Mac come back with news. She vaguely recognized the grey-haired woman standing on the threshold but the man was a stranger. He thrust a hand towards her.

'I'm Tim,' he said. 'Friend of George's. That is, we found him at the airfield.'

Karen was utterly bewildered. 'He's not here,' she said. Tim and Rina, George had talked about them, said they were nice.

'We know he's not,' Rina said quietly. 'Tim has just received a very disturbing phone call and we need you to come with us. Now.'

'This is about George?'

Rina nodded. 'A man calling himself Edward Parker has him. I'm assuming you know who that is?'

Karen swallowed nervously. 'Let me grab my coat and bag,' she said.

She dodged back inside, leaving the door ajar and her visitors standing on the tiny landing. She didn't dare let them in, scare her mother even more.

'I've got to go out,' she told Carol.

'You're going to fetch George?'

'Yes, I'm going to fetch George.'

'He'll probably be at Paul's house,' Carol said. 'He's always round there.'

'Yes, Mam, he probably is.'

Collecting her coat from the peg, Karen caught sight of herself in the mirror by the door. She looked a mess. Red-eyed and blotchy. Even her hair looked untidy.

She opened the door and gestured for them to go down ahead of her, there not being room for three on the landing. Closing it quietly, she hoped her mum would be all right on her own, feeling as she did so that this was such a permanent departure but not fully knowing why.

'Tell me,' she demanded. 'You've not gone to the police, have you? Useless lot.'

Tim and Rina exchanged a glance. 'No, no police, though I think we ought to,' Tim said. 'The man on the phone said there'd be someone watching, but I don't know if we should believe him. I saw nothing out of the ordinary coming over here.'

'Tell me, what did he say? Why phone you?'

'He must have found my card,' Tim said. 'I gave one to George. I'm a magician,' he confessed, as though that would explain everything. 'Anyway he said his name was Edward Parker and that he had George but that he'd trade for you. He wanted you and that this was all going to happen now. No argument. Then he went on for a bit about how much this was your fault.'

Karen nodded. 'Sounds like our dad,' she said. 'So, when and where?'

'You can't be serious about going?' Tim said. 'He sounded crazy to me. I mean, not that I'm an expert or anything . . .'

'Tim, you're gabbling,' Rina told him sternly. 'Of course we have to go. This man has threatened his children. Something is going to be done about it.'

Tim nodded. When she put it like that it seemed obvious. Kind of.

'We?' Karen questioned.

'My dear,' Rina said. 'We are involved now. You don't think we'd let you do this on your own, do you?'

* * *

They reached Peverill Lodge. Rina lifted the cordless phone from its cradle in the hall and directed Karen and Tim into her sanctuary. The Montmorencys and the Peters sisters had gathered in the hall.

'Lunch is late,' Rina announced. 'Steven, do your bit with that wonderful sauce of yours, will you, and ladies you can do some pasta. No, not for us; I'll tell you everything at tea.'

Listening from inside the cozy little room, Karen turned to Tim and whispered, 'Is she for real?'

'Oh, very real,' Tim whispered back. 'Oh yes, she is very real.'

Rina sat down in her usual chair and directed Karen to the other. 'Now,' she said. 'What does he want and why? Truth now, no misdirection. If we are to protect young George and keep you away from that dreadful man, then I need to know it all. And I suggest you keep it brief; he's due to call very soon.'

Hesitant at first, Karen explained about their past. The violence, the need to escape and how he had found them again.

'Which doesn't tell me why he hates *you* so much,' Rina said bluntly.

Karen stared down at her feet. 'I wanted him dead,' she said. 'After that last time. I couldn't bear it any more, being afraid all the time, seeing Mum and George going through so much.'

'And you too?'

She shrugged. 'Me too. I got George out of the way and I went to find our father. I knew he'd be in the pub; I could have told the police that and had him arrested, but they'd arrested him before and then Mum chickened out and I knew if I was the only one willing to speak out no one would really take any notice. Oh, they'd all said the right things, but . . . Look, I just wanted an end to it all.'

'So . . . ?' Rina prompted.

'So I checked which pub he was in and I waited outside. I knew I didn't have long and if he'd not come out in time I'd have to get back for George, but he did come out and he did cut through the alley and he didn't see the knife I had until I'd cut him twice.' She shrugged. 'I even wore a pair of Mam's washing-up gloves. I left him there, thought I'd killed him. Got rid of the knife and gloves on the way home and then went to finish clearing up before George got back. Then we packed our stuff and left.'

Tim stared at her. She'd not looked at anyone while she'd been telling her story, staring instead at the laces on her shoes. She looked up now, her expression defiant.

'I'd do the same again,' she said.

Rina nodded slowly. 'So now we know what happened,' she said. 'Right. His is the next move.'

On cue the phone began to ring.

'Pick it up, Tim.'

Reluctantly, he did as he was told. 'Yes, this is Tim Brandon. Yes, I've got her with me.' He held out the phone to Karen. 'Wants to talk to you.'

Karen took the phone. 'Hello, Dad,' she said. 'Still an absolute bastard, aren't you?'

Looking at Rina, Tim saw her flinch at Karen's bluntness. Not, he figured, quite the way to handle this.

'Hurt my little brother and I'll really do for you this time. Oh, I don't need an army. Only mistake I made last time was I should have made sure you were bloody dead.'

She listened then, nodding slightly, her lips pursed and white, then she handed the phone back to Tim. 'You'll have to drive me,' she said. 'You do drive, don't you?'

Tim nodded anxiously.

'Listen to him then,' she said. 'He needs to tell you where and when.'

Tim listened, repeated the instructions. 'Why there?' he wondered when he'd finally got off the phone.

Rina shrugged. 'Because you can see anyone coming for miles,' she said. 'I suppose that must be one reason. What puzzles me, though, is why such a rush? It's almost as though he's on a schedule. Karen, we really should call the police.'

She was on her feet, cheeks blazing. 'No, absolutely no. You don't know him like I do. He'd kill George at one sniff of police.'

Rina waved her back to her seat. 'Sit, let's think this through. Karen, why all this elaboration? He could have found you, had his revenge. He didn't need to take George to get to you.'

Karen shook her head. 'I don't know. He showed up at the school last week, but the police reckon he moved down here a few months ago. He must have known where we were, or more or less where we were. I thought at first it was just part of his method. He likes people to be afraid. He knew if George had seen him, George would be afraid and that he'd tell me. He must have realized we'd just move on again.'

'Sounds as if you suddenly became the priority for some reason,' Tim speculated. 'But if you'd known he was around, wouldn't you have reported him, got an injunction or something?'

She shrugged. 'We'd probably have tried.'

'So, you'd have drawn attention to him,' Rina said thoughtfully. 'Maybe that was something he definitely didn't want. Maybe he had to stay in the background. Maybe whatever reason he had for staying hidden no longer applies.'

THIRTY-FIVE

George tried to work out what time it was. He'd spent what seemed like hours staring out of the window watching the sky change from dark grey to pale blue and back to grey.

He'd been let out once to use the toilet in the bathroom next door, and the blond man had brought him a sandwich and a drink, so he guessed it must have been lunch time, but what did that mean? Twelve? One, even two? The pale and watery sun had moved out of sight behind the house and he tried to visualize how the sun shifted in relation to Frantham. He knew it set down past Marlborough Head but he'd never observed its movement closely enough to guess the time.

George had passed most of the time in speculation. Why was his dad so angry with Karen? Just what was going on? After a while, getting nowhere, he switched to wondering what Paul was doing now, fantasizing about what they'd do together when all of this was done. He was surprised to find that even the daily monotony of going to school seemed oddly comforting and inviting.

George left his perch and lay down on the bed, staring at the cracked plaster on the ceiling, wondering if he should try and sleep. He understood now why his mum and Paul had found that activity so appealing. Voices from the stairs attracted his attention. He slipped off the bed and pressed his ear against the door, recognizing his father's voice and that of the blond man. He guessed that the three of them were alone in the house.

'I know time's bloody short,' Parker senior was protesting. 'But he can spare me an hour or two. That's all it's going to take.'

'Better be all,' said blond man. 'Look, he's been tolerant, Ed, but try his patience, take too many risks, and he'll drop you just like that. He doesn't like it when personal matters get in the way of business.'

'And I've not let it, have I?'

George backed away from the door. His dad was shouting and he could hear him clearly enough now.

'Just so long as you remember.' George was struck by how unconcerned blond man sounded. 'You miss the boat; no one's going to wait.'

The door opened. His dad was holding George's coat and his other belongings. He dropped them on the bed.

'Twenty minutes and we're leaving,' he said. 'Be ready.'

'Where we going?' George asked, but his dad ignored him and George was soon alone again.

He checked through his stuff, glad to find that Tim's card and his watch had been returned to him. His watch told him that it was two forty-five. He put it back on his wrist, tucked his belongings back into his pocket and put on his coat.

* * *

Mac had returned to the flat to tell Karen that he'd got some bodies looking at the camera footage. Knocking but receiving no reply, he let himself in, calling out that it was only him. He'd leave a note for Karen.

Carol didn't look up as he came in, staring at the television; she didn't seem to have moved since Mac last saw her.

'Carol? Is Karen not here?' Receiving no response, he came over to the sofa. 'Carol?' He touched her hand, a cold chill in his stomach. 'Carol!'

Her hand was still warm, but Mac noted the pallor of her face. He touched her wrist, her throat. She slipped sideways, away from him, her head striking the arm of the sofa. 'Carol!' What had she done? Had she taken something? Karen kept her pills hidden. But not here; maybe there was no hiding place here. No pulse, she was not breathing—should he try CPR? Instinct told him it was far too late for that.

'Oh, God. No. No, you can't do this to them. You stupid woman, don't you know what this will do to them? What reason have you got to kill yourself now?'

He stared at the prone form of Carol Parker and felt the same sense of utter despair he had encountered that night on the lonely beach, watching the little girl die. But this time the despair was tempered with slow-burning fury. How dare she choose to cop out now? How could she choose to die when her kids were doing everything they could to live?

He pulled his mobile from his pocket and called an ambulance, then called Eden. He'd been kneeling by the couch but he got up now and paced the room, willing Eden to pick up, scanning the floor for anything that would give him a clue as to what she'd done.

Bending, he could see that a glass had fallen beneath the sofa, fallen from her hand. He schooled himself not to touch it, but he could see traces of milk coating the inside. Stuffed beneath the cushion beside the dead woman he saw the box, the bubble pack, nothing left inside. How many had she taken?

Eden's voice came on the phone. 'Mac, Andy's just spotted your boy on the CCTV footage. Shop under your flat. There was a man with him, looks like Parker senior but he doesn't show us his face unfortunately.'

'She's dead, Eden.'

'Who? Mac, are you OK?'

He took a deep breath. He was beginning to feel like Jonah. He'd come here and brought the taint with him to a place that hadn't known a violent death in more than two decades.

'Carol Parker,' he said. 'I can hear the ambulance. Overdose, I think.' A sudden calm seemed to have descended upon him, the panic and fury fading as suddenly as it had come. He closed his phone and went to open the door for the ambulance crew, wondering again where Karen had gone and aware that the brief note he had planned to leave when he came to the flat just couldn't begin to cover this.

THIRTY-SIX

Despite Karen's objections Rina had used a trip to the bath-room to try and contact Mac. He was out, she was told. Something had come up unexpectedly and no one knew when he'd be back. She considered trying Eden but Karen was calling from the bottom of the stairs that it was time to go, and Rina, peering at her watch, was inclined to agree.

This was her lucky watch. It had a tiny, elegant little face and a pretty leather band. Her husband had given it to her on their first anniversary and Rina would not dream of doing any-thing important without slipping it on. It was her touchstone.

'I'm going to need you watching over me this afternoon, love,' she whispered. 'This is going to be a tough room.'

Karen was pacing impatiently. 'Tim's gone to get the car. We'll be in time, won't we?'

'My dear, we've got plenty of time. We'll get there well ahead of them.'

She heard Tim's car pull up outside and hustled Karen through the door. Matthew Montmorency stuck his head around the living-room door.

'You off out, then?'

'Yes, won't be long.' She checked that Karen was out of the way and then placed a piece of paper by the phone, putting her finger to her lips as Matthew opened his mouth to ask a question.

'Bye, Matthew,' she said, hoping he would do as she asked and just keep on trying to reach Mac, hoping he would understand the brief message she had left.

* * *

It was a ten-minute drive to the hotel at Marlborough Head. They parked in the car park and then made their way on to the cliff path. Tim remembered the day he had come here with Rina. He consulted his watch. 'High tide soon,' he said.

She nodded. 'I thought I heard a boat engine a minute ago. It's a bit hard to tell with this wind.'

'Where are they?' Karen fretted.

'It isn't time yet,' Rina reminded her. 'We got here ahead of time.'

Tim shivered. He could see that the women were cold too, their faces pinched and reddened by the stiff breeze. Karen's strawberry-blonde hair whipped around her face. Impatiently, she pushed it back, but had nothing to keep it in place. She turned, trying to escape the worst of the blast, but the wind had other ideas and just tugged the hair free of her grasp, flailed at her again.

It's going to chuck it down, Tim thought, looking up at the rain clouds. He caught the sound of a boat engine again and squinted out to sea. A motor launch sat halfway between the shore and the horizon, but the sound he had heard sounded closer in, nearer to the cliff. A boat could land at high tide, he remembered.

'They're here,' Rina murmured.

Tim looked back towards the hotel. A black car swung into a parking space and three people got out. A shock of bright red hair disclosed the smallest figure as George.

'Oh!' Karen made as though to run towards them but Rina took her arm.

225

'Wait,' she said. 'Don't make sudden moves, we don't know how he's going to react and it looks to me as though he's got a gun.'

'A gun?' Tim was horrified. He studied the three figures and realized that Rina might be right; something was pressed against the boy's side, something his father held. How could a parent threaten his child that way? Tim, whose parents had been gentle, sweet, if slightly ineffectual at times, found it incomprehensible.

'What do we do?'

'We wait,' Rina said. 'And we play our cards the way they fall, Tim. The aim is to get ourselves and the children out of this safely, nothing more.'

Children, Tim thought, looking sideways at Karen. Was she a child?

He eyed the two men warily. The other one, the blond one, looked ex-military to Tim. His uncles were, and so were both his grandfathers. He knew the look. It occurred to Tim that he and his father really were the odd ones out in their clan. His father was an artist and he was a . . . well, just now he felt more like a failed clown than Marvello. It occurred to him too that it had never mattered, not to any of them, that he and his father had taken a different path.

'I must go home,' he said. 'When this is over. See the folks.'

'Good idea.' Rina approved. 'I've been telling you that.'

Karen blinked at them, uncertainty and disbelief reflected in her eyes. She clearly thought that they were both ever so slightly mad. Right now, Tim was inclined to agree.

'You brought your nan with you,' Parker senior said. 'What's with the old woman?'

Tim could see Rina bristle.

'Well, you can both clear off. This is nothing to do with you. It's between me and the kids.'

'You've got five minutes,' the blond man said.

'Plenty of time.'

Tim watched, bemused as the blond one pushed past Rina and headed for the steep little path he and Rina had climbed down that day after the kids' party. Parker senior was now waving the gun towards Karen.

'Get over here.'

'Why, can't you hit me at that range? Lousy shot then, aren't you?'

'I said get over here.'

'Not until you let George go. Not until she's taken him out of here.'

'Like you've got a choice.'

'Oh, she has a choice and she's making it,' Rina said. 'You want her dead, shoot her now. You want them both dead, then you'd better shoot young George as well, and us two witnesses, and I don't think you want that, do you, Mr Parker? Just too many deaths to explain away. And the police will know it's you. I can't think your employer will be too impressed, you drawing that much attention to yourself.'

Parker had turned his attention to her now, brandishing the gun in her direction. Rina backed off steadily as he advanced, gesturing slightly to Tim that he should move aside.

Puzzled, Tim did so, and then it became clear. Rina was drawing Parker closer to the edge. He remembered that day when they'd slipped and slithered their way down the cliff path. The rocks below. The cold sea. Inwardly, he shuddered.

Parker was paying him no attention. He had one arm round George, across the boy's chest. Tim caught his eye, wondered how much nerve the boy actually had. He bared his teeth, grimaced; he opened his mouth and snapped his teeth shut, silently.

George's eyes widened, but he nodded almost imperceptibly. They had moved now, on to the path itself, and Karen was talking to her father.

'I'm here,' she said. 'So what now, we dance around on the cliff all day? That bloke said you had five minutes. That must be almost up. That boat waiting for you, is it?'

'You're coming with me,' Parker senior said. Tim watched him, waiting for the moment when the gun was furthest away from George, pointed nowhere. The man's eyes were hard as blue chipped ice. *He's the one that's crazy*, Tim thought. *He's truly lost it.*

Catching George's eye again, he nodded. George lowered his head and bit down hard on his father's hand. Parker senior yelled out, shook the boy, raised his gun and brought it down hard on George's shoulder, aiming for the head but missing as the boy struggled aside. Only then did George let go.

Rina threw herself at the man's chest. He stumbled back, the gun firing into empty air as Tim swung George aside then ran to Rina's aid. He flung himself at the hand holding the gun, praying that something of his martial forbears might just have filtered down and into him. He knocked the arm up and back, his full weight already committed. Parker stumbled, but he was so much stronger than Tim. With a roar that chilled Tim's blood he swung round, gun still in hand, and put his right foot down into empty air.

For a moment he hung on, slipping sideways over the grassy edge of the cliff, his hands grappling for purchase, gun falling to crash on to the cliff below. His fingers dug so deep into the tussock and the clay that Tim thought he might just save himself.

'Dad!' Despite himself, George was horrified.

'Help me, son. Help me now.'

George took a step and Tim grabbed him by the coat sleeve, pulled him back. Then the moment was lost and Parker was gone. Below them they heard a boat engine roar into life and a small launch speed away.

The sound George made was feral, bereft, appalled.

'Nothing you could have done,' Tim said softly. 'He'd have taken you over with him.'

'No, but you could have,' Karen said. 'But you didn't, did you?'

She was smiling.

THIRTY-SEVEN

A week passed in Frantham. The media circus departed, satisfied that Mark Dowling, murder victim two, had been the killer of Mrs Freer and so the young man was now of less interest than he might have been.

Mac had read most of the reports. Many were, to his mind, tainted with a faintly satisfied inflection. Many of the additional officers had left too. No leads, no forensic, no suspects equalled no process. Their services were required elsewhere.

It was, Mac thought, the week for funerals.

He'd been surprised at how many people turned up to give Mrs Freer a good send off. Saddened by the thought that few of them had visited her in life, though he suspected a sense of collective guilt that just slightly assuaged that. She was cremated and, there being no living relatives, Rina scattered her ashes in the garden of remembrance. Mac found some solace in the knowledge that her husband's remains had been scattered there too.

Mark Dowling's body had been released for burial. Mac attended that too. The gathering was smaller. Family, close friends. Mac kept apart, not wanting to intrude, not welcome or belonging.

He watched as the parents wept over their lost son and recalled the mother, the slash of red lipstick on the tired face when she had answered the door. Her evident dislike of the boy playing too-loud music in the upstairs room and of Mark himself. Threatening and feral and thoroughly unpleasant.

No one had money to pay for Carol's funeral and so it was a sad, simple affair organized by social services, though Rina had provided food for the wake and the Montmorency twins cooked with flair and aplomb.

Carol was cremated. Her children attended, along with Paul and his family and Rina and her entire household. And Mac. Neither George nor Karen wept. They seemed beyond that.

'What will you do?' Mac asked.

Karen shrugged. 'I don't know. Work, try to keep on with my studies. Social services say there are benefits I can claim and such. We'll get by.' She was cool with Mac since that day at the flat when George had been abducted. Unforgiving.

Later, Mac sat in Rina's sanctuary and drank some very good scotch.

'I think she did it,' he said. 'I can't prove it, of course.'

'No,' Rina said. 'You could prove it if you had a mind to. You just don't know if you want to yet.'

'That isn't true.'

'Isn't it? Look, Mac, no one's that clever; no one commits murder and leaves nothing behind. The proof is there. You've just got to want to find it.' She paused. 'Have you shared your thoughts with anyone else? Has she appeared on anyone else's suspect list?'

'No, to both,' Mac said. 'Rina, what really happened that day on the cliff? Did he really fall?'

'He lost his footing and he fell,' she said. 'Yes, I pushed him, and yes, Tim grabbed his arm and tried to take the gun. He was very brave. But no one could have done anything to help Parker, even if we'd wanted to.'

'Ah, there's the thing,' Mac said. Rina proffered the whisky and he accepted gratefully. 'She's all George has.'

'But is she *good* for George?'

'She loves him.'

'Undoubtedly, but such a love! One day George will want a life of his own. He won't want or need his sister's protection. Might come to resist such obsessive love.'

'Is it obsessive?'

'Oh, I would say so.'

'But to lose her too . . . Rina, I couldn't do that to him. There've been so many lives lost and ruined already.'

'So, you'll let a murderer go free?'

He swallowed the last of the scotch in his glass. He was drinking far too much, especially after such a long period of abstinence. He really shouldn't be drinking at all, should he? Rina leaned over and refilled his glass.

'The boys,' she said. 'What about them? They broke into Mrs Freer's house. What will happen?'

Mac shrugged. 'The family court will deal with it in time. They've been cautioned. There's mitigation. We'll have to see. I can't see either of them re-offending. Paul's seeing a counsellor. George refused . . . I should go. Did I tell you I have the flat for another month? Suicide and holiday lets don't go together, I understand. Bad publicity.'

'And how do you feel about it?'

He shrugged. 'How should I feel? I still can't believe she did it. It seems so . . . pointless. She came all this way, she survived so much, and suddenly she just decides to end it all. Just like that.'

'You don't think Karen might have . . .' Rina began. 'No, forget I even uttered the thought.'

'Yes, I think Karen might just have forgotten to hide the pills,' Mac said.

THIRTY-EIGHT

Mac had spent a sleepless night at Rina's, sleeping in the little bed in the cramped room. Not that the location had anything to do with his restlessness.

Morning brought clarity, along with a thumping hangover. Rina was on hand with painkillers and coffee. He refused breakfast.

'I have to be off early,' he said.

'You've decided, then?'

'Did I even really have a choice? I'm going to talk all of this through with Eden, get a warrant to search the house. Bring her in for questioning. She still killed a man, Rina, and I'm being a fool if I think I can let that go.'

Rina nodded. 'You have to follow your conscience,' she told him.

Mac laughed harshly. 'Duty,' he said. 'Not conscience. Thankfully, that doesn't even come into it.'

Rina watched him leave, sitting quietly at her table and sipping her morning tea. She wished Tim was here, but he'd made good on his promise and gone home to visit his kin. It was about time, she thought.

Then she too made up her mind. She went through to the hall and collected her coat then walked up on to the still-deserted promenade and used the public phone. Nothing would happen for a few hours, she thought. Enough time.

* * *

Mac arrived at the Parker house just a little before noon. He drove. Andy was in the car with him and a patrol car followed, a scientific support van drifting in their wake.

George and Paul were in the street, playing football. They were not yet back at school but both looked much better. Mac's conscience needled that he was about to cause more pain.

George came over, Paul trailing a bit behind. 'You've come to see Karen,' he said.

'Yes.'

'She said you'd want to talk to her. She said she'd see you later. I'm staying the night with Paul while she goes to see her boyfriend. She's not seen him much lately.'

'When did she decide to go out?'

'Oh, I think he phoned her this morning. She said she'd like to stay over. I didn't mind.'

Mac nodded, pushed the suspicions away. He didn't even want to acknowledge they were there. 'George, I have to . . .'

The boy was feeling in his pocket. He produced a front-door key. 'Here,' he said. 'OK if I go back to Paul's?'

Mac nodded and George turned to go, then he swung around and looked Mac in the eye. 'She did it, didn't she? She isn't coming home.'

He didn't wait for a reply, just turned back to his game, but Mac could see from the set of his shoulders and the stiffness in his limbs that the tears were not far away.

EPILOGUE

The morning post brought a padded envelope addressed to Mac and delivered to the police station. It was postmarked Exeter and contained a brief note and a mobile phone.

'I don't want to risk anyone else getting the blame,' Karen's note said. 'You'll find the evidence on the phone. Just don't let George down. He's your responsibility now.'

'So, that's it then,' Eden said as he looked at the pictures lifted from the phone. 'Case closed.'

Mac nodded. *But not for George*, he thought. *Not for George*.

* * *

A young woman with a neat, dark-red bob smiled at the driver when she got on to the Manchester bus.

'You look cold, love.'

'Freezing,' she laughed and her blue eyes sparkled.

'Never mind. Nice and warm in here.' He watched her in his mirror as she took her seat. *Nice-looking*, he thought. Then he closed the doors and made ready for his journey, just another passenger to be noticed and then just as quickly forgotten.

From the window, Karen gazed out into the gathering dusk, finally leaving all of her past behind.

THE END

ALSO BY JANE ADAMS

RINA MARTIN MYSTERY SERIES
Book 1: MURDER ON SEA

MERROW & CLARKE
Book 1: SAFE

DETECTIVE MIKE CROFT SERIES
Book 1: THE GREENWAY
Book 2: THE SECRETS
Book 3: THEIR FINAL MOMENTS
Book 4: THE LIAR

DETECTIVE RAY FLOWERS SERIES
Book 1: THE APOTHECARY'S DAUGHTER
Book 2: THE UNWILLING SON
Book 3: THE DROWNING MEN
Book 4: THE SISTER'S TWIN

DETECTIVE ROZLYN PRIEST SERIES
Book 1: BURY ME DEEP

STANDALONES
THE OTHER WOMAN
THE WOMAN IN THE PAINTING
THEN SHE WAS DEAD